KT-409-513

ROSEMARY AITKEN

The Cornish Blacksmith's Daughter

First published in Great Britain and the USA in 2016 by Severn House Publishers Ltd

This edition published in the United Kingdom in 2023 by

Canelo
Unit 9, 5th Floor
Cargo Works, 1–2 Hatfields
London SE1 9PG
United Kingdom

Copyright © Rosemary Aitken 2016

The moral right of Rosemary Aitken to be identified as the creator of this work has been asserted in accordance with the Copyright, Designs and Patents Act, 1988.

All rights reserved. No part of this publication may be reproduced or transmitted in any form or by any means, electronic or mechanical, including photocopy, recording, or any information storage and retrieval system, without permission in writing from the publisher.

A CIP catalogue record for this book is available from the British Library.

Print ISBN 978 1 80436 546 5
Ebook ISBN 978 1 80436 049 1

This book is a work of fiction. Names, characters, businesses, organizations, places and events are either the product of the author's imagination or are used fictitiously. Any resemblance to actual persons, living or dead, events or locales is entirely coincidental.

Look for more great books at www.canelo.co

Printed and bound in Great Britain by Clays Ltd, Elcograf S.p.A.

1

To Kathy, with much love.

Part One

October 1915

One

The woman who opened the police-house door in answer to her knock was so unlike anything that Verity had expected, that for a moment she could not find her tongue.

Surely this couldn't be the wife of Constable Dawes? Verity had heard that he was married, naturally. But she had a mental picture of what policemen's wives were like. She had vivid memories of the last one: Sergeant Jeffries' missus, always dressed in black, skinny as a rake, with a prune face and a disapproving stare and grey hair scraped into a bun. This woman was only a few years older than Verity herself, pretty as a peach, with glorious chestnut hair swept up around her face, and wearing a fawn costume – skirt and coat to match – that fitted beautifully. Must have been made to measure, and what policeman's wife could possibly afford to dress like that? No, this must be a caller to the station, like herself.

'Can I help you?' the woman said, and Vee realized with a start that she'd been goggling.

'I was looking for that young policeman that I spoke to once before. Name of Dawes. You come to see him, too?' She found that she was nervous and her tongue – as usual – was rushing on all of its own accord. ('Fluent, imaginative and intelligent', they had said at school – though Mother

3

said she simply talked too much.) 'Some nice young man, he is.'

'You think so?' The young woman smiled.

'I know so,' Vee said stoutly. 'Saved me a walloping when I lost my mother's purse. Helped me trace my footsteps and we found it by the path with all Pa's weekly wages still inside.'

'That sounds like Alex,' the voice was pleasantly amused. 'Very keen on footprints and fingerprints and things.'

'Well, it saved my hide that day – he walked me home and never said a word to Pa, 'cept that I'd had a nasty fright out on the path. I'm sure he would remember.' Vee stopped short with a frown. 'But if he isn't back, I can't well stop tonight. If you see him, tell him it's the girl that lost her purse. Verity Tregorran – though they call me Vee for short. When they're not calling me "larks legs", that is, on account of I'm so thin.'

The woman was giving her a peculiar little smile. 'Well I'd tell him, Miss Tregorran, and with pleasure too, but I'm afraid that you're too late. Constable Dawes is not here any more.'

'Don't tell me he's already gone and left for France!' Verity exclaimed. 'I heard some talk that he was planning to go and join the war – but I never thought that it would be so soon. My father said that they weren't asking for married men to go.'

'They will take any fit man who volunteers. I'm sorry, Miss Tregorran. He left here months ago.' The face was rueful now. 'Would you like to speak to Sergeant Jeffries instead?'

Vee shook her head. 'That wouldn't do no good! He thinks I'm flighty.' She spoke with feeling. Sergeant Jeffries had known her since she was two years old, when she took a fancy to go and see the fair. She went off walking without telling anyone and was halfway to Sennon before he brought her back. It had earned her a good hiding for frightening her folks and the Sergeant had thought her 'flighty' ever since. 'Besides,' she went on, 'he used to be friendly with my family – and Pa'd be madder than a bull if he knew that I'd been here. Toby Tregorran – keeps the smithy, up Rosvene. Know him, do you, or are you a stranger hereabouts?'

The woman laughed. 'Oh forgive me, I should have introduced myself. I'm Effie Dawes, the constable's wife.'

'Oh!' Vee said, stupidly. Of course, she should have realized all along. She'd heard the rumours like everybody else. The police-house had been offered when the husband took the post – came as part of it – and that's what allowed the Daweses to get married, people said. Old Sergeant Jeffries had been rattling round it, since his missus died, and had been more than happy to make room for them. 'I heard you were to live here while your husband learned the ropes. Sergeant's retiring in a few months, isn't he?'

'Should have done last Christmas, according to the plan, but then the war came – and Alex volunteered. So the Sergeant delayed his retirement and agreed to hold the fort, at least until my husband gets back home again.'

'You're never living in the police-house with the Sergeant here?' It sounded scandalous.

Mrs Dawes laughed. 'No. The Police Authorities have agreed to let the wives of volunteers stay on in their cottages rent-free, but I hardly think they would approve of that! I've moved into his retirement cottage down the street.' She waved a hand at it. 'You're lucky to find me here, today, in fact. I've only come to pick up a few things I'd left behind.'

Vee nodded, she knew White Cottage well. 'Old lady used to live there, didn't she? Had a wooden leg – used to wave it out the window, just to frighten us.' Then she wished she hadn't said that. It sounded impudent.

'Sergeant Jeffries' mother-in-law, that was.' Mrs Dawes did not quite suppress a smile. 'Came to him when she died, years ago, and he always intended to end up there himself. And it is only yards away. So he was happy to let me stay there, in the meantime anyway. Quite my Sir Galahad – without his kindness I would probably have had to leave the area and go to Alex's people right up Falmouth way.' She sounded as if the prospect did not please her much.

Verity tried to imagine Sergeant Jeffries in the role of knight protector – she'd read about Sir Galahad in school – but try as she would she couldn't manage it. 'So, with your husband gone, there's no chance of me talking to anybody else?'

Mrs Dawes shook her head. 'The Sergeant's doing the policing on his own, again. Though that may not be for long. He's finding it an effort, these days, cycling up the hills. They're going to send a volunteer reservist to help out, when they can. But they're so short of men that even that is difficult – so for the moment, he is all there is.' She flashed that smile again. 'So what was it that you wanted? Or would you rather wait and see the new man when he comes?'

Vee thought about her errand and wondered what to do. 'Thing is, something's happened which don't seem right to me – and I ought to tell someone in authority. Not Sergeant Jeffries, though, if there is any choice – he won't pay no heed to me. But perhaps it shouldn't wait until this other policeman comes. I think it might be connected to the war.' You heard such dreadful stories: how spies were everywhere and the Germans were likely to invade at any time! The Government had even handed pamphlets out, about what to take with you if the Hun arrived. 'Could I talk to you?' she added, hopefully. Talking to a kindly face would make things easier.

'I don't think I could help you,' Mrs Dawes replied. 'You should see the Sergeant really, but he isn't here just now – he's out on his bicycle doing his patrol. But perhaps if you tell me what the problem is, I could advise you what to do. Come in for a minute.' And she led the way inside.

Verity had never been inside a police station before and she was rather nervous as Mrs Dawes ushered her across the hall. Was she going to be taken to a cell to wait?

But no! The room they entered was an ordinary one, plainly furnished with a table and three chairs – and a sideboard with a photo lying flat on top of it. Was this the room they used for questioning criminals? Likely not – that photograph was obviously personal. Vee managed to get a squint at it as she went past. It was in a fancy frame and it showed a man she recognized. It was that nice young PC Dawes, though in the picture he wasn't a policeman any more. He was sitting on a horse and wearing army uniform – a fancy one with lots of braid on it.

The other woman had noticed what she was looking at and Vee turned scarlet to her very ears. 'Your husband, isn't it?'

'That's right,' the woman said. 'He had some portraits taken before he went to France but I couldn't find this one when I came to move. I came back today to look for it, and found it in a drawer, up in the attic with some furniture we left. Alex must have put it there by accident.'

Verity nodded, but her mind was following a different train of thought. 'He's not an ordinary soldier than?' she said. 'Ned Chegwidden, who used to live next door, has just gone off to join the army too. Sent home a photo but he doesn't look like that.'

The minute that the words were out, she wished them back again. What had possessed her to mention Ned, and to a stranger too? Suppose that news of it got back to Pa, or – worse – to Grandfather? They'd guess that she and Ned were sweethearts on the sly, and then the skies would fall because the Chegwiddens weren't Strict Adherent Christians, like themselves. Might as well be heathens, as far as courting went. That would be the end of her going anywhere alone, so she'd never get a chance to speak to Ned again – and serve her right, maybe. Besides, her unguarded comment had sounded rather rude.

But Mrs Dawes was not affronted in the least. She picked up the photograph and looked at it herself. 'He's in the dress uniform of his father's regiment.'

'His father has a regiment?' Verity was stunned. 'Like the Duke of Devonshire?'

Mrs Dawes laughed outright, not unkindly though. 'No! But my father-in-law always calls it "his" – or just "the regiment" as though there were no others in the world! Alex's elder brothers are both in it as well, so when Alex volunteered, that was naturally the regiment he joined. And with his background in the police, he was given a commission straight away.'

'So, is he in the trenches?' Vee enquired, remembering the letters that Ned had sent home to his ma. He tried to be cheerful, though he could not say too much – and even then a lot was crossed out with censor's pencil – but you could tell the trenches weren't a pleasant place to be.

'No!' Mrs Dawes was looking at the photo, still. 'They sent him on attachment to the mounted military police, so he's escorting the wounded back to hospitals or riding guard for prisoners on the march.' She put the picture back. 'Personally I'm relieved to know he isn't at the front, but from his letters he isn't very pleased. Feels he's "shirking danger", which is obviously rot – but it's not what he joined up for, I suppose.'

Vee nodded, but her thoughts were still with Ned. He had talked about the military police the last time that they met, when he came home on embarkation leave. 'Blomming redcaps – made up from the ranks just so they can boss us round!' he'd said. But perhaps PC First Class Alexander Dawes was different from the rest. She rather hoped so: she had liked him very much. 'He was a lovely policeman!' was all she could reply.

'Well, sit down,' his wife was saying, pulling out a chair. 'And then you can tell me what this is all about. Did I understand you thought it might concern the war?'

Vee perched on the wooden seat and took her bonnet off, twisting the pink ribbons between nervous hands. Suddenly her mission seemed a stupid one. 'I'm not sure. I don't know where to start.'

But Mrs Dawes said, 'Start at the beginning.' So she did.

'Well, it's like this, you see. I'm the third one in the family...' And out it all came in a rush. 'We're nine girls altogether and the last one's only small, so someone has to stop home and give a hand – but Ma has views about us taking turns. She was the eldest in her family, you see, and her own ma went on expecting her to stop and help at home, while her two sisters went in service and got paid for doing less. Unpaid skivvy Ma became, she says – and she isn't going to let her own girls do the same.'

'I see,' said Mrs Dawes. 'And what has this to do with whatever brought you here?'

'Well, that's how I came to be up on the cliff. My next sister, Constance, she's just got old enough to give up school and take my place at home and I was hoping I could join the older two, working up at the steam-dairy factory out towards St Just – I 'spect you know the one?'

Mrs Dawes nodded. 'I've heard of it, of course. They're taking girls, now, are they – with so many men away?'

'They've always taken women, it's cheaper I suppose, and now – with the Government putting females on this War Register – they're taking girls from there. But they've put in new machinery...' she tailed off. Ma would say that she was running on again.

But Mrs Dawes was clearly listening. 'I think I've read about it. To sterilize the milk?'

Vee shook her head. 'They already did that – have done for several years – but now they're expanding into other things. Used to do just fresh butter, cream and cheese and that was that – 'cept sell a bit of whey back to the farmers for their pigs – but with this new equipment they can evaporate the milk, or turn it into powder to send it to the troops. And salt down butter and put it into tins. All sorts of things like that. It makes a lot less waste, but it calls for extra hands. So one way and another there are often vacancies, but you can't wait until you hear that there's a job come free.'

'Because they'll just take someone from the War Register?'

'Exactly! So I thought as how I'd go up there and ask – tell them I had sisters working there and see if there was any positions going. Our Patience (she's the eldest) said it was a good idea, but I ought to try and see the general manager. Young Mr Radjel – that's the supervisor of the creamery – doesn't really have the final say. So I was to ask for Mr Grey, in person.' She glanced at Mrs Dawes, in case she had that glazed look that Mother always got, when Vee was trying to tell her anything. But Mrs Dawes was smiling. 'And did you?'

Vee shook her head. 'Not first off, I didn't. I went up yesterday and asked to talk to him, but he wasn't there. The factory's working all the hours God sends, the fellow said, and the manager can't be there all the time. More than likely he'd be back later on, when the night shift came on at seven o'clock, to oversee the loading of the carts. Well that seemed a bit awkward, first off, cause it would be dark by then and I didn't have a lamp, and there wasn't time to go and get one, so I nearly gave it up.'

She paused to make sure Mrs Dawes was following, but instead of saying, 'Well get on with it!' like Ma would probably have done, the policeman's wife said, 'But you did wait in the end?'

It was proving easy to talk to Mrs Dawes. Verity let out a long sigh of relief. 'Well, it struck me Pru and Patience would be coming out, and if I found them and let them know to wait, I could walk back home with them. So I told the man I'd do that and went out along the cliff road – to fill in time by calling on my aunt – and when it came to half past six, I started back. It was getting dusk by then and coming on to rain, so I stopped to shelter underneath a wall, trying to make up my mind what I would say to Mr

Grey. Just by the top crossroads where there's that Cornish cross and stile. And that's when I saw this feller...'

–

After the story had come tumbling out, Effie stared at her young caller in surprise. 'A man was standing on the cliffs, you say, and started signalling to someone with a lamp?'

The girl nodded. 'Thing is, I wonder can he have been a spy? Everybody says that there are German spies and sympathizers around and we should all be on our guard because they might be anywhere.' She obviously believed in every word of this unlikely tale. Her freckled little face was pink with earnestness and her tawny eyes were shining with sincerity.

Effie frowned. The story was unlikely, but such things were possible. There were reports of spies. And showing lights along the coast was a criminal offence – one that could earn a very heavy fine. Even the light ships and lighthouses had been turned off for weeks – though that had been rescinded since, for fear of accidents. But here in Penvarris Cove?

She said gently, 'You don't think he was signalling to a fishing boat? Pointing out a shoal of pilchards to the crew, perhaps. The older men can spot them from the clifftop miles away, from how the water moves – it's quite amazing, but I've seen them doing it, myself. I know they're not supposed to do it, with the war, but I expect that they still do.'

'It was too dark for that. And if there was a boat, there was no light on it.'

'Then perhaps he was guiding someone to where the crab pots were, if it was getting too dark to see the floats?

Or indicating that it was safe to land?' There was a little shingle beach down there, with a steep path leading to it from the clifftop by the cross. She and Alex had scrambled down there once, and boats did haul up there sometimes when the tide and wind was right.

Verity Tregorran shook her tousled head determinedly. 'Must 'ave been some sort of stranger then. Fishermen round here know every rock and channel like the back of their own hands, and how would anyone forget where he had put his pots?'

'But in the darkness...?' Effie said. 'You said yourself you hadn't seen a light.'

'Well, that is what's peculiar!' Verity exclaimed. 'If fishers d'go out at night, they've all got lamps aboard – of course they have, even if it's only a dark lantern nowadays. How do you suppose they manage else? Don't know much about fishing, do 'ee, Mrs Dawes?' She was looking at Effie with a forgiving sort of smile. 'Besides, if he was local I'd have known him, sure as eggs. By sight, at any rate. My Uncle Terence (the one that's married to the aunt I went to see) he goes out regular – got part shares in a fishing boat, like lots of miners do – and I used to sneak down sometimes to help him with the fish, so I know all the fishing folk from round the Cove. But I didn't know this man, he was tall and thin – a beaky sort of face, I saw it in the light. And I'm as near as certain that he had a bowler 'at. Who ever knew a fisherman to wear a fool thing like that?'

'So you saw a stranger on the cliff path with a lantern in his hand. What made you think that he was signalling? Didn't you say that he was beside the stile? Isn't it more likely he was simply holding up the lamp to see where he

13

was going?' Effie was aware of sounding sceptical, but this story did lack substance, the more you heard of it.

'Then why was he acting so suspicious-like – looking up and down the road, trying to make sure that there was nobody about? And I'm not dreaming that. When Farmer Crowdie came past in his cart, the fellow covered up his lantern with his coat and hid behind a rock.'

'And it wasn't just that he was anxious not to scare the horse and sheltered by the rock to get out of the rain? Just as you yourself had hidden in the shadow by the hedge?' This time she tried to soften the questions with a smile. 'I'm only asking to make quite sure what we are dealing with – the sort of things the Sergeant would ask if he were here.'

The girl turned scarlet. 'You don't believe me either! I should have known, I suppose. Stupid to have come here. But I thought about it all last night, and felt I had to come. You aren't allowed to wave a light from on the cliffs these days. And there was something about the way he sneaked about – he was up to something or I'm a Dutchman's aunt.' She glanced at Effie from under downturned lids. 'Mind, there might be a way that someone could find out. I'm almost certain that he'd dropped something by the stile – I heard him mutter something and search about for it – but in the end he just gave up and left. I went to have a look for it – when he had gone – but in the dusk I couldn't see a thing and anyway I had to hurry to get back to Mr Grey. But perhaps if somebody went out and made a search—'

'You heard him saying something?' Effie interrupted, with sudden interest. This was something new. 'Did he sound like a German? Was that why you think he was a spy?'

'Don't know what a German sounds like,' the girl mumbled, turning an even darker shade of red. 'But I suppose it wasn't foreign talking, come to think of it. Sounded more like "Now where have I gone and buggering dropped the damty thing?"'

The laugh which had been hovering for several minutes now, almost defeated Effie and burst out at this, but she managed to bite it back and say, politely, 'You didn't know the voice?'

Vee Tregorran looked affronted. 'Well, of course I didn't. Wouldn't have thought it was a spy, else, would I now?' She stopped, looking thoughtful. 'Though if somebody you knew turned out to be a spy, I suppose you wouldn't know he was one – till someone found him out.'

The convoluted logic of that last remark did make Effie smile again, but a more serious thought occurred to her. 'It might have been a smuggler, I suppose,' she murmured suddenly. Such things had happened in lonely Cornish coves for centuries and they could occur again – even in the twentieth century, possibly. All sorts of things were getting short just now, and prices had been rocketing since the war began. There would be money in importing alcohol again – or even coal and meat. Not from France, of course, but possibly from Spain. And strangers might require a signal in the half-light, mightn't they? Why had she not thought of that before?

She gave herself a mental talking-to for having been so slow of wit and so rudely doubtful of her visitor. 'I think that you should tell the Sergeant what you've just told me. Smuggling is a serious matter in a time of war. He should be here directly if you would like to wait. Perhaps in the meantime, you would like a cup of tea?' But the girl just shook her head.

'Perhaps you'd tell him for me, Mrs Dawes. He'd hear you out, but pay no creed to me. And I had best be off. I was only sent out to Crowdie's farmhouse for a bag of swedes – and I called here on the way. My pa will be asking questions, as it is!'

She sounded so hunted that Effie murmured, 'Never mind your father, you did right to come. You can tell him that I said so, if you think that it will help,' and escorted the poor thing to the door. She'd delay a few minutes until the Sergeant had come back – she might even make him cocoa, the way she knew he liked. It would give her time to find a few more oddments from upstairs and it would be nice to catch up with police gossip once again. In the meantime, there was this photograph to wrap.

Alex's mother had asked to have it sent 'to remind her of Alex' as though one needed a starchy photograph for that! Well, Effie could spare it – she had much better ones – and Alex hadn't liked it either. 'Makes me look a pompous idiot – just like Papa!' he'd said. She smiled at the memory, then fetched a cloth, wrapped up the photo frame and set off for the attic to rummage a bit more.

It did not occur to her till she was halfway up the stairs, that she had not asked whether Verity had got the hoped-for job or not.

–

Sergeant William Jeffries was sitting at the table in the police office, sipping the cup of cocoa that Effie Dawes had made and trying – discreetly – to keep it out of his luxurious moustache. He looked at Effie kindly.

'Course there's nothing in it, Mrs Dawes. What did she see except a fellow with a lamp, apparently looking for something he'd dropped beside a stile? I'll take the trouble to question her myself – of course I will, since you have asked me to – but when it comes right down to it, that's really what it was. All this talk of signalling! The girl's too fond of reading silly tales – the chap was obviously moving the light about to look for what he'd dropped. And it can't have been all that important, even to himself, because he seems to have gone off without it in the end. At least according to Vee Tregorran – though you can't be sure of it. Wouldn't surprise me if she'd imagined the whole thing.'

Effie Dawes said stiffly, 'I'm sorry, Sergeant Jeffries, if you think I'm wasting time. But it might have been smugglers and I thought you ought to know.'

She was a pretty young woman and he liked her company. He'd miss her when this new young policeman came – perhaps there'd be another cottage vacant she could rent. He'd keep an eye out for one. Meantime, he beamed at her. 'Now, now, Mrs Dawes – you mustn't blame yourself. You were not to know what kind of girl she is – but I've known her since she was no higher than a blade of grass, and she's always been the same. I remember when she was five or six years old – gone off missing, like she often did, when she was sent off with her sisters and the barl to fetch water from the peath.'

Will glanced to make sure that Mrs Dawes had understood the local terms. 'Bringing home the water from the spring in a water barrel?' she confirmed.

He'd forgotten that she'd once been a villager herself. He nodded. 'They sent for me cause she'd gone running off and not been seen for hours – but by the time I got there, she had turned up again, telling some story about a dragon on the path and how she'd had to walk the long way home to keep away from it. There had been a lizard, so her sisters said. But no, it was a dragon where Verity was concerned – she'd seen a picture in some storybook and this looked just the same, no matter that the creature was only inches long. But that's typical of Vee. Flighty then and flighty she remains.'

'Flighty?' Effie was giving him an embarrassed little smile. 'That's what she said you'd say.'

He took a sip of cocoa. If she weren't here he'd dip his piece of bread in it – make up for the butter which was hard to get these days – but that might offend her, she was rather ladylike. His wife would never let him do it, either, while she lived. Well, never mind, he'd save a bit of crust and dunk it when Mrs Dawes was gone. She was bound to leave directly, before it got too dark, leaving him to finish up his notes and lock up for the night. In the meantime he gave her a sympathetic smile, surreptitiously wiping his whiskers on his hand.

'I'm not saying that Vee does it purposely,' he said. 'Believes her own nonsense half the time, I'm sure. She's not an outright fibber, the Tregorrans aren't that sort. Very Christian family. Strict Adherents, I believe they call themselves. Brought up a bit severe – no cooking on a Sunday and that sort of thing – but all of them as honest as the day. It's just that Vee has got a lively mind, I suppose. Just like her mother did, when she was young. Matter of fact...' He stopped himself in time. He'd been about to say that if he'd been a younger man, he'd have made a play for Martha Tregorran in those days himself.

Martha Warren, as she used to be. Pretty as a picture and sweeter than a rose – he'd seen that on a card once and he'd thought of her. He sighed, remembering. But she was twenty years his junior and it would not have 'done'. And then he'd married Ivy and it was far too late – and just as well, perhaps. You'd have to be a braver man than he was, to have dared to court that girl, with a father like she had – dreadful old fellow, always dressed in black with bristling side-whiskers and a ferocious frown. The man she married was out of the same mould – a Strict Adherent too, old-fashioned, righteous and a Bible-thumper – but quite mild-mannered in comparison. But Martha Warren…

Mrs Dawes was looking at him in surprise. Perhaps she'd heard the sigh. 'Matter of fact…?' she prompted.

Sergeant Jeffries smiled. 'I was only going to say about the family. Quite religious they are, father especially but the mother's side as well. That's how the girls all came to have those names: Prudence, Patience and all the rest of it. Called for Christian Virtues, all the lot of them – and the father won't have drink or playing cards or singing in the house, unless it's hymns – and has strict opinions about everything. Don't think they approve of storybooks in fact – it's only that Vee won them when she went to school. For prowess in reading, so I understand. Perhaps that's why she liked them quite so much, and her aunt had no more sense than to encourage her.'

'Would that be the aunt that lives out on the cliff?' Effie had risen to her feet, and was putting out a hand to clear his cocoa cup away.

He shook his head, shielding his cocoa and looked at her – surprised. 'You've heard about that business? Verity's mother's sister. Dreadful fuss it was. Married Terence Jones – against her father's wish. Decent fellow, Terence – Methodist and all – but not the right kind of Christian in the old man's view. He has never spoken to his daughter since – though she's made a few attempts to heal the breach with him, I know. But it didn't do no good. From that day to this, if she comes into a room where he is, then he'll walk out of it. And he expects the whole family to behave the same.'

'But Verity is still in touch with her,' his guest remarked. 'She told me so, today.'

Will Jeffries nodded thoughtfully. 'That will be her mother's doing, I expect. Doubt that her father very much approves.' Although perhaps he tolerated the visits, secretly. Martha could wind any man around her little finger. Always could. Hadn't she quoted some scripture, something about 'the churning of milk bringing forth butter', and persuaded her husband to let those girls of theirs go down to the dairy factory and work? No doubt she had her own way over other things as well, even with a husband like Toby Tregorran: big as an ox and blinkered as a horse. What did she see in him? Waste of a good woman!

Will brushed imaginary breadcrumbs from his uniform, suddenly aware that Mrs Dawes was looking expectantly at him. 'And I'm damty sure her grandfather don't know they've been in touch!' he finished. He lumbered to his feet. 'But enough of that! I see it's getting dark. Give me a minute and I'll light the bullseye lantern and I can see you home. I want to make a last patrol in any case.'

She laughed. 'Nonsense, White Cottage is only a stone's throw from this door.'

But she permitted him to escort her, all the same. At her door she turned and touched his arm. 'You won't make trouble for Verity, will you, Sergeant? With her Pa, I mean. I sort of promised her.'

He held the lantern high so she could see him tap his nose. 'You leave that to me. I'll call in there tomorrow, when he's likely to be out – working in the smithy – and see what she has to say.' It would give him a chance to talk to Martha, too. 'And I'll even go and take a look out by the stile, make sure there's nothing there. Now here's your door. G'night then, Mrs Dawes.' He touched his helmet in salute and watched her safe inside. Then he walked on down the street and back up through the lane – though it wasn't strictly necessary to make that last patrol.

By the time that he got back home his cocoa had gone cold and he had to make another cup to dunk his breadcrust in.

Two

Will Jeffries kept his word and rode over to Rosvene forge next afternoon, though by the time he got there he was puffing and panting so much from cycling up the hill, he was seriously regretting that he'd been so quick to promise to call by. However, here he was, and there was the smithy with the cottage next to it.

Carefully approaching from the side where he was invisible from the forge – from whence the roar of the fire and a reassuring hammering could be heard, suggesting that Toby Tregorran was in there hard at work – Will dismounted and walked the last few yards. He leaned his bicycle against the whitewashed wall, mopped his brow with his copious handkerchief, adjusted his helmet and pushed open the gate. A thin girl with copper-coloured plaits was in the yard, sitting on a stool beside the door, stringing beans into a saucepan. She leapt up from her stool as he approached.

'Ma!' she called, across her shoulder, though without for a moment ceasing to stare at him, 'there's that policeman come!'

Martha appeared behind her at the door, wiping floury fingers on her dusty pinafore. 'Sergeant Jeffries! Well, as I'm alive! Constance, where's your manners? How don't you show him in?' She smiled at Will. Same smile as ever, though the face was tired and the eyes a little faded. 'Come in, Sergeant, do!'

He took his helmet off and followed her inside. 'How are you, Martha?' He knew his face was pink, and not just from exertion. 'I swear that hill gets steeper every day,' he said, to disguise the effect that her presence — embarrassingly — could still have on him.

She hadn't noticed. She was moving damp washing from a line above the fire, to clear a space around the only chair; there was no room for more, in that tiny whitewashed room, what with the dresser and the table with a long bench either side. It must be very crowded with eleven people here, even if most of them were skinny girls, he always thought. As it was there was scarcely room for him to sidle to the seat, though Martha had placed a lumpy homemade cushion on it now and was patting it invitingly.

'Sit down and catch your breath. I'll set the kettle on.' She picked up the battered object and put it on the trivet over the embers as she spoke. 'Not seen you for months. Pity I've only just put this bit of saffron cake to rise. Only a small one, cause things have got so short, but if you'd've come later this afternoon, you could've 'ad some with your tea. As it is I can only give'ee bread and jam, if you've a mind to it?' This last was shouted from the scullery, into which she had briefly disappeared, though she was now emerging with three saucers, cups and plates.

He shook his head, balancing his policeman's helmet on his knee. Jam would be a luxury in this house, you could see. 'Just a cup of tea would do me grand. Don't want to run you short. But, nice and all as it is to see you — this not a social call. Your Verity about, is she?'

Martha gave him an astonished look and sat down abruptly on the nearer bench. 'No, not here she isn't. Gone down the dairy with her sisters. Started there this very day. Constance is stopping home instead now, giving me a hand.' She nodded at the girl, who was standing on tiptoe to reach the milk and sugar from the shelf. 'What do you want with our Vee, anyhow? She's not in any kind of trouble?' She scarcely waited for him to shake his head, before she rushed on, her voice sharp now with anxiety. 'There's not been an accident, down that factory?'

'Nothing like that, Martha. It's just...' He cleared his throat. He had been deciding what to say the whole time he'd been pedalling up that confounded hill, and now the time had come. He got out his notebook, licked the end of his pencil, and went on, trying to sound as policemanlike as possible: 'It's come to our attention that there may have been some questionable activity on the cliffs the other day, and it seems your Verity—'

He was interrupted by a roar from the doorway. 'Verity! I saw the policeman's bike outside and wondered what was up. I might have known that if there's trouble, she'd be bringing it. What has she been doing now?' Tobias Tregorran was standing at the door, still in his leather working-apron, and he'd never looked so huge. One massive hand was resting on the jamb, while the other was balled into a fist, and being shaken in a threatening fashion – though at no one in particular.

Martha, dismayed, had risen to her feet and would have said something but her husband cut her off.

'Woman, don't shake your head like that at me. I know you've got a soft spot for that girl, but I wasn't born yesterday and I've got eyes and ears. I heard exactly what was being said. Something questionable going on, that's what the sergeant said. And on the cliffs at that. Loose morals, very like. And obviously serious, or we'd not have policemen calling here.' He turned his piercing blue-grey eyes on Will. 'You tell me who the chap is, and I'll sort him out myself. And don't you worry, Sergeant, we'll have her home again – none of this working in the dairy factory. Verity's not steady, like the other girls. She isn't wicked – I aren't saying that – but there are too many notions in that head of hers, it makes her easy led. I should have known better than to let her go down there to work!'

Will was on his feet by now. 'It isn't what you seem to think, Tobias. It's nothing that your daughter's done at all. You're making ogres out of shadows!' It was unexpected to find himself defending Verity, but Martha was giving him such a grateful look that he went on: 'As I was saying to your wife, when you came in, we've had information – I can't disclose exactly what about or who reported it – but it looked suspicious, and it seems your daughter happened to be passing at the time. I'm hoping she can give us further details – that's all.'

'There you are, Toby!' Martha sank down with a deep sigh, like a collapsed balloon. 'Though, Sergeant Jeffries, you had us worried then. But if all you came for was to talk to Vee, you've had a wasted journey, I'm afraid. It's sure as God's in heaven that Verity can't help. Her tongue would not have stopped wagging for a week if she'd seen any impropriety going on.'

Toby had stopped gesticulating now and somehow managed to insinuate his frame in behind the table and sit down on the bench. 'Martha's right!' he said, gruffly, as his daughter hurried to pour him a cup of tea. 'Anything like that, Vee would have said as soon as she got home. That girl runs on like Pentargon waterfall, if there's anything to tell – and very often even if there's not. Pass a horse and cart and she'll create a drama out of it.' He put half a spoon of precious sugar in his tea and drank it greedily. 'She can't have seen anything that would interest you. Anyway, what would she be doing on the cliffs?'

'Oh, she went out there, Toby – the day before yesterday at dusk – while she was waiting for that interview.' Martha turned away to add more water to the pot. 'Don't 'ee remember?'

Toby grunted. 'First I've heard of it!'

Martha's cheeks had turned a little pink, but she answered steadily, 'Well she mentioned it to all the rest of us – must have been while you were doing something at the forge. She wasn't making any secret of the fact. She had to wait for hours to see this Mr Grey, and it was threatening rain – so very sensibly she called in on my sister for a while.' As she spoke she refilled her husband's cup. 'She was telling about it for at least a half an hour – you know what Vee is like – even to the jam that Dorcas gave her with her tea!'

'I don't know why you encourage her to go down there so much,' Toby grumbled. 'Your father would be proper vexed if he found out.' He took another slurp of tea, but he seemed mollified.

Martha turned back to her visitor. 'But, Will, that just proves what we were telling you. She didn't say a word about peculiar goings-on – and, knowing Verity, she would have burst with it if she'd've noticed anything.'

The Sergeant gave a private smile, disguised by his moustache, partly because he knew what they did not – their daughter had clearly held her tongue this time – but also because Martha had called him 'Will' before she thought. She hadn't called him by that name for years

27

– not since he was a strapping policeman in the prime of life and Martha was no older than Verity was now. And nobody had since. (His wife had always called him Billie as though he were a goat, or William if she was annoyed with him.) It took him back. Did Martha ever think about those times as well? He didn't look at her, but he could feel her eyes on him. He sipped at his drink, crooking his little finger as Ivy taught him to: 'makes you look a bit genteel', she used to say.

He glanced up. Both Tregorrans were gazing expectantly at him. He put down his cup quickly and licked his pencil end again. 'But she was out there, that evening? You can vouch for that? Thing is, it might have seemed quite innocent to her, but if I could talk to her a bit – find out who she saw and where they were – it might even remind her of something she'd forgot. Perhaps I could find her down the factory?' It came out as a question, and – perhaps because Tobias was such a massive man – Will found himself adding, 'If you've no objection?' Though of course, as a policeman he had every right to interview their daughter if he wished. He put his notebook carefully away.

Toby set his cup and saucer down and pushed them both away. His hands were huge and roughened with hard work. If he'd crooked his little finger while he drank it would have looked absurd. Will hid his own plump ones under the tabletop.

The blacksmith heaved a sigh that shook his massive frame. 'Well, I'm glad it isn't worse. I've been too quick to judge. The Lord be praised, there's nothing to forgive. Yes, talk to 'er by all means – I can't object to that. Want to call back this evening and see her here, do 'ee?'

Will was about to shake his head – Verity would never talk freely with her parents there – but he caught Martha's eye and some inspiration made him say, 'I might do that very thing – if I can't find her down the factory. But, since she's not here now, I'd best be on my way. I've got other things to do,' he added, rising to his feet. He smiled at Martha, 'Thank you for the tea' and then to Toby, 'and thank you for your time. I didn't mean to interrupt your work.'

Tobias spat into the fire. 'Not much to interrupt. I've left young Sam Chegwidden in there to blaw the furnace – he's too small to be much use for anything, but with this war you take what you can get – and I came in to see had Martha made a pot of tea. By and by I'll go back out and make those hooks she wants, but that won't pay the bills. Not much paid work to speak of, the way things are these days.'

'Shoeing horses, surely?' Will was startled into speech. Toby was not given to confidences, much.

The blacksmith shook his head. 'Army's requisitioned half of them – and it's not just the shoeing that has disappeared. No horses means there aren't the chains and cartwheels to mend – or make – and with so many men away to war, I don't get tools so much. More forks and shovels on the farms than hands to work them, nowadays.' He shrugged his massive shoulders. 'Mending fire irons for a widow – that's all I've done today. And what kind of living can you make from that?'

'Always be work for blacksmiths,' Will said, cheerfully. 'Or what kind of world would we be living in?' He was already sidling to the door, which Martha was holding patiently ajar.

'Don't worry, Father. Something will turn up. The Lord will provide — isn't that what you are always telling us?' Will had forgotten about the girl with plaits, but she spoke softly from the shadows by the stairs.

Tobias clearly half-suspected that she was mocking him. 'Well, let's just hope He does so, Constance!' he retorted. 'And don't quote Scripture back at me. Honour your mother and your father, that's what the Good Book says.'

There was a dreadful silence. Martha caught her breath, but the girl's face was a mask of innocence. After a few seconds, though, she said, 'I'll go and see to Faith,' and scuttled up the stairs.

Toby nodded, looking satisfied, as if he'd won a battle of some kind. He leaned back on his bench and said, quite heartily, 'Well, Sergeant, let us know when you have spoke to Vee!'

The moment of family tension had passed, but it had been an awkward one and Will was relieved to find himself outside the house again. He crammed his helmet on his head, then climbed onto his bike and a moment later he was streaming down the hill — a lot more quickly than he generally did.

—

Martha made the excuse of fetching fresh water to go into the yard, so that she could watch the sergeant down the hill and out of sight. Poor man, he'd been embarrassed, she could see. And not just by Toby either, she thought with a smile. Never could stop his face from showing what he thought.

No, she told herself severely. She was imagining things — thinking she could flutter hearts at her age! She made a rueful face and dipped the ladle-pot into the water butt. There had been a time when he was sweet on her – but no good to think of that! Her family would never have permitted it, even if Will had been nearer to her age. Father'd had his eyes on Toby for her from the very start. 'A good, godly Strict Adherent, and a steady sort of man.' And that was that.

Mind, things were different then, nobody asked a girl's opinion much and there was none of this free education, like her own daughters had. Even the boys round here didn't have much schooling in those days, on the whole, and if you were a girl you learned to read at Sunday school, or not at all. She paused in her ladling, remembering her early struggles with the spelling books and *Bible Stories Retold for the Young*. But she had stuck with it and done very well in time – prizes and scholar's tickets to the Tea Treats every year.

Now everybody learned to read and write, it seemed, though none of the girls but Verity seemed to value it. Didn't know their own good fortune, Martha thought. Her own ma had never learned to cypher all her life, and had to write a cross to sign her name, right up until she died, though she could add a bill up in her head as quick as wink.

But, what was she up to, daydreaming like this? The bucket was so full it would be hard to carry in. Martha let the ladle dangle on its string and put the metal-grid lid back onto the water butt. Toby had made the cover, to his own design – it let in the rain but helped to keep the birds and creatures out. She picked up the water pail. It was very heavy – she'd filled it to the brim and in any case it was a metal one. Her husband had made that for her as well.

Toby was like that – he was clever with his hands. He'd been a good provider, never drank or swore and had never lifted a hand to her, and rarely to any of the girls. Father had chosen well for her, according to his lights – and she had grown fond of Toby, in his way. Something to give thanks for, really.

'Here, woman, let me have that, do. You're spilling half of it!' Her husband's voice startled her into spilling more, but she relinquished the pail with some relief from her two hands into his enormous one.

'I'll put it in the scullery, where you can easy get to it,' he said, carrying it inside as though it had no weight at all.

How many husbands would do as much, she thought as she followed Toby back into the house. She should be thankful for her lot – not having ungrateful thoughts about widowed police sergeants! 'I'll see if me saffron's risen,' she said with a smile, moving the old teacloth that was covering the bowl. 'And you can have some with your bit of supper later on. Yes, it's looking handsome. You can taste the mixture, if you like, though I 'spect you'll be wanting to get back out the forge? Even Sam Chegwidden will have blown the fire by now.'

But her husband didn't take the hint and go. He stood in the doorway of the scullery, filling it and looking at her keenly with his deep grey eyes. 'What was it kept you at the water butt so long? I was feared you might have dropped the pail, or tripped and hurt yourself.'

She laughed. 'Just daydreaming as usual. I'm worse than Verity!' Dreaming about Will Jeffries, she thought guiltily.

Toby smiled his slow smile. 'S'all right then. I'll get back to me work.' He turned away – then suddenly turned back. 'Anythin' happened to you, Martha, I don't know what I'd do.'

She'd turned the saffron dough out and was punching it. 'Silly!' she said, as lightly as she could. 'What you think is going to 'appen? Fall in the fire and bake myself along with these 'ere buns? Get along with you, or I won't get this baking done before the younger girls get home. They'll want some bread and jam when they get in from school. Grace has only been down the schoolhouse for a week or two – poor little mite will be worn out with listening and copying letters on her slate. Then Faith will wake up any minute, crying for her feed. And don't forget, you've got those hooks to make.'

Her husband nodded and turned away again. But still he did not leave. 'Don't like that policeman coming here,' he said.

She was about to protest that Sergeant Jeffries was of no account to her, when Toby went on: 'You don't suppose that Verity saw anything, do you? I wouldn't want her mixed up in it, if something nasty happened and it came to court.'

Martha laughed aloud, though partly from relief. 'Oh, Toby! Course she didn't. She'd have told us, if she had. When did Verity ever learn to hold her tongue?'

To her surprise her husband shook his head. 'Our Vee can keep a secret when it pleases her. She thinks that I don't notice how she looks for an excuse to call round to the Chegwiddens every whip and while – but, not being a horse with blinkers, naturally I do.'

Martha said, 'Well, what is wrong with that?' although she knew quite well, of course. 'They're neighbours, after all. And isn't their Sammy working in the forge with you?'

33

'It isn't Sam she's after, it's that Ned of theirs. Goes to find out if he's written home – and Edna Chegwidden has no more sense than to read his letters out and even show the pictures that he's sent.'

'Who told you that?' said Martha, remembering just in time that she mustn't add, 'It wasn't me!' and prove she'd known herself. 'Young Sammy, I suppose?'

Toby nodded. 'He says his mother's glad to have her come, so she can share her news with someone. I wish she wouldn't, it encourages the girl. I do believe our Vee is rather sweet on Ned. If he was living nearer, I'd be quite concerned.'

Martha kept her eyes fixed on her baking tray. 'The Chegwiddens are nice people. Good chapel folk, as well. Verity could do a great deal worse,' she said.

But her husband's mood had altered. 'And a great deal better, too. You know as well as I do what the Good Book says "be not yoked with unbelievers"!' He hadn't raised his voice, but you could tell he was displeased.

'They're not "unbelievers" – they're good chapel folk – at least the mother is...' But it was too late. He'd gone out through the kitchen and she heard him slam the door.

Martha made a little face and put the buns to do their 'second rising' by the kitchen fire. Hardly had she done so than Constance came downstairs, holding a red-faced, crying infant in her arms.

'Faith's woken up,' she murmured, handing her sister to their mother as she spoke. 'Have you got some water on? She needs a wash and change. I'll do it if you're busy.' She was already at the hearth. 'There's not much in the kettle. What's happened to the pail?'

34

'Out in the scullery,' Martha said, pushing Faith's damp hair back from her face and bouncing the child so the sobbing stopped. 'Your father put it there.'

But Constance had already disappeared. She came in with the refilled kettle and put it on the trivet by the fire, then turned to her mother and made a little face. 'I heard him slamming out. It woke the baby up. What was that about? Not me, again, I hope?'

Martha shook her head. 'No you're a good girl, Constance. As I'm sure he knows. Your father's not a bad man, it's just he fears the Lord. And that policeman coming here about our Verity upset him – that's all.'

'Oh!' Constance had rummaged in a pile of clean, washed rags and laid one on the table. 'I thought I'd vexed him earlier, with quoting scripture back. But if it's only Verity, I needn't fret. Let me have the child.' She laid Faith on the table, stripped off the dirty cloth, sponged the little bottom and pinned on a clean new rag. 'There now, that's better, isn't it? We'll find some milk for you. You got it ready, Ma?'

Martha nodded. 'I'll put a bit of tea and sugar in, to help her sup it up.' She went out to the scullery and brought back the metal feeding cup. It had a clever sort of spout that let the infant drink. Toby had made it when their firstborn came and all the girls had used it in their turn. She filled it with the mixture and handed it to Constance, who gave Faith her feed. 'You're some good with babies, Constance,' she said, gathering up the dirty cloths to boil. 'Better than I am myself, I think.'

Con turned pink with pleasure at the compliment but she answered with a laugh. 'Better than Verity in any case. I've seen her feeding Faith. Forgets what she is doing, and half drowns the little mite. "Never make a proper mother"

35

– that's what Grandpa says – always got her mind on something else. Wonder if she likes it down that factory?'

Martha said, 'I 'spect so', but her thoughts were somewhere else. For some reason it had popped into her mind to wonder what Ned Chegwidden was doing as they spoke.

–

Ned Chegwidden was crawling through the mud. He and Davy Warren had been sent out to mend the wire. There was too much mist for snipers, but there was always random fire and the possibility of falling into craters in the murk, so they were wriggling their way back to the safety of the trench. To add to their misery it was raining solidly.

Davy snagged himself on something and Ned heard him curse. It still shocked him sometimes, the language Davy used, but there were things round here that would make a saint blaspheme. The dratted mud, for one. Ned had been raised a country boy, of course, so he was better off than some – there were lads who had never so much as walked across ploughed land until they volunteered. But this wasn't honest farm mud, or bog – like on the moors – this was horrid French mud and it got everywhere: down your neck and in your boots and even in your tea. And it stank to high heaven – though no wonder, perhaps, considering what got sucked down into it. There was half a corpse emerging from it just outside their trench – legs which still had boots on, sticking sideways in the air. Just legs, very rigid, but no body visible. Ned was not even certain if the owner was attached or had been blown to pieces on the way to Kingdom Come. The sight had made him almost sick at first, but now – like everybody else – he had got used to it.

A shell went screeching overhead and he flung himself face down, trying to drive himself deeper in the mud. It hardly mattered, he thought bitterly. He could not be more muddy than he already was. The shell exploded somewhere far away, sending up a sullen red glow that pierced the gloom. A form rose, white and eerie in the mist from a crater nearby.

Ned felt his blood run cold, but it was not a ghost. It was a mud-caked soldier, struggling with a limp. 'Are you B compa—?'

Suddenly the rat-tat of machine-gun fire rang out. The solider gave a cry and fell back in his hole. Then there was silence and the day was still again, except for the distant moaning of some poor fellows further up, whom the stretcher-bearers had not managed to collect. And this was what the Major called a 'lull' and 'a quiet portion of the front'. Ned had overheard him making a report.

Another shell went shrieking and Dave gave a shout. 'The mist is thinning and they've got our range. They're going to start bombarding – we'll have to run for it. Bloody Huns!' And he was on his feet, half-crouching, half-slithering and running for the trench. Ned waited for a moment, wondering if he should go and help the soldier in the hole – he shouted, but there was no answer from the man. The machine gun spoke again. Dave was right. Another minute and Ned would be sniper-fodder, too. He chose his moment, squatting, till the light had passed, then set off scampering, bent double at the waist.

Twice he lost his footing, once tripped across a corpse, but finally he made the entrance to a trench. He was not sure it was his own, but he dived into it – just as a bullet pinged beside his hand. He sank down on a sandbag, wiping mud out of his eyes and rubbing his leg where he had gashed it nastily.

'Cocoa, soldier?' Someone handed him a mug – and mud or not, it seemed the best drink that he'd ever tasted in his life.

It was the right trench, but the other end of it, and it was a long, stooping scuttle down to his own outfit, trying to keep his head down all the way. He reported to the Major, a young, bluff, hearty man, who was sitting in a widened portion of the trench with what they called a GI cover over it – meaning a piece of galvanized iron serving as a roof. It was big enough to take a table, like a proper room, and the Major had an oil lamp and an inkstand close at hand.

He looked up from his writing. 'Well done, Chegwidden. I hear you fixed the wire. Glad to see you safe. Private Warren said he'd lost you in the mist.'

So Dave was safely back. Ned gave a weary smile.

The Major looked at him more closely. 'Very well, Chegwidden, permission to stand down. You are excused from sentry duty for today. Get yourself cleaned up and have a meal, then get yourself some rest. You look done in and we'll be moving at first light.'

'Yessir! Thank you, sir!' Ned saluted and made his way along the trench. He saw Davy Warren, sitting on a fire step with a little group of other off-duty Tommies. Someone had a ukelele and they were singing bawdy songs. Dave waved to him to join them, but he shook his head.

He'd have to get up and join the others later on and heat up a ghastly meal of lukewarm stew (you couldn't warm things properly on the mess stove in your kit, and Maconochie was horrible in any case – tinned lumps of something disgusting that they claimed was beef and unrecognizable vegetables in a sort of gravy soup). There was no mess kitchen this far up the line. They'd brought the only water in old fuel cans, too, so things tasted of petrol – even tea, unless you put your rum ration into it.

He grinned. What would they say at chapel if they knew that he had rum? Not that he ever drank it on its own – it was too strong for that. And he didn't touch his cigarette ration at all – though he always took his share. You could swap it with people who were dying for a smoke. Sometimes they'd even give you chocolate – or a piece of a cake that somebody had sent.

He was glad to retire to his allocated space – what they called a dugout: just a hollow in the wall, where you wrapped your coat around you and did your best to sleep. He took out the tin in which he kept his things, found a candle and a pencil stub and wrote his daily letter to his ma. (They only got posted now and then, of course, but he knew his family were reading them to Vee – and writing a bit daily made him feel in touch.)

'Dear Ma and everyone,' he wrote, 'I hope this finds you well. I am doing well and in good health. Thank you for the parcel with the home-made vest and socks.' He broke off as a rat went splashing through the mud and disappeared beneath the duckboards which were all the floor there was. He watched it out of sight, then sucked his pencil and began again. 'Both very welcome as it is sometimes damp at night...'

He grinned as he folded up the note and put it in his box. Probably the censor would cross that last bit out. It didn't really matter. No one at Rosvene could imagine this mud hole anyway. Just as well, perhaps. Because, surely, this must be what Hell was like? Wouldn't it surprise the chapel folks at home, he thought, if they discovered that Hell was made of mud, and wasn't a fiery furnace after all?

And then he didn't think anything at all, because he was so weary that – despite the mud and the shells which were falling nearer now – he'd dropped his pencil and was fast asleep. Dave had to wake him later to come and warm his tin of stew.

Three

Vee washed her hands with carbolic in the big white cloakroom sink. She took off the new overall and cap that they had issued her and hung them on the hook where they had written up her name. She was copying her sister Prudence, who had just done the same, so she didn't show herself up, first day, and get teased like new girls did.

'How did you get on then?' Pru was asking, in a friendly offhand way.

But Vee didn't answer. She had caught sight of Sergeant Jeffries through the open door. He was standing at the gate, leaning on his heavy policeman's bicycle. He was pretending to watch the other girls as they streamed through the gate, but Verity knew at once that he had come for her.

Her heart sank to her neatly mended boots. Drat that Mrs Dawes, she muttered inwardly. 'Drat' was the strongest word she knew, but it was well deserved. All smiles and promises, that policeman's wife – and now look what she'd done! There was the Sergeant – everyone would see, and the news would be all over the factory next day. Verity would be lucky if she kept her precious job!

Not that it had been as much fun as she'd hoped, packing pats of butter into tins for hours with someone breathing down your neck if you so much as spoke a word – but there was the prospect of that pay packet in a little while. True it was only half the normal rate – she'd be on 'trainee wages' for a month at least – and most of that would have to go to Mother for her keep, but Vee had never had money of her own before. Of course they stopped a little for your uniform, until you'd paid for it, so that was another three or four pence gone, but suppose she had a penny or a ha'penny left each week – even allowing for the collection plate on Sunday and paying for things like mending her own boots – it could add up to sixpence in a month or two.

She was already making plans about what she'd do with it. Spend it on a notebook and pencil, perhaps – or there was a paper magazine that was published just for girls, with letters and stories and all sorts inside. The teacher at her school had shown her, so it was respectable. Even Grandfather could hardly disapprove. Course, it came out monthly and she couldn't run to that, but she might save up and buy the Christmas issue, perhaps? No end of reading there would be in that.

And now here was Sergeant Jeffries, come to ruin it all! Mr Grey would never keep you on, if you were thought to be in any kind of trouble with the police. And news would reach him, sure as eggs were eggs. What was worse, she'd brought it on herself. What had possessed her to go rushing off to the police station like that, just because she'd seen that fellow signalling? Though, of course, she'd meant to speak to that nice young PC Dawes, who might have had some tact – not awful Sergeant Jeffries with his whiskers and his sneers.

'Here, Verity, what on earth's got into you? Packed your senses up in one of the butter tins, or what? Aren't you coming home? Or are you going to stand there staring like a witnick half the night?' Pru gave her a sharp nudge with her elbow as she spoke. 'What is it that you're looking at, in any case?' She poked her head in front of Vee to look out of the door. 'Oh, I see. That Sergeant. Wonder what he wants? Bringing bad news for some poor soul, I 'spect – probably an accident down Penvarris mine.'

Verity brightened. 'You think it might be that?' She felt instantly ashamed of being pleased.

'That's what brought him last time,' Pru said, with a shrug. 'Though I never heard the siren this time, come to think, so there can't be many dead. Still, if it's your pa, I suppose it's as bad to you as if there's dozens killed. Now, are you going to put on this shawl and come home, or what?' She was shaking it in front of her sister as she spoke, like a housemaid with a tablecloth.

Vee allowed herself to be wrapped in the warm plaid. 'Aren't we going to wait for Patience?'

Pru gave a little laugh. 'I shouldn't think she'd like it if we did. Wants to stop and talk to someone, I expect.'

She said it in such a peculiar tone of voice that Vee whirled round at once. 'You don't mean a man?'

Pru laughed. 'I didn't say that, did I? And don't you go saying anything at home. In any case, suppose it was a man? Where would be the harm? Patience is eighteen, near enough. Lots of girls of her age are married, with children of their own.'

'So it is a man? A Strict Adherent?' Verity was torn between amazement and a kind of shocked delight at being entrusted with this secret. 'Pa would not allow it otherwise!'

'Don't ask so many questions – and you won't be told no lies. What Pa don't know he can't complain about,' Pru said. 'Besides, there aren't that many Strict Adherents, especially not our age – wait for one of those you could be waiting all your life.'

'Or end up with some frightful widower like old Ephraim Tull,' Vee said. 'Terribly holy but never known to smile. Though I've thought he had an eye for Patience once or twice.'

'More than that. Came round once to ask Pa could he offer for her hand!' Pru gave Vee a wicked little nudge. 'Can you imagine! Patience was horrified, of course, and couldn't answer him. Pa had to say she was too young to marry yet – and when she was he wouldn't force her to marry anyone. I was on the landing and I heard it all – though no one knows I know. So Ephraim went away. But I think he still has hopes.'

'Here! You don't suppose that's what she's frightened of – and that's why she's busy looking out for someone else?'

Pru laughed. 'Don't be daft. You're spinning stories in your head again. This is nothing. Just a bit of chat. Now, come on home – forget I ever said. Patience will catch up with us along the road.'

So Verity jammed her old grey bonnet onto her head and followed her sister outside. But she knew in her heart that there wasn't a mining accident down at Penvarris mine. Sergeant Jeffries had come to talk to her.

–

The Sergeant was doing his best to look 'avuncular'. (It was the word the police commissioner had used, during his training, and it had stuck with him. 'Like a kindly uncle' – that was what it meant, and it was desirable when dealing with young ladies, it appeared, provided you did not suspect them of a crime.) And Verity Tregorran was in employment now, so she was a young lady – not a wayward child.

He bestowed his best kind-uncle smile on her. 'Miss Verity Tregorran? Could I have a word?'

She did not seem pleased to see him, despite his best attempts. 'Sergeant Jeffries!' she mumbled with a frown.

The pretty dark girl with her looked appalled. 'Lummy, Vee, what have you gone and done!' That would be her sister Pru, Will realized. He had not seen her for a year or two, and she'd turned out handsome. Martha would be proud. And wasn't there another, older girl, as well? Though there did not seem to be any sign of her.

Verity was pushing back the curls which strayed out from her hat. 'It's all right, Pru, I know what it's about. Just something I said to Constable Dawes's wife the other day.'

The girl called Prudence dug her in the ribs. 'And now you wish you hadn't, by the look of you!'

'Well, are you surprised? Everybody's staring!' Verity's cheeks had turned a flaming pink. She turned a pair of furious eyes on Will. 'If we've got to have this conversation, let's go down the road a bit where we won't be on view – though I suppose, it's too late now. There, Mr Grey has seen us – now I'll lose my job I 'spect. How could you be so daft as to come and find me here? Too late, he's coming over!'

The girl was right, he realized. Everyone in the factory yard had turned to stare at them, including a stout man in a dust-coat and incongruous bowler hat, who was hurrying towards them with a ledger in his hand and was clearly a person of some authority. 'Now then, young lady, what exactly is going on?'

45

'I need to question Miss Verity, that's all!' Will tried to sound important.

Grey looked at her again. 'Why it's that new girl that I took on yesterday! Wanted for questioning? Well, young woman, you can see me afterwards. I'll give you what's owing, but that's the end of it. We can't have our employees bringing policemen to our door. It creates a bad impression for our customers!' He gestured to the courtyard where a horse and dray was being loaded with crates of butter tins, milk powder and cheese. The driver and assistant – like everybody else – had stopped to watch the little drama at the gate. 'And Miss Prudence, I'm surprised at you. Letting your sister bring us into disrepute.'

Will cursed himself for being such an idiot. Now one of Martha's girls was likely to lose her post and another had a scolding – and Verity was right, it was all his silly fault. He'd only thought of finding her alone – without her father breathing down his neck – and (admittedly) of giving her a fright, so that she wouldn't come bothering Mrs Dawes with foolish tales. He hadn't meant to get her into trouble with her boss. Well, he'd have to do his best to get her out of it.

'Mr Grey – I understand that is your name? You are quite mistaken in your attitude. Miss Verity is, if anything, an ornament to your establishment. She has – quite rightly – tried to contact me because she saw something that she thought suspicious on the cliffs. Exactly what any citizen should do in time of war. You would not wish to punish her for doing that, I'm sure?'

Grey clearly held the police in gratifying awe. He took his hat off and turned the brim between his hands. 'Well, officer, if you put it that way, I suppose! But couldn't

46

you have interviewed her somewhere else? What do you imagine our customers will think?'

Will put on his most important face. 'I'm sorry about your customers, but it was particularly convenient for me to come and find her here. This factory is not far from where the incident occurred. I am hoping she can show me exactly where it was, so that we can launch a search and full enquiry.' He was improvising wildly – he hadn't really intended to waste more time by going out there at all – but Grey seemed to be impressed.

The man was still nervously fiddling with his hat. 'And what am I to tell them?' he gestured at the cart.

Will had an inspiration. He winked and tapped his nose. 'You can tell them anything you like – but keep this to yourself. This whole affair may prove to be quite inno-cent – indeed I hope it does – but in times like these...' He let the sentence hang. 'I rely on your discretion.'

'You can count on me, officer!' Grey, as he'd hoped, was flattered. 'And I'm sorry, Miss Verity, if I was quick to judge. We'll see you both tomorrow and I'll say no more of it.' He turned to Will again. 'And never fear, I know how to keep things underneath me 'at!' And, as if to prove the literal truth of that, he jammed his bowler on and hurried back towards the factory. 'Now then, move along there – there's nothing here to see. Bit of bad news for those girls that's all.' And, as if he'd pushed a button, there was a general shuffling and everyone resumed what they were doing earlier.

Will turned to Verity. She was staring at him as though she could not quite believe what she had heard. 'You're really taking it serious, what I said to Mrs Dawes? I thought you'd only laugh.'

He found he was impatient suddenly. 'I said I'd take a look with you, that's all.' He whirled to frown at Prudence. 'Not you. You can go off home. And mind you hold your tongue about what happened here.' He didn't want Martha learning that he'd nearly cost her daughter her position, or that he'd had to make a proper song and dance of things.

'Oh she can keep a secret, can't you, Pru?' Verity's green–grey eyes were sparkling now. With excitement, probably, he realized ruefully. But he'd have to go through with this foolish expedition to the cliffs – though of course there was nothing to be found.

There wasn't, either – just a trampled patch beside the stile where people had been walking, like they always did. Nothing more sinister than a broken cycle clip and an apple core.

'That's where he was standing, signalling with the lamp!' Verity said, pointing. 'Just about this time of day, it was. A little earlier, perhaps, but it was darker with the rain.'

Will pushed his helmet further back. 'Well, he isn't here now, is he? Supposing there was ever anyone at all. It seems to me that your imagination's been at work again, my girl. I promised Mrs Dawes I would come to talk to you – she thought it might be smugglers you saw – but there's no sign of anything. Not even any recent footprints on the cove that I can see. There's been a deal of trouble for nothing much at all – cost me a whole day's effort and nearly cost your job. So next time that you fancy that you've seen a spy – or a dragon, come to that – just make sure you catch him before you come to me. Do you hear?'

Verity looked chagrined. 'But you told Mr Grey that I—'

'I know what I told him. And now I'm telling you. There's too much imagination in that head of yours. So now, you get off home before the day turns any darker than it already is.' He ought to offer to accompany her, he knew, but he didn't have a lantern and it was getting dusk – and he had his cycle which he couldn't ride back without a lamp. Serve her right to walk home in the gloom, this once. He threw his leg across the crossbar, 'You mind what I said!'

And he cycled off without her. The last thing that he saw, she was hurrying forlornly in his wake along the road.

–

'Joe Martin, can't you talk a bit of sense? Of course our Effie isn't looking down on us. This was her home for seven years. How wouldn't she bring us a bit of something, now and then? Shop butter and jam is getting very scarce – and such a price I'd never think of paying out for them. Effie only means it as a bit of a treat, that's all. If you don't want it, leave it – just means more for all the rest of us.'

Effie sighed. She had called in to see her aunt and uncle for an hour. She ought to go more often, she was aware of that – after all, Madge had taken her in when Mother died (with Pa in lodgings and working down the mine, he couldn't cope with a young daughter on his own), and when Pa'd had that awful accident Madge and Joe had given up their own room to nurse him back to health while they slept in the best parlour on the horsehair chairs. Effie had plenty to be grateful for.

But though she was a married woman, and with social standing too, she was still treated in this house like the child she used to be. And nothing was ever right for Uncle Joe.

Take this afternoon. If she hadn't brought them something he'd have grumbled about that! Though he was spreading the bought butter on his bit of bread, she saw. No jam — nobody in this house ever had them both at once, unless it was Christmas or their birthday. They would be scandalized if they'd seen Alex eating toast — they were scandalized enough when she married him. Not only was he 'from a hoity-toity family' but he was a 'bloody policeman' and Joe hated them, after they'd broken up a protest at Penvarris mine.

Funny to think she'd once lived in this crowded little house. Of course there were fewer cousins to cram it nowadays. Peg was married, and Meg in service now — and even little Samuel was old enough to work down at the mine, even if only as 'kiddlyboy'. He had been doing the most menial jobs, like taking tools to be sharpened, though today it seemed he had progressed to holding the bore-piece in the hole while someone hammered it.

'Force of it goes right up through you — makes your teeth rattle,' he reported proudly now, sinking his own into a slice of bread and jam. 'Some nice taste, Effie,' he added, through the crumbs. 'Which reminds me, I saw your pa today, working at the shaking-tables.'

Effie nodded. Her pa had to be content with a surface job these days. His accident had left him with a weakness in his leg that made it near impossible to go back underground. But he'd grown skilled at what he did, and had almost grown resigned to grading tin instead of mining it. 'I called to see them yesterday,' she said.

Uncle Joe made a hurrumphing sound. 'Why he had to go and marry that Mrs Richards, I shall never know,' he muttered, holding out his plate while Madge cut more bread for him. 'Man of his age! Ought to have more sense.'

He was only being awkward, because of course he knew. Pa had felt so guilty when her only son was blinded in that same accident – Pa had been the leader of the team – that he'd tried to support the pair of them in the best way he knew. And truth to tell, it had worked out very well. Pa had lived in rented lodgings half his life, while Jilly Richards was a widow with a cottage she was struggling to keep, so the marriage suited both of them.

'Don't be so cussed, Joe,' Madge was saying now, as she and Effie folded clean washing after tea. 'Walter is looking happier than he's been for years. To say nothing of him being better fed, and his laundry better washed.' She winked at Effie. Was it imagination, or was Madge mellowing, now that she was not rushed off her feet all day with all those mouths to feed? 'But I'm glad you drop in now and then to see your pa,' she went on, with a sly glance at her niece.

'Which reminds me, you'll never guess who called in here and was asking after you.'

'Who?' said Effie, although she guessed at once. 'Not Peter Kellow?' Poor Peter, they had been childhood sweethearts years ago – he'd given her a kiss in the school-yard when they were six and, though they'd grown up since and she married Alex Dawes, he'd never looked at anybody else. Cousin Meg had thrown her cap at him, in vain.

'Course it was Peter Kellow,' Joe said. 'Came in purposely!'

'He never did,' Madge contradicted. 'He was telling about a high-up fellow who's been going around Cornish mines, wanting skilled men to sign up in some special Tunnellers Brigade. Badly needed for the war apparently, and anyone who's skilled with dynamite can earn six bob a day. He thought your uncle might be interested – though it would take more than that to stir Joe to anything.'

'It's a lot of money, though,' Effie said, covering her surprise at how this news had chilled her heart. 'Most soldiers only get a shilling, don't they?' She knew her face was scarlet but she didn't care. She was worried enough about Alex as it was, without her oldest childhood friend going off to war as well. And underground tunnelling with dynamite? What would that be for? Undermining enemy positions, probably? That sounded wickedly dangerous – as if it wasn't bad enough above the ground, with Germans shooting cannons at you all the time.

'That's a damty sight more than we're earning down the shaft,' Joe said. 'That's why he came to say. They're specially looking for experience, he said – but I'm too old for tricks like that and I've a wife and family to think about. Surprised he didn't go himself, though – he's a single man.' He shot a look at Effie as he spoke.

Effie found that she was breathing out, in her relief – though she hadn't been aware that she'd been holding in!

But Aunt Madge was speaking. 'He told you, Joe – there's wolfram in the big shaft down Penvarris pit, and that's essential for making armaments. They aren't looking to take men who are extracting that. That's why this general didn't go recruiting there – though several fellows heard and signed in any case. But Peter'd rather stay round here, at any rate, I 'spect.' She gave Effie that knowing grin again.

'The Lord knows why he bothers,' Uncle Joe replied. 'Broke his heart, you did, my girl, marrying that damty policeman. Think yourself too good for common miners, I suppose.'

'If you can't say something nice to Effie when she comes to call, then don't say anything,' his wife exclaimed. She turned to Effie. 'Born finding fault, he was. If angels were showing him into Paradise, he'd find something wasn't right! Suppose he ever got to Paradise at all, what with his language and his visits down the Tinner's Arms!' Madge had been brought up Methodist, like Ma, and did not approve of alcohol – though, to do him justice, Joe only went to the Tinner's after union meetings, once a month at most, and even then he only had a single glass of ale. Effie had never known him come home 'worse for wear'.

But Joe (as if to prove Madge right) turned argumentative. 'Good God, woman! What do you expect? Have to wash my mouth out if I say "damty" or permit myself a drink? Worse than those Strict Adherents, the way you carry on!' He was stirring his cup of strong brown tea. 'And can't a man run to a bit of sugar now and then? Can't be that expensive, surely?'

'Yes it damty can!' Madge slammed down the folded teacloths with a bang.

Any minute there was going to be a row, but Effie had learned long ago how to stop an argument. 'Talking of Strict Adherents, I met one yesterday.' She told them about Verity and the lantern on the cliffs. 'Could it have been smugglers, do you think?'

'Shouldn't think so for a minute.' Her uncle made a face. 'Why did she come telling you about it, any'ow?'

'She came to talk to Alex,' Effie said. 'But of course, he wasn't there.' She tried to keep the sudden quaver from her voice, but failed.

Joe must have realized she was genuinely upset, because he changed the subject hastily. 'Well, better get you home before it gets too late,' he said. 'Wait while I get a lantern. I'll need it coming back.'

He wasn't usually so thoughtful, and Effie was quite touched – though of course Joe had to spoil it by grumbling all the way.

Four

Verity was hot and breathless by the time that she got home – though Crowdie had passed her in the farmcart and given her a ride to the bottom of the hill. By the time she reached the smithy it was almost dark, with just the faintest moon to help her see her way.

She braced herself for trouble as she raised the latch. The rest of the family were sitting round the table, eating soup, and they all watched in silence as she hung up her shawl and hat.

Her father put his spoon down and she waited for the onslaught of jawing' to begin. But all he said was: 'Sergeant Jeffries came to see you, then?'

She sank down at her place by Constance on the bench. 'You know about all that?'

Pa broke a piece of bread and mopped his plate with it. 'Told me he was going to. Called here to see you – but you weren't home, of course.' He raised an eyebrow at her. 'Seemed to think you'd seen something awkward on the cliffs? Pru said he took you out there to point out the place to him.'

'Pa knew about the policeman, anyhow,' Prudence muttered scarlet-faced. 'Had to say something, how you were so late.' Vee glanced around the table. All her sisters were still staring up at her, except for Patience who refused to meet her eyes. In fact, her eldest sister was

55

looking very odd, pinker than Hope's school pinafore and carefully concentrating on her empty bowl. Verity shrugged her shoulders. Perhaps there'd been trouble about her chatting to that man. If Pa had found out there would be the deuce to pay. But she herself had got off lightly, for a change. Pa and Ma knew everything it seemed and there was no need to fear a row – or lines and lines of Bible verses to be learned by heart.

'The Sergeant must've thought it was important,' Pa was saying now. 'But you hadn't said anything to us.'

'Well, it was really nothing,' Vee answered, with a laugh.

Best to make as little of it as she could. 'I saw a man out by the stile, the other night, that's all. Trouble was, I spoke to Mrs Dawes, and she thought it might be smugglers – though it doesn't seem it was… Why, what is it, Pattie?' Her sister had made a strangled noise and jumped up from her chair.

Patience, more red-faced than ever, sat down and shook her head. 'Nothing! Swallowed a bit of something the wrong way, that's all.'

'But…' Verity began, and saw Pru shake her head. 'Shall I fetch you a bit of water from the pail?'

'Please,' Patience managed. 'Then I'll be all right. Just a bit of onion or carrot, I expect.' But of course, it was nothing of the kind. Patience had not been eating at the time, and there was nothing left inside her bowl for her to choke on anyway.

Vee shook her head as she went out to the pail. Just one more strange thing in a day of oddities. First Sergeant Jeffries standing up for her and seeming to take her story very seriously, and then suddenly losing interest when they got out to the cliff. And as for saying that there were no footprints in the cove – did he think she didn't know that the tide would rub them out? But you couldn't argue with a policeman, or with an elder sister either. She filled a glass tumbler – it had once held jam – and took it to Pattie who drank it greedily. But after that she seemed to be avoiding Vee as much as possible.

Apart from that, the evening ran its normal course. Each of the girls had their own chores to do – Verity's was darning, and helping Charity to read – and there was no time or space for sharing secrets, with their parents there.

But when Vee went upstairs, taking a candle, to help get the younger girls to bed, Patience stopped her on the landing and hissed furiously at her, 'What were you thinking of! Getting the story all around the factory that there was trouble in this house!'

'It wasn't my doing,' Vee replied, with truth. 'It was that Mr—'

But her sister cut her off. 'And as for what you said to Pa when you came in! Do that again, and I shall swing for you, I swear!' And she stormed downstairs again.

Vee was completely mystified, but Patience could sometimes be horrid when she chose – especially if she'd had a jawing about something from their pa. In the meantime, there were tasks to do. She and Prudence had their hands full, too, with four little nightshirts to put on, and four lots of hair to brush. There was always an argument, in any case, about whose turn it was to have the pillow end – which two were at the bottom and which two at the top, leaving just space for Vee and Constance either side. (Pru and Patience shared the narrow bunk next door and Faith was in Ma's room in the cradle still, of course.)

But at last all the schoolgirls were in bed and the night-light safely on the windowsill. Vee gently closed the door on them, then turned to Pru and said, 'What's up with Patience?'

Pru just shook her head. 'Not here,' she murmured. 'They won't be sleeping yet. Small pitchers have big ears! Besides, it might be better if you didn't know – you'd blurt the truth to somebody before you thought.' And she led the way downstairs. She had the candle, so Vee had to follow her – and that was clearly all the explanation she was going to get.

–

There was a little bit of awkwardness when they got to the dairy factory next day. Patience had been right. The story of 'bad news' had clearly spread and some of the other girls were frankly curious – and Verity's attempts to shrug off their questions only made things worse.

Of course you couldn't talk once you were in the packing room – young Mr Radjel prowled around and saw to that – but when it was time to pause and eat your lunch (apart from three timed 'pass-outs' to the cloakroom in the day, the factory allowed you fifteen minutes for your meal) several people who were off at the same time huddled together on the far side of the yard, whispering and looking sideways at the Tregorran girls.

Patience was mad as hops with Verity. 'Now see what you have gone and done. Look at everyone – nudging each other and gossiping behind their hands!' She jumped to her feet and off she stalked, her face as red as fire – which only made things worse.

It was Pru who had the inspiration which put paid to it. She left her bit of crowst and sidled up to one girl who had been her friend at school. 'Here, Gloria Tresize! Don't upset our Verity by asking her too much. Her friend's gone for a soldier and his mother's just had news – and well... I won't go into details, but let's hope that he'll pull through!' She spoke just loud enough for other folk to hear.

Vee felt herself turn scarlet – more than Patience had – and hurried back to work before she'd even eaten all her bread and scrape. But it worked like magic – people understood about the dangers of the war. The whispering stopped at once, and when the day was over several people came and asked Vee quite kindly how she liked the job, and telling her little tricks to make it easier. Nobody mentioned soldiers, though, to her relief.

'I can see how that was a clever thing to say,' she remarked to Pru as they went through the gate and turned for home. 'Except I feel a fool because it wasn't really true!'

Pru whirled around to face her. 'What wasn't true about it? Ned Chegwidden is a soldier, isn't he? And he's a friend of yours, and his mother has got news – you told me just the other day that she had heard from him. And of course you hope that he'll survive the war. I never told them one word of a he. If they made something different of it, that is up to them.'

'But now everybody supposes that he's been hurt or killed.' Verity could not leave the subject there. 'It's almost like wishing it on him.'

'Don't be ridiculous. That's superstition, and you know that is a sin!' Pru said.

'And telling whoppers isn't? I don' know what Grandfather or Ephraim Tull would say. Besides, lots of folk round here know Ned – what are they going to think of me when he comes home unscathed?'

'They're going to think that I meant someone else, of course. I never mentioned anybody's name. You ninny, do you suppose that everybody knows that you are sweet on Ned? I thought it was a secret?'

Verity turned red again. 'So did I,' she murmured. 'But it doesn't look like it. You seem to know, for instance.'

'I wasn't sure until this moment,' Pru said, with a leer. 'But you've just admitted it, so I am certain now! So you make sure you help me with my chores from time to time, or I might forget and mention it to Pa.'

Vee looked at her appalled. 'You wouldn't!'

Pru was laughing at her. 'Course I wouldn't, silly goose. Although…' She was interrupted by a shout from behind them in the lane.

'Here, you two. Can't you stop and wait for me?' It was Patience, calling and hurrying after them, though her voice had gone peculiar and strained. She had thrown her cloak and hat on all haphazardly and her face was red and shiny as if she'd been in tears.

Vee said, in genuine astonishment, 'I thought you'd catch us up. Don't you want to stop and…' She trailed off in dismay.

Patience was glaring at her. 'Don't I want to stop and what…'

Vee looked to Pru for guidance but her other sister would not meet her eyes. 'Stop and talk to someone,' she said, in misery. 'I thought you had a friend.'

Patience stamped a buttoned boot. 'Well, I haven't, so there's an end of it. And if I haven't, it's no thanks to you!'

'Oh Pattie!' Prudence sounded quite upset herself. 'He hasn't…?' she bit her lip and stopped.

'Thrown me over?' The older girl was bitter. 'That what you meant to say? Well, he hasn't – cause there wasn't anything to throw. Not that I'd tell you anything, even if there was – you'd only go and blab to Verity. How could you go and do that, when you know what she's like? Mouth bigger than a catfish – and you are just as bad.'

'Oh come on, Pattie,' Pru exclaimed. 'Of course Vee had to know, once she was down the factory and walking home with us. Else she'd have been asking questions where you'd got to every night – and then there would have been proper ructions, wouldn't there?'

Patience tugged her cloak and bonnet straight. 'And aren't there ructions now?'

'Well, it wasn't Vee's fault, Pattie, she didn't say a word. It was the policeman who started all the talk – he really came about some smugglers, and he didn't want it known. I tried to tell you yesterday, only you were too het up to heed. So whatever Vee reported seeing on the cliffs, it wasn't you.'

Verity was so astonished that she blurted out, 'Of course it wasn't her. What would Patience be doing on the cliffs – in working time at that?'

For answer Patience snatched her bonnet off and threw it at the stile. 'Pru Tregorran, now look what you've done. Have you no sense at all?'

Pru shook her head. 'It's all right, Pattie. You leave this to me.' She took Vee by the arm. 'The thing is, Verity, Pattie's done some private errands for young Mr Radjel, now and then.' She made a face at Patience who had tried to interrupt. 'No, let me tell her, Pattie.' She turned to Vee again. 'Shouldn't have asked her really – but she couldn't well refuse, with Mr Radjel being who he is. He arranged the shift so she would not be missed and promised her a little something in return, so the other girls would only get spiteful if they knew. Isn't that so, Pattie?' She waited for Patience to nod reluctantly before adding, 'And it's certain that Mr Grey would not approve – so that's why it's a secret, do you understand?'

Vee was flattered to be in their confidence. She nodded solemnly. 'I won't tell anyone. Cross my heart and hope to die!' It was a vow she'd learned from other girls at school.

The assurance seemed to work. Patience was impatient, but no longer furious. 'Nothing to tell, now, is there? It's all ruined after this. He can't have people gossiping, he said, and that was that. I shan't be going again. So let's say no more about it, and we'll get off home.' All at once, her voice was quavering and there seemed to be angry teardrops standing in her eyes. She picked her battered bonnet up and jammed it on again. Then, without another word, she stormed off up the lane.

Her sisters exchanged glances and hurried after her. Pru tried to soothe her, but she would not be soothed and they all three walked in silence until they reached the house.

–

Ned was feeling something of a fraud. Or he would do, if he wasn't feeling so peculiar – hot and light-headed and his leg was sore besides.

It must have happened on that scamper in the mist back to the trench. He knew he'd gashed himself on something, but it hadn't bled a lot and he hadn't really paid it much attention at the time. He'd cut himself a score of times much worse when he was home, and at first he'd been more concerned about his uniform – though he'd been too tired to bother to sew it up that night.

He managed to take part in the next day's exercise, in which no ground was gained. He was not among the wounded (unlike Davy, who got a bullet in his arm) and he got back all right, but he wasn't moving freely and he was feeling very strange.

But next day his leg was throbbing something terrible and when he rolled his trousers up to look he was alarmed by what he saw. The calf seemed to have swollen up to twice its size and turned a funny colour overnight – and, worst of all, there was a horrid smell. With so many shot and wounded he hardly liked to go complaining, for such a tiny thing, but in the end he had to – he was swaying on his feet.

The Major was emphatic. 'Nothing so useless as a soldier who can't walk. Report to the MO and get that attended to.'

'I can't believe it's got like this so quick!' Ned found himself saying, in the first-aid post.

The Medical Officer took one look and shook his head. 'Got an infection in it – I've seen these things before. Pity you didn't get here earlier, I could have cleaned the wound – but I'm going to have to send you down the line to save your leg, I think.' He was doing something to the wound by now and his voice seemed to be coming from somewhere far away, but the last words jolted Ned.

'Save my leg?' His own voice sounded strangled; the pain was terrible.

'If there's a deep infection in it – and it looks as if there is – it will need debridement or it will spread throughout the limb and I don't have the facilities to do that properly. I've done what I can with it – got a metal splinter out

63

– but the gangrene has gone deep so we'll bathe it with carbolic and bind it up for now.' He put something wet and stinging on the wound. 'You're still fit enough to travel, and there's a relay ambulance, so we'll see what the CCS can do with you.' He turned away, and muttered to an orderly – though Ned was just aware enough to take it in: 'Write down "gas gangrene". No, nothing to do with poison gas, its just a kind of wet gangrene that can spread rapidly. We've got classic symptoms here – high fever, brown-red discharge, putrid smell. But we need to move him fast.'

The orderly murmured something. Ned didn't catch the words. By now he was slipping sideways on the inspection bench, finding it impossible to sit upright.

The MO turned back and took his legs and, with the orderly, moved Ned to a stretcher-bed nearby. 'Of course we've got worse cases, and he's not the only one,' he said, across Ned to the orderly. 'There's so much filth and ordure in the ground – farm manure and rotting corpses, to say nothing of the rats and what seeps from the latrines – that any wound's infected instantly. But get him on transport as soon as possible. There is some hope for him. Gas gangrene is a killer and he could be dead by dusk – but the wound is not too deep. With proper treatment this one could recover and come back to fight. But only if we're quick. He's already losing consciousness.'

But he wasn't quite sure he had heard the words. He did not really want to fight again, but it was a hope he clung to through the mists of pain as he was loaded onto the horse-drawn ambulance and jolted down the ruts to the Casualty Clearing Station, further from the front.

Part Two

January 1916

One

Something was seriously wrong. Verity realized it just in time, before she opened the back door. Somebody was getting a terrific fuss.

She paused. Nobody was expecting her home at this hour anyway – especially with the factory working round the clock these days and keeping open all the weekend too, to meet the extra orders that poured in for the troops. But there was a fuss on there as well. Something troublesome had been found in the accounts – a 'grave discrepancy', whatever that might be (something to do with Penvarris churchyard perhaps?) – and people had been sent home while they looked for it.

'But I thought they'd already found it?' Vee's neighbour on the packing-line had whispered in her ear, when Old Mr Radjel first came in and read the notice out.

Vee had laughed and dug her discreetly in the ribs, but they didn't laugh for long. Whatever this thing was it was clearly serious and there was a lot of muttering about the loss of pay.

Then some brave soul asked what a 'dishthreepency' might be and Mr Grey himself had come, white-faced, and explained it properly. How things had been going missing, over several months – supplies which had been packed, and checked off as being sold but had not arrived at the distributors. The management had been trying to sort it themselves – at first they'd suspected the carters who moved the goods about – but now they were sure the problem was in the factory itself.

'And this is not simply petty pilfering,' Mr Grey declared, 'though we would not have tolerated that. This is serious. All told it mounts up to several hundred pounds – all of it food which should have been sent to our brave boys at the front.'

So now the management had called in the police and – on the advice of Sergeant Jeffries – were closing down each portion of the line in turn, while they searched the premises and interviewed the staff. The newer employees were permitted to go home, but anyone who had been there since before last July (when this had first been spotted) was to remain for questioning. That meant Pru and Patience had to stay, but of course Vee had only joined in October and – since the police had started with the packing room – she was unexpectedly free to finish for the day.

So here she was back home, and it could not be three o'clock. She had been dreaming of a dozen ways she'd like to spend the time – calling into the Chegwiddens for news of Ned perhaps – though Ma would doubtless find some chores for her to do. But even as she put her hand upon the latch, she was aware of voices from within.

Ma's first, in an urgent whispering: 'What do you mean, it's not your fault? Who else d'you think's to blame? You ought to know better, and there's an end to it. No one forced you to it, from what I understand?'

'No,' came a tearful murmur in reply, so soft that Vee could not work out who the speaker was. Though it was certainly not Pa, as she'd imagined first – Ma did give him a private jawing now and then. This sounded high-pitched – like a woman or a child. Had Sammy Chegwidden let the fire go out while Pa wasn't there to watch? That was possible. You needed a permit for everything these days, and Pa had gone grumbling into Penzance to deal with forms. And, come to think, there was no hammering or hissing from the forge, so probably he'd miss his hoped-for lift on someone's cart and was having to wait for the horse-bus, or even walk back home. If Sammy was 'for it', though, she mustn't interrupt. Better if she turned around and tiptoed off again! Bother! What a waste of a lovely afternoon!

But somehow she didn't tiptoe anywhere. The next words had her rooted to the spot. 'Exactly!' That was her mother's voice again. 'It's no good blaming anybody else. You are responsible for what you do – and what you did was sin! And you raised a Strict Adherent all your life, brought up in godly ways!'

A Strict Adherent? So it wasn't Sammy then. It must be one of her own family – Constance, possibly? Had she been saying mocking things again? But no, it couldn't be. Constance had taken little Faith down to her Aunt Dorcas for a treat – a special privilege for birthday girls – and was going to call in at the village afterwards and walk home with the others when they came out of school. That had been arranged for days, supposing it was fine. And today was bright and cold, without a sign of rain. So whoever was it? Grace, Joy or Charity sent home by the teacher in disgrace? Somebody sobbing, that was evident, so much that Verity could not hear the words.

Mothers answer, though, was clear enough. 'You're going to tell him what you've just told me. What else are you to do? And you'd better do it quick. You just wait till your father hears of this! He'll be down that factory, sure as fire is fire, and knocking sparks off everyone in sight – that is if he doesn't wash his hands of you!'

Down the factory? Verity was perplexed.

'You think I haven't? I told him just today. Went to see him specially.' That was Patience, surely? But Patience was down the factory being questioned by the police. Or was she? Vee had not seen her eldest sister since first thing – not even at the meeting, come to think – but she'd thought nothing of it because Pattie worked in the evaporator room and not on the packing-line like herself and Pru. But Patience couldn't have been sent home with the newcomers like Vee, she had been down there longest of them all. Only – wait a minute! What did Ma mean by 'sin'? Surely Pattie couldn't be involved in this 'dishthree-pence' thing?

Vee found she was leaning forward to listen at the crack. Her sister was still speaking. 'And you know what he said? Nothing to do with him and I couldn't prove it was. It was my own stupid fault and I'd better hand my notice in as soon as possible. And if I didn't go away and hold my wicked tongue he'd see that I was thrown out on my ear, at once, without a character. And then I'd never get a job again with anyone round here. Or a husband either!' She broke into sobs again.

'Is that what he told you?' Ma's voice was dangerous.

'I tried to plead with him, but he wouldn't pay no heed. Just rang the bell and had the clerk come in and usher me away. I was crying my eyes out by that time, of course, so I couldn't go back and join the other girls – just told the clerk I wasn't feeling well and came straight home to you.'

'So you left without permission?' Ma sounded scandalized. 'As if you aren't in enough trouble as it was!'

'Well, I only said the truth. I was feeling terrible and Mr Grey was in some meeting with the police, so I couldn't talk to him. Besides, if they turn me off for leaving without a proper chit, what does it matter now? I can't well go back there in any case, not even to work my notice out and get what I am owed. The girls will all be wondering where I've gone and why, and I don't want to tell them – though no doubt they'll work it out. And the Strict Adherents will call me out in chapel, I suppose – and never mind my health. I shall be the talk of Rosvene, by and by.'

Vee made a private sympathetic face. Being 'called out' was a terrible disgrace – made to stand in front of everyone in penitential clothes while the preacher read out what your sin had been. No wonder Patience had been off her food for weeks, snappier than a dragon, and looking pale and drawn. This must have been on her conscience all that time. And no wonder! Imagine stealing from the factory – it seemed impossible. Pattie of all people! Verity was shaken to the core. Well, this was not a moment to go in and interrupt.

She thought of popping into the Chegwidden's house to see if there'd been word – Ned had picked up some awful infection at the front and had been very ill, so he couldn't write himself, but the last report had said that he was rallying. But Mrs C had seen her pass, and would obviously want to know why she'd not gone in at home – and that would reach Ma and Patience, who'd guess she'd overheard. Best go somewhere else entirely until it was proper home-time and Pru was there as well.

But meanwhile, what to do? There must be at least two hours of daylight left. Go and see her aunt out on the cliffs perhaps, and join Faith and Constance as they picked the schoolgirls up? Yes, there would be just time for that and – with it being Faith's birthday afternoon – it wasn't altogether an unlikely thing to choose to do.

She turned away, trying to make as little noise as possible, and hurried back down Rosvene hill again.

–

Effie Dawes was strolling back along the path across the field from the cliff. The day was gusty and tearing at her skirts but she was not sorry for the walk. She had been visiting her father and his new family, today – he'd been working night shifts so he was free this afternoon – and much as they made her welcome and pressed her to stay to tea, she'd suddenly found the stuffiness of the little cottage overpowering.

It was just the damp washing steaming by the fire, she told herself. Nothing at all to do with Peter Kellow happening to call. He often seemed to do that when she was visiting – almost as if he knew that she was there and had somehow arranged his shifts to suit. Although of course, that wasn't possible, she made her visits random – purposely – and you could hardly choose your hours when you were working down a mine.

Though she wouldn't put it past him to arrange it if he could! Peter had been sweet on her since they were six, and he had never got over it from that day to this – though she'd never knowingly encouraged him again. When she'd married Alex, she'd disappointed him, she knew. Not that Peter had ever said a word.

He'd even sent an unexpected marriage gift: a hand-turned bowl he'd made himself, together with a note to say he wished them happiness and if 'they two ever needed any help and it lay within his power, he would be "onered" to be asked'. She and Alex had been rather touched, but Alex's mother had laughed and wrinkled up her nose.

'How totally absurd. It's not as if he worked on our estate or anything. A miner, who dared have hopes of Effie at one time! Has he no sense of what's appropriate? Besides, the thing is hideous. You'll send it back, of course.'

Alex, of course – dear Alex – had understood at once. 'Mater, we've no intention of returning it. The gesture was generous and sincere. And jolly dignified. If I'd lost Effie to someone else, I hope I'd have the character to behave half as well.'

Effie could not help but smile, remembering. Alex would no doubt tell her that she was being foolish now – allowing that childhood friendship to embarrass her so much. It wasn't that Peter meant anything to her – not in that way, at least. He was hardly a romantic figure, after all, with the red hair and freckles that all the Kellows had, and great hands 'like mining shovels' as he used to say himself.

No, Peter was a really lovely chap – one of the best around, if you liked the solid type – but part of a life that she'd left far behind. So she never knew quite what to say to him, these days. Like this afternoon, for instance. She had made excuses and come away as soon as was polite, though there was no horse-bus at this hour of day and she'd had to plead a headache as an excuse to walk. Even then she'd had to dissuade Peter from accompanying her part-way.

Though all in all she'd quite enjoyed her unexpected stroll. When she was younger she had walked alone a lot (it was the only way of getting anywhere) but respectable married ladies did not do so as a rule – especially wives of policemen who could afford to ride. But now the fresh wind had whipped colour into her cheeks, and she felt invigorated by the sea air in her lungs, the sight of the white-capped waves that lapped the shore below, and the smell of the windswept grass and heather at her feet. There was even one lone, brave golden bud of flower on the furze. And as she clambered over the stile to join the road, she saw another unexpected sight.

Verity Tregorran was hurrying down the hill ahead, bundling her cape around her to keep out the wind. Yet, wasn't she working at the factory these days? According to Sergeant Jeffries, anyway. So why was she not there? Effie hadn't seen her since the day that she had called in at the police-house, looking so distressed. And she wasn't looking very happy now.

Effie paused and looked around her, up and down the hill. It wasn't ladylike to shout, but there was no one else to hear. She placed a firm hand on her hat and used the other to cup against her mouth. 'Verity Tregorran?' she called, against the wind.

Her voice must have carried. The blacksmith's daughter turned, then – obviously recognizing who was shouting after her – paused politely at the corner of the road, though she did not look altogether pleased at being forced to stop. But it was too late to retreat. Effie began to hasten down to her, but she had only gone a pace or two when something whooshed past and forced her to the hedge.

It was a young woman, of all things, on a bicycle – not wearing those scandalous bloomers, but freewheeling down the hill, with her ankle boots showing underneath her skirt and with her hat tied underneath her chin with a swathe of gauzy stuff. It was outrageous enough to make people stop and stare – if there had been anyone but Verity and Effie there to see.

Effie had stepped back, startled, and almost tripped into the ditch. She looked up, crossly, ready to complain; but instead of pausing to apologize the rider swooped on by, with an enormous smile on her young glowing face and her fair hair streaming out behind her in the wind – not even glancing in Effie s direction as she passed. She did however give a cheerful wave to the Tregorran girl.

'Yoohoo, Miss Verity!' she caroled and was gone around the bend. Verity seemed to know the apparition, too, because her face lit in a sudden smile and she returned the wave – too late – and stood staring in the direction that the bicycle had gone.

Effie started down the hill once more – conscious that she'd muddied her pretty ankle boots. 'Good afternoon,' she proffered, when she was near enough to speak in normal tones.

'Oh, Mrs Dawes, it is you! I thought I heard your voice, but it's hard to be certain over all this blaw, and then I saw the bicyclist and thought that it was her.'

Effie looked at her with curiosity. 'You know that person?' It wasn't a polite enquiry perhaps, but there weren't many young ladies who rode bicycles in the whole of England, let alone Penwith. Effie could not remember seeing one before! She could just imagine what Uncle Joe would say. 'Tisn't natural!' she could almost hear his voice. 'A woman racing round the county, like a man, showing her legs up almost to the knee. Wanton, that's what that is. Girl wants locking up for her own good.'

But Verity was answering the question by this time. 'I only know her more or less by sight. Vicar's daughter, over to St Erne. He used to bring a horse to Pa for shoeing now and then, and she'd come with him on the trap – but we haven't seen them since the war began. Lost the creature to the army probably. We did hear from Crowdie that the vicar had a bicycle these days – uses it to visit the parishioners and things – but I never thought I'd see his daughter riding one. Looks some fun, though, doesn't it?' Her face split in an enormous impish grin.

Effie nodded. Truth to tell, she'd thought the same herself. Imagine the freedom! Better than a horse. You could go to visit Pa and be home in half an hour – or even venture all the way into Penzance and not have to worry about what time the bus was due.

'My husband used to ride a police bicycle,' she said, conscious of sounding something of a prig. Though it was true. Alex had ridden it for miles when he was stationed here – though he'd always been far happier on an animal. In fact he had been keen that she should ride as well – his family would doubtless have approved – but somehow she had never mastered it; it wasn't the sort of thing her folks had ever done and horses were so big they rather frightened her. And they were wilful with it.

But a bicycle, perhaps? You could park a machine and it would stay where it was put. It wouldn't come round behind you and try to bite your bottom if you turned your back. Looking for sugar, Alex had declared, but he'd thought it was funny, you could see it in his eyes.

'…haven't you?' a voice was saying in her ear, and she realized with a start that Verity was talking and she hadn't heard a word.

Effie smiled and murmured, 'I'm quite sure you're right!' wondering what on earth she was agreeing to.

'Though I expect they'll clean,' the Tregorran girl went on. 'Don't see many people hereabouts in lovely boots like that. Or that costume, come to that.' She nodded at Effie's matching pale-blue skirt and coat. 'Mind, you used to work in a haberdashers, one time, so my sister said?'

'Briefly, before I married Alex,' Effie said, politely. 'Though I was in service before that. But I was always interested in needlework.' She was about to add that she had won a prize for it at school, but Verity did not give her a chance.

'Most I ever did was sew new ribbons round my Sunday skirt when it was handed down from Prudence and my mother turned the cloth.' She gave a little laugh. 'Though here I'm talking out of turn, again! Sorry, Mrs Dawes, you don't want to hear all that. You wanted me for something?'

Effie shook her head. 'Only to ask if anything came of that potential smuggler? Or if you had ever seen that man out on the cliffs again?'

'Never been out there, since,' the girl replied. 'Though matter of fact, I'm on my way there now – meet with my sisters. That's how I'm in something of a rush. Probably wasn't anything suspicious about it, any case – or so Sergeant Jeffries says. Tell you I'm being flighty, I expect.'

She sounded so resigned that Effie smiled and said, 'Now, don't let me delay you, if you've got folks to meet. But if you ever hear or notice anything again – never mind Sergeant Jeffries – you come and let me know.'

The thin face lit up in a delighted smile. 'Thank you, Mrs Dawes. You at least believe I aren't an idiot. But now, if you'll excuse me, I'll take the cliff path here!' And off she scampered, bonnet round her neck and blue skirt, plaid shawl and wild curls flying in the wind.

Effie watched her with a thoughtful smile. There was something very likeable about that young scatterbrain – perhaps because she reminded Effie of herself. Like the way her eyes had lit up at the thought of bicycles. A foolish dream for both of them, of course. Verity could never have afforded such a thing and respectable married ladies had to be more decorous.

Though, if vicar's daughters had begun to cycle around the lanes, it could not be entirely disreputable nowadays. One of the things that had altered with the war, perhaps – like women taking tickets on the railway trains. And bicycles must be available for sale.

She shook her head. It was impossible. Whatever would Alex and his mother make of the idea?

–

Martha Tregorran pushed her hair back from her eyes and put the kettle on the trivet by the fire to boil. In a crisis, it was what she always did. Not that a cup of tea was going to help this time – but Strict Adherents did not keep alcohol about, not even for medicinal purposes. Though the Chegwiddens did. She was almost tempted to go and beg some from next door, claiming a headache, and it would have been no lie. Patience had given her the biggest headache of her life.

She looked across at her eldest daughter now, sitting at the table in a sobbing heap, her hair dishevelled and her face all red and streaked. 'Dear Heaven!' she said aloud (it was the strongest oath that she allowed herself). 'Pull yourself together. Don't sit there snivelling. We've got to think what you are going to do.'

Patience raised tearful eyes. 'Do? What on earth can anybody do? Except tell Pa – I suppose he'll have to know?'

Martha gave an exasperated sigh. 'You think you're going to hide it and pretend the fairies came? Don't be ridiculous. Of course he's got to know.'

'He'll throw me out, I know it. I'll end up in the workhouse!'

Martha did not answer. It was a possibility – Toby held strong views about immoral girls.

Patience began to weep hopelessly again. 'Well, if I do, I just hope the factory don't turn off Pru and Vee as well. Scandal sticks to families, that's what they always say. Oh, why was I so stupid?'

'First sensible remark I've heard you make today,' Martha said tardy. 'A bit less self-pity and bit more penitence, that's what you need, young lady. But you're thinking about other people now, and that's a start, I suppose. Not that I expect your father to agree.' She shook her head. 'Fair break his heart, you will. Always hoped to live to see you wed and happy with a family of your own. But not like this – without the marriage first. If your young Mr Radjel was not already wed, your father would be down there like a bolt of lightning – though the man is barely Christian from what I understand.' She meant it. Old Mr Radjel was generally liked, but his son was a scandal – to the Strict Adherency at least. In fact he had once been 'prayed against' for his father's sake, because Satan had tempted him to gambling, and he didn't hardly show his face at church or chapel any more, except for feast days, weddings and funerals – which didn't really count.

'Not the kind of husband we'd have chosen for our girls, but better that than nothing,' Martha said bitterly. 'But even he is not available, so it's nothing – it appears.' She sighed. 'Whatever possessed you to get mixed up with him – a married man?'

The question was enough to start the tears again. 'Told me that he loved me and that we'd run away and start again – in London, possibly. He was putting away money to pay the fare, he said – but...' She let out such a piercing sob it touched her mother's heart. 'And I believed him. I must have been a fool.'

'We aren't about to disagree on that, I don't suppose!' Martha said. 'But perhaps if your father went to talk to him?' Old Radjel was a decent sort of man. They might make an allowance for Patience, possibly? Something that would enable her to go away in fact – somewhere like Launceston, where she would not be known. And later, perhaps, if Toby could be talked around to it, they might take in their grandchild and pass it off as theirs. Such things were not unknown – and little Faith was just a toddler still, so another baby would be unremarkable.

Her mind was working overtime by now. Suppose she wore a few extra layers for a bit? Of course it was deception, of a kind, and Strict Adherents shouldn't do that sort of thing, but if nothing was actually said, it was not exactly lying, was it? And this was clearly an emergency.

'It wouldn't do the slightest bit of good.' Patience's voice broke into her thoughts. 'He'd say it wasn't him. He's already said as much to me. And how could I prove it? He took some proper care to make sure that we weren't observed – we'd leave different times and meet up on the cliffs, out of sight of everybody else. Supposed to be on different errands for the factory – Mr Radjel had it sorted out. And no-one ever saw us – 'cept, nearly, Verity.'

'Verity?' Martha was startled.

'On about seeing something suspicious on the cliffs. I could have killed her, but turned out it wasn't us. But when I told him – thinking that he'd laugh – he did the opposite and took a proper fright. Said it was over, it was far too dangerous, and since that day he's never even looked at me again. That is, until this morning, and you know what happened then.' She shook her head. 'Don't let Pa go down and see him, it won't do no good, just make trouble for the other girls. Stephen Radjel's like that, I can see it now. How didn't I realize he was a liar and a cheat?'

'You might have guessed that when he cheated on his wife,' Martha said sternly. She was torn between anger and worry for her girl. 'I wish I knew what I could do to help.' She shook her head. 'Might go down the chapel and say a little prayer – or look in the Bible and find a guidance text. That's what your grandfather would recommend.'

'Well it's no good looking in the box of promises!' She nodded towards the round container by the hearth – it was full of little rolled-up tubes of paper, each of which contained a cheerful text, and you took a pair of tweezers and selected one. 'Grandfather would say I needed a penitential text. "Therefore I will wail and howl, I will go stripped and naked, I will make a wading like the dragons and mourning as the owls"!' Patience – like all Strict Adherents – knew many such scripture passages by heart.

Martha looked at her. 'That's from the prophet Micah! And you know what follows next! "Declare it not in Gath, weep ye not at all: in the house of Aphrah roll thyself in dust." Don't mock the Good Book, Patience. Aphrah must mean Ephraim. We've had guidance after all. Ephraim Tull has offered for you more than once – he's been looking to marry since his first wife died. And he's a Strict Adherent, which would make things easier…'

'Ephraim Tull? But he's as old as Pa, and he's got warts all down his nose and everything! Besides, he wouldn't have me – not after what I've done.'

Martha, for the first time, found solace in her tea. 'He might do, since the Lord is on our side. Course we'd have to tell him that you were in the family way – but you picked the text yourself – "tell it not in Gath". We don't have to tell him everything, it seems. But if he thought somehow that it was Christian charity – that you'd been set upon by a stranger on the cliffs perhaps – he might be persuaded that he was saving you from harm.' She put her cup down with a clatter suddenly. 'That must be it. And didn't he always hope that he might have an heir, someday? And that text says, just a few verses on: "yet I will bring thee an heir unto thee". Patience, seems the Lord is good to you. He's given us a sign. Perhaps you won't end in the workhouse after all.'

But Patience did not look comforted at all. 'You mean I'll have to marry that awful Ephraim Tull?'

'My dear girl, have you got no sense at all? Ephraim Tull would be a saviour to you, after what you've done. If he agrees to have you, you'll take him and be grateful – do you hear? Fortunately he's a great believer in the Word, and if I go and tell him how it was a guidance text…' She stood up abruptly. 'I believe I'll do it now. Sooner the better, if it's done at all. It isn't very far, and he's generally in his farmyard of an afternoon – and if I can persuade him to agree, it will make things much easier with your father later on.'

Patience looked a little hopeful, suddenly. 'And what should we tell Pa? About how this happened?'

Martha unhooked her bonnet from the door and tied the ribbons underneath her chin. 'Tell him the same as Ephraim, I suppose. T'isn't all the different from the truth – by what you say it did 'appen on the cliffs, we just won't mention that you knew the man. Though your pa will likely give you a dreadful walloping for not telling him about it at the time.' Patience said nothing, just sat in misery.

Martha took down her cloak and wrapped it round herself. 'But perhaps that's a blessing in its way as well – it's no good his asking the police to find the man, which he'd be bound to do, else – because it's months ago and any stranger would have gone away.' She sighed. 'Now, it's getting time the others will be coming home. You go out to the water butt and wash your face in it, try and look a bit more normal. There's sprats out in the wash house, you can fry them up for tea. Tell them I've gone for cabbage, I'll bring some home with me. And I'd best be off and do it, if I'm to be back here before your father is. And when he does come – you leave your pa to me.'

'Oh Ma!' Patience leapt up and tried to give her an embrace, but Martha shook her free.

'I aren't doing this for your sake, Patience. You've sinned and that's a fact. I'm doing it for your father's sake, and for the other girls.' And for that unborn baby, she added silently, as she set off to talk to Ephraim Tull.

Two

It was a steep walk across the fields to where Ephraim kept his farm — though 'farm' was rather a fancy word for it these days. Since his wife died of fever, many years ago, Ephraim had taken little interest in the place. Crowdie (who was not a Strict Adherent, naturally) had once remarked that if Ephraim Tull spent fewer hours on his knees and more on his harrow, he would please the good Lord more, and — though she had been scandalized — Martha could see exactly what he meant.

The whole place badly needed a coat of whitewash on the walls and through the open doorway she could see a woeful mess within — piles of unwashed cloam was piled up in the sink, graying laundry drooped from a line above the hearth and nobody had taken a broom or duster to the place for years. The flypapers that dangled from the beams were thick with the insects they had trapped and even the framed texts on every wall had smeary glass. In his place, she thought, she would have been ashamed — how could a godly man have let it get like this? No wonder he never invited anyone to call.

'Ephraim! Brother Tull?' she called, and tapped the door, but there was no reply.

She looked around. There were a few bedraggled chickens clucking in the yard — Ephraim clearly kept them for the eggs — and a bad-tempered sow was grunting in the pig's-crow opposite, but there was no sign of their owner or even of his dog. Not that he could have much use for the poor thing nowadays; it was said that he only kept a dozen cows and half-a-dozen goats – and apart from a few carrots and potatoes for himself, he only bothered with cabbage and broccoli to sell. It was fortunate that the farm had been handed down to him, and he was not a tenant – like most folk hereabouts; any landlord would have had a thing or two to say.

'Sister Tregorran! Greetings in the Lord. What are you doing here?' And there was Ephraim, rising from behind a corner of the wall, where – judging from the piece of stone he held – he'd been repairing it. He was a tall, gaunt man with dark unsmiling eyes, and such a habitual disapproving frown that for a moment Martha almost wished she hadn't come. But he had seen her now and there was no escape.

He dusted off his hands and came around to her, taking off his cap in deference. He wore a waistcoat, open to the waist, a shirt without a collar and a pair of brown trousers tied close around his heavy boots – quite a contrast from the suit and tie he wore to Sunday Meetings. 'Come to tell me that Toby's changed his mind and will consent to let me marry that eldest girl of yours?' His voice was deep and rasping but it was not fierce today and there was even the vestige of a smile around the deep-lined lips.

The remark was intended as a bitter joke, of course. Ephraim had offered for Patience more than once – but even Toby had seen that it was not a perfect match. In fact it was Martha who had dissuaded him, 'There's no affection there. He just wants a wife to wash for and clean for him,' she'd said, and Toby had agreed. And now she would have to argue just the opposite!

But the jest had given her an easier opening than she could have hoped. Martha gave the man her brightest smile. 'I think the Lord put those words into your mind, Brother Tull. That is exactly why I've come to call. I need to talk to you. But not out here, perhaps?' She gestured vaguely to the farmhouse.

Ephraim looked doubtful. 'It is not good for a man and woman to be alone together in a house – save they be married.'

Martha shook her head. That was not a text – she knew her scriptures and was fairly sure of that – but Ephraim always managed to make the simplest things sound like biblical quotations. 'I aren't going to lead you to temptation, I suppose. Besides, "blest are the pure in heart" the Good Book says,' she countered.

Ephraim looked nonplussed. 'Well then,' he said, after a moment, 'you'd better come inside.' He led the way into the kitchen she'd already glimpsed. The room was earth-floored and smelt of damp, but there was a vestige of a fire in the stove, and evidence that the man had tried to make a meal. He moved some mending to clear a chair for her, running his arm across the seat and table as if conscious of the dust that lay on everything.

For a moment Martha felt a pang. Not only for Ephraim, but for Patience's sake – yet hadn't the guidance text foretold this very thing? 'In the house of Aphrah roll thyself in the dust.'

That recollection strengthened her resolve – this match was clearly 'meant' – so when Ephraim said, 'So what did you want to tell me? Patience changed her mind?' she was so convinced that things would be all right that she simply told him. Not quite everything, of course, but the gist of it – with no actual untruths. 'And when we found the guidance text I came to you at once,' she finished, breathlessly.

There was a long silence, then Ephraim got slowly to his feet. 'And you came here supposing I would marry her, now defiled and carrying some stranger's child? Have you not read the scriptures, woman? "A bastard shall not enter the courts of the Lord".'

Martha was so astonished that she could hardly think. This was not what she'd envisaged. 'But it would not be a bastard – not officially – if you gave it a name. And Patience—'

'That girl has brought this on herself!' the farmer said. 'Haven't I seen her, Sundays, with ribbons on her skirts? What's that for, if not to flaunt herself? And showing her petticoats by crossing on the stile. And I've seen her pinch her cheeks, when she thinks that you aren't looking, just to turn them pink. Outside chapel too – and we all know that vanity's a sin.' He had already reached the open door and he stood beside it gesturing her out.

'Then how come you offered for her, Ephraim Tull?' Martha was also on her feet by now.

He made a lofty face. 'I felt that she was young. I could have forgiven her and taught her otherwise, but now she's lost her virtue. And a fallen woman is a snare. "Remove thy way far from her and come not nigh the door of her house." So, there's your answer Martha. I'm surprised you came. I think you'd better leave.'

'But what about the guidance texts? I thought...' she faltered. 'A Christian man like you—'

'Should not keep company with fornicators,' he retorted, bitterly. 'That's what the Bible says. And if you follow it, Sister Tregorran, it's clear what you should do. "If your eye offend thee – pluck it out." For the sake of your salvation! Turn this reproach away. "A good name is better than precious ointment."'

'It's our good name that I am thinking of! If you took Patience, who would need to know, except the three of us – and Toby, I suppose? But now the world will be full of wagging tongues, laughing at Strict Adherents I wouldn't be surprised!'

He didn't move. Just gestured to the door. 'I will pray for you. And for that unborn babe.' He didn't mention Patience, who most needed it!

Martha found that she was very angry, suddenly. She marched past Ephraim and – once outside in the yard – whirled around to look him in the eye. 'Well, Brother Tull, I'm leaving. But I'm surprised at you. I've thought you a Strict Adherent through and through, but you are nothing but a hypocrite. Did I not hear you preach, this very Sunday past, on succoring the widow and the fatherless? And what is the unborn child but fatherless? Yet when I come to you – following the very text that we'd been given – you wash your hands of us. I've heard you pray to God to have a wife and heir – and when God provides one, almost ready-made, you turn it down because it's not in the form you hoped. Well, God moves in a mysterious way. You're always saying so. But if that's the kind of man you are, our Patience would be better in the workhouse than doing penance here. And penance it would be!' So saying she turned and stomped off to the gate.

'Those who twist scripture do so to their own destruction, Sister Tregorran,' Ephraim shouted after her, but she did not look back.

She was breathing hard and fighting back the tears as she walked home. What had she done? She had been so confident! And now, Ephraim would call Patience out for sure and shame the family in front of everyone. News would be all round the village in an hour. And she hadn't even had the chance to talk to Toby yet!

At her own gate she paused and braced herself, straightening her shoulders before she went inside. The younger children had come back from school – together with Verity, apparently, and Patience was obediently frying sprats.

It was not until that moment that Martha realized that she'd forgotten to buy a cabbage and bring it home with her.

–

Peter Kellow walked glumly down the street towards Nancarrow Village Institute. He was rather early, because he hadn't stopped for tea. He had no appetite. Cap'n Maddern always arranged his shifts for him, so he could get off sooner when it was evening class. Usually Peter enjoyed his night-school – he was good with a slide-rule and his marks were excellent. But tonight the prospect held no joy for him.

It had been a mistake to call on Walter Pengelly and his wife, though he'd been welcomed at the house. The older man had become a sort of friend during the long months which followed his awful accident. Peter had visited him very often then, brought him news and stories from the mine and even helped him find his feet again when the splints had been removed and the damaged leg had set. But even then, if he was honest with himself, it had been Effie who had drawn him to visit quite so much – just as she'd drawn him to pa's present home this afternoon.

Of course he'd known that she was likely to be there. Walter had mentioned it, a day or two ago. So Peter had hurried over as soon as he was free.

For what, he asked himself? So that she could be embarrassed and refuse to talk to him, then scoot off home far sooner than she would have done if he had not been there? What kind of idiot did tactless things like that? And it was not the first time either.

It wasn't dignified. For her, as well as him. Each time he did it, he swore that he would stop. Effie was a married woman, and a happy one. It was like putting your tongue into a sore place in your teeth – painful, but somehow you kept on doing it.

He had to face reality, he told himself. She loved that Alex, and the policeman loved her back. You only had to see the two of them together to know that. She was out of his league now, anyway, with a maid and everything! And that would just get worse. One day that Dawes would inherit a small fortune, wouldn't he? Anybody decent would be pleased at that. It meant that Effie would be well provided for.

Peter had done his level best to be pleased on her account – even made a wedding present with his own two hands. It had been wrong, of course – PC Dawes's awful mother had made that very clear. 'The thing is hideous!' he'd overheard her say, when he ventured to the police-house to deliver it. And he hadn't even had the chance to talk to Effie then – though she had kept the bowl, and even sent a nice note thanking him. He still had that, folded in the pocket of his coat. The only bit of Effie he was likely to possess.

He was so busy with his thoughts as he walked down the street, that he scarcely noticed the woman in the hat who crossed the road and was approaching him. He went to step aside, but she moved in front of him.

'This is for you, you coward!' she declared, taking a white feather from a basket on her arm and thrusting it towards him with a black-gloved hand.

For a moment he was mystified. He looked around. There was another woman on the far side of the street, just as stout and red-faced as the one confronting him, watching with folded arms and nodding her approval of the little scene. She had a basket too upon her arm, and was dressed in the same kind of long coat and monstrous hat, except that hers was trimmed with feathers rather than a bow. Both of them were strangers, whom he'd never seen before.

'You tell him, Mildred,' the feathered one said. The voice was from up country, not a local one. 'Show him what we think of cowardice. Should be at the war, a strapping lad like that.'

No point in explaining that wolfram was a precious war resource, or that tin was needed for cans to keep the soldiers fed – these two were not disposed to argument. The bow-trimmed woman took another feather out and stuck it in the upper button-hole of his coat, where it was visible. 'You look at that, wherever you are going,' she said, in a voice that was clearly intended to be heard for miles, though there was no-one in the street except the three of them. 'And think about our sons and nephews at the front, and see if you feel quite so smug about your evening, then!'

And with that she turned and joined her companion on the other side. Peter stuffed the feathers in his pocket out of sight, and went on walking to the institute.

His friend Jack Maddern from the mine was there awaiting him. 'What's up with you then? Lost a shilling and found sixpence?'

Peter shook his head. 'Don't know why I bother coming here at all. What good does it do me?'

Jack looked astonished. 'Weren't you just telling me last week, how you were hoping to be made up leader of your pare? You said how they were picking younger men these days, if they had certificates, on account of some older ones have gone away to war!'

'Only wish I'd done the same,' Peter said morosely. 'Joined that Tunneller Company – while I had the chance.' He took out the crumpled feathers and showed them to his friend. 'Here I am, working my eyes out, doing doublers half the time – two shifts in succession to meet the war effort – and what's the thanks I get? Some fat goose of a woman shouting names at me. Better off in France. Specially if they're still paying six shillings every day. 'Tisn't even as if I've got a wife to think about – or likely to have one, either.'

'Here, boy, what's the matter?' Jack put his hand on Peter's arm. 'You're some down tonight. Don't let they two daft biddies spoil your day.'

Peter shook the hand away. 'T'isn't only that. I'm fed up anyway.'

'Romantic troubles, is it?' His friend made a sympathetic face. 'I know you lost that girl you were so keen about, but there are other women.'

Peter turned away impatiently. 'Not for me,' he said. 'Now you coming into class or aren't you?'

Jack said nothing further and followed him inside. But after the lesson – in which Peter did not shine as much as usual – he sidled up beside his friend again.

'None of my business really, and you can tell me so – but if you're serious in what you said, might be a chance that you could join that unit yet. Well, next best thing, at least. I heard today they're going to form another company – looking for people who can deal with dynamite. Have to go to London probably, and it might be already too late, but there is a recruiting office in Penzance. They could tell you, if you went and asked. If you're really serious, I mean.'

Peter felt inside his pocket, where the feathers were – and a folded piece of paper that was Effie's thank-you note. He screwed the items – all of them – into a savage ball and threw it into the waste-paper basket by the door.

'I do believe I might,' he said, as coolly as he could. 'Mother won't like it, but there's nothing for me here.' He managed to keep his voice from wavering.

–

'Here, Vee! Wait a minute,' Pru muttered in her ear that evening, when they had finished putting the younger girls to bed.

It had been a strange, strained household over the bread and sprats tonight, what with Patience looking more woeful than a sheep, Ma strange and silent and Pa demanding what was wrong with everyone. Even the younger children had picked up the mood and there had been no laughing and gossiping tonight. The girls had simply done their chores – boots and spoons were polished, ironing damped and rolled, squares of paper threaded onto strings to put out in the privy, and Mercy's spelling for tomorrow checked – all in virtual silence for a change. And when the clock struck seven the young ones went to bed, scuttled off at once without the least complaint, as if glad to be out of the atmosphere downstairs.

But now Pru paused on the landing with the nightlight in her hand and was tugging at Vee's sleeve. 'You were home here earlier,' she whispered. 'You must have heard. Whatever is going on?'

It ought to be flattering to be asked for news and treated like an equal by the older girl for once, but suddenly Vee didn't want to talk to anyone. 'I aren't altogether sure, myself,' she said. 'I was here earlier but I never came on in. I just heard voices in the kitchen – Patience having a wigging by the sound of it – so I turned and went again.'

'But what was it about?' Pru whispered, so fiercely that she almost blew the candle out.

Vee shook her head. 'I decided it was better to keep out of it. I went over to Auntie's, met up with Con and Faith, picked up the others and then came home with them. So I don't know much more than you do.' She wriggled from Pru's grasp. 'And you haven't said what happened down the factory, come to that. Have they found this "dish-threepence"?' She didn't mention her fears that Patience might have been involved.

Prudence shook her head. 'They still can't work out where the stuff is disappearing from. Our packing-room, they think. The bosses have been in and they've started a new system of checking orders out – something the police suggested, it appears. From now on every chitty will be double-signed – and they're going to put another supervisor on. That ought to put a stop to it, but they don't have the slightest notion who it was – and...' she broke off as there was a tapping on the door.

95

A visitor? At this hour? Whoever could it be? The policeman about that business at the factory perhaps? Vee felt her blood run cold but Pru was unconcerned, giving her a gleeful glance and sneaking across to peer down through the banisters. Vee followed slowly, though she too was careful not to make a sound.

Pa had already opened the kitchen door by now and was standing on the step, while beyond him a dark figure could be seen, holding a lighted lantern high. 'Why, Brother Tull!' Pa sounded thunderstruck. 'What's happened? I suppose you'd best come in.' He stood back to admit the visitor.

Pru glanced at Verity in the candle-light, raising astonished eyebrows and pulling an exaggerated face. But it was Ephraim Tull, indeed, dressed up in his going-to-chapel clothes and his cheeks red-raw in the lamplight where he'd been shaving them.

'Sister Tregorran! Brother Toby! And Miss Patience too.' Ephraim had politely taken off his hat, but he kept on his coat as he came inside.

He put his lantern down and went across to stand on the only vacant bit of floor, beside the window. He did not take the proffered chair, but went on standing there, facing the family who were huddled by the fire. He was not in full view of the landing any more, but Vee could still glimpse the bottom half of him – a pair of big hands fiddling with his hat, which he held across his stomach like a shield.

There was an awkward silence, then Pa said again, 'Can we help you, Brother?'

Ephraim cleared his throat. 'I've been on my knees for hours, Sister, thinking what you said, and I b'lieve you might be right. I might be guilty of spiritual pride.'

Pa said, 'What's all this, then…?' But Ma interrupted him.

'Not now, Toby. Let Brother Ephraim speak. It's true, I went to see him earlier today. I'll explain why later, when we are alone. And Constance, I think you should go upstairs. Tell the other two to stop up there as well. This is private business between Patience and ourselves.'

There was a shuffle and a flounce as Constance grabbed a candle from the shelf, lit it from the fire and did as she was told. There was almost a commotion when she reached the top and saw her sisters there, hiding in the shadows, but Pru held a finger to her lips and made room for Constance to come and watch as well.

There was a moment's silence downstairs, until Pru opened and loudly shut the bedroom door, then Ma said, 'There, she's gone to bed. You were saying, Brother Tull?'

'T'isn't all the girl's fault, rightly, and – if she's penitent – I could see my way to doing as you ask. Did not Judah acknowledge Tamar when she was defiled, and from her was born the house of David?'

There was the noise of Pa rising sharply to his feet. 'What is this, Ephraim?'

Ephraim raised a hand. 'I turned to Jeremiah, and what did I find? "Only acknowledge thine iniquity, that thou hast transgressed against Lord they God and scattered thy ways to the strangers under every tree." Well, it was clear who that applied to – but the very next verse says, "I will give you pastors according to my heart, which shall feed you with knowledge." Now, there is a guidance text if ever one was found. I am to be the means of her redemption by study of the word, if she acknowledges her sin. If the Lord has laid this on me, I must follow his command. So,

Brother and Sister Tregorran, I have come to offer for Miss Patience after all.'

Then Mother's voice, shaky with emotion. 'Oh, thanks be to God! Patience what have you to say to Brother Tull?'

Pa said, 'Will someone please tell me what this is about?' But Patience – unbelievably – was saying, 'Yes, I will. Brother Tull, I accept your offer!' though she sounded close to tears – more like someone ordering a shroud.

Pa was just asking sharply, 'Patience, are you sure?' as Constance dropped the candle in astonishment. Mercifully it blew out as it fell, but the candlestick escaped and rolled noisily away.

There was the sound of a stool being pushed back on the flags and Ma came storming to the bottom of the stairs. 'Here, what's going on up there? Don't pretend there's no one there. I hope you've not been listening to what's none of your concern. You're supposed to be in bed.'

It was no good hiding in the shadows now. The candlestick had given the game away. Pru, as usual, was the first to act. 'It's just me and Verity,' she said, taking a step forward and moving into sight. 'Wondering should we bring the dirty water downstairs? But Constance said there was a visitor and we wouldn't want to come down in our nightdresses.'

Vee looked at her in wonder. Pru could think so quickly in a scrape! And what she said was reasonable enough – they did bring down the water from the washstand every night, but generally only after they had washed in it themselves!

Ma, though, seemed less than totally convinced. 'Never mind the water – you leave it where it is. Patience can see to it when we have finished here. And you two

98

get to bed, you hear me! Straight away. Or I'll come up and tan your hides myself!'

So after that there was nothing they could do but creep away to bed, Vee lay for a long time, straining every nerve, trying to hear what was being said downstairs, but she couldn't make it out – though Pa seemed pretty furious when the visitor had gone. (Vee could tell when that was, from the backdoor squeaking closed.)

It was a long, long time before Patience came upstairs, and even when she'd done so Verity could not sleep. So Pattie was going to marry Ephraim after all. Disappointed in her other friend perhaps. And Pa did not seem pleased. Did that mean that he'd had someone else in mind? Was there a Strict Adherent chapel in Penzance where he'd found a likely beau? Or had Pa come to realize – at last – that there weren't sufficient Strict Adherents to go round, and that if his other daughters were to marry anyone, they might have to look for husbands somewhere else?

Husbands like Ned Chegwidden, possibly? She was still thinking about that when the dawn began to break and it was time to rise and start another day.

Three

Ned Chegwidden was lying on a stretcher in a train. Half an hour ago, roused to get in the motor ambulance at dawn, he'd been excited at the prospect of being transferred back to a Base Hospital at last. However, he was still weaker than he'd realized, and simply getting here had almost jolted him to death. The rest of the journey promised to be misery, despite the neat bunks, clean sheets and pretty Queen Alexandra nurse who watched as he was transferred to his berth. (Quite a change from the straw-filled cattle trucks he'd heard about from men who had been wounded earlier in the war.)

There were other bunks above him and a lot more behind, and more men were being stretchered in to fill the tiers across the aisle, so there was quite a hubbub in the carriage where he lay. It was hot – they had obviously tried to warm the train – and there was the usual unpleasant smell of wounded men, but at least there was a moment where he could just lie still and rest. Two of the men were calling to each other from their upper bunks – cheerful optimistic chatter – but he wished that they would stop. He was glad when a stretcher-bearer stopped and chided them. 'No shouting in the ward!'

He could understand their cheerfulness, of course. He had been itching for this moment for at least a month himself. You would think that a Clearing station would be exactly that, clearing the casualties on within a day or two, but it hadn't proved that way. After the operations on his leg – there had been several, including 'irrigation' of the wound – he'd spent what seemed for ever in the evacuation tent, waiting to gain strength enough to be moved on anywhere.

Too fast a move would kill him they'd decreed to his dismay, and they were no doubt right – once or twice he had not expected to pull through. Much of the first few weeks had been a kind of fevered dream, in which he drifted in and out of agony. Who would have imagined that a tiny scratch could cause such pain or result in the huge wound that now covered most of what had been his lower thigh?

'You just be thankful, soldier,' the medical orderly had said, quite recently, when changing the blood-soaked bandages had made Ned shout aloud. 'A good sign, this is. When the cavity bleeds all over we know that it is clean. It'll leave a nasty hole for ever, I expect, but it's digging out the dirt and damaged flesh that saved your life – if this had happened a year or so ago, you'd have been very lucky to survive. They didn't understand these problems then. They'd have put a dressing on it, and left it as it was – and the gas gangrene would have killed you within a day or two. So hold still while I bind it up so it can heal.'

So Ned bit his lip and managed to endure it without crying out again, though something – was it iodine? – stung the raw flesh damnably. But the orderly was right. Since that day his health had gradually improved, there were no more fevered nightmares and he'd begun to eat (mostly beef tea, which he did not like, but which seemed to do him good) and he could feel himself getting a little stronger every day. Though not as strong as he had thought, apparently.

'There you are then, soldier!' The pretty nurse cut across his thoughts. She was holding out a mug of something warm and sweet and helped him sit forward so he could sip from it. 'We'll soon be on our way. Just waiting for our escort… Ah, and here they are!' She broke off as a group of mounted military policemen drew up outside the open door. 'I'd better go and tell them that everyone's aboard – we've already checked the lists. Then we should be off.' She gave him a quick smile and disappeared, closing the carriage door behind her as she went.

Ned leant back on his pillow. He was very tired and only dimly registered the voices from elsewhere. But he'd barely shut his eyes before he heard the door again, and the nurse's voice was saying. 'He's in here, officer. Private Chegwidden!' She came and shook his shoulder with a gentle hand. 'Someone here to see you.'

Ned blinked himself awake. She was smiling down on him, and behind her was a redcap standing at the door, brandishing a document and looking quizzical.

'Private Chegwidden? I saw the name on the list and thought it might be you. You're from Rosvene, aren't you?' The officer climbed into the carriage and came across to him. 'You don't know who I am?'

Ned shook a weary head. The face was familiar somehow, but he was too tired to work at placing it.

'It's Alex Dawes. Don't you remember me? I used to see you sometimes at Rosvene. Even once caught you scrumping apples, I recall.'

'My dear life!' Feeble or not, Ned raised himself an inch or two on one elbow. 'That policeman chap! Of course! Heard from my girl that you were in the forces, sir. Well, I'll be blowed! PC Dawes, who'd have thought of seeing you!'

'It's Major Dawes, these days,' the man said, with a smile. 'But I'm glad to have made contact with you, young Chegwidden. You get well, you hear? Bit of an ordeal this journey back to the Base hospital, but it's the first step back to Blighty, eh? Think of it that way. And when you get there, you go tell my wife that you've seen me, and I'm well and thinking about her. Will you do that for me?'

Ned managed a wan smile. 'A pleasure, Major.'

'Good man,' Dawes said, and closed the door again.

Back to Blighty. Talking to Mrs Dawes and Verity. Really home! Somehow, till that moment, it had not seemed possible. Ned leaned back on his pillow and closed his eyes again. Whether it was the effort of the journey to the train, or whether there had been something in the tea, he never knew, but within a moment he was fast asleep – and not even the shell that rocked the train awakened him, though it wrecked the next carriage (killing several men) and caused a huge delay.

So Ned didn't know – until a long time afterwards – how close he'd come that day to being blown to bits.

–

Will Jeffries was feeling pleasantly important. This business at the factory was serious, of course – those supplies had been intended for the troops. The Quartermaster General for War Supplies took a dim view of crimes surrounding food, so when the culprit was apprehended he could expect to be hauled off to London for a public trial – and – though not even Will could pretend this was a capital offence – the miscreant could expect a hefty prison sentence and an even heftier fine, to say nothing of a mauling by the national newspapers. 'A deplorable business,' as Will had said to Mr Grey.

But there was something secretly satisfying, all the same, in doing something real to assist the war effort. There had been lots of 'special directives' from above, of course, and Will had dutifully done the rounds, making a list of all homing pigeons in the area, ensuring that licensed premises were shut by nine, or that the 'no-treating' law was properly observed and people were not buying one another drinks. He'd even visited the local farms to check that no-one was feeding precious bread to animals or fowls – though for the life of him he could not really see the sense in that; the creatures created food for people in the end!

But there'd been no opportunity here for the more exciting tasks – like stopping and questioning suspicious strangers – and although the local station had a modern telephone, there'd not been a single aircraft – marked or otherwise – flying overhead for him to report to the Admiralty, though he kept the telephone number written in his notebook, just in case.

But here at last was a significant affair and he had actually been called on to investigate. It was distinctly gratifying – and it was pleasant, too, to dispense advice about what kind of security measures should be put in place. He almost wished that Ivy was still here so that he could tell her all about it – modestly of course.

Though, perhaps not! He could almost hear her voice. 'Hardly a crime of national importance – a few hundred-weight of tinned butter, milk and cheese!' And she would have sniffed and gone on knitting those horrid lumpy socks, her four steel needles flashing as she worked.

But it was a matter of local consequence, he told the ghost of Ivy inwardly. Even the Borough Chief of Police had been involved, responding to the Sergeant's telephoned report with a special phone call of his own, asking to be kept informed about developments. 'Good man, Jeffries. Keep up the sterling work!'

'Don't worry sir, we'll catch him! I'll go down there first thing,' Will had answered, almost bursting his tunic buttons with pride.

And of course, he'd done so – though in truth, there was not a great deal more that he could do. He'd questioned everyone, with no results at all, and his system of gate-checks and double signatures had been introduced at once, but – though it would doubtless put a stop to future theft – it had slowed down deliveries so much that the waiting carters were beginning to complain.

Perhaps that was why, after a swift visit to the dairy earlier, he had decided to leave matters there to Mr Grey, and allowed his bike to carry him up Rosvene Hill. He was not conscious of having such a plan, but somehow he reached Forge Cottage without really meaning to. He dismounted by the gate, left the bike against the tree, and let himself into the yard to tap the kitchen door. When there was no reply he pushed it shyly open. 'Anybody home?'

But if he'd been hoping for a cup of tea and a sympathetic chat, he was disappointed.

Martha was in the kitchen with her eldest girl, surrounded by piles of damped washing. Sheets and petticoats drooped from every stick of furniture, while a box-iron heater stood hissing on the brandise at the fire. Both women whirled around as he appeared.

'Sergeant Jeffries. Well, as I'm alive! You gave me quite a turn!' Martha looked flustered, perhaps because she was surrounded by female undergarments. She gathered an armful, of various sizes, into a rough heap and thrust them at her daughter as she said, 'Please excuse the mess. I'm all three scats behind here, like Jan Trelawny's band. Pattie, you take these things upstairs to sort, and help Constance keep an eye on Faith!'

Patience took the clothes and scuttled off, seeming quite relieved if anything. She was pale and sickly-looking and her eyes were swollen red. Under the weather by the look of it – presumably the reason why she was not at work. Though Will was quite surprised. Hardworking people, like this Strict Adherent family, didn't usually stay home for common ailments – not without they were too ill to stand. Perhaps Pattie's malady was more serious than it looked. He was about to ask Martha, but she cut across his thoughts.

'But what brings you here, Will Jeffries, any case? Not Verity again? Is there some sort of problem?' She didn't meet his eyes, but turned away and spread a scorched sheet across the table as she spoke.

He shook his head. 'Only that business down the factory. I'm sure your girls have said.'

'What business?' For a moment Martha sounded sharp. Then she nodded vaguely. 'Oh, I know what you mean. Pru mentioned it last night. Goods going missing or something, wasn't it?' She did not sound especially impressed.

'Goods intended for the army.' He found he was using his most serious policeman's voice. 'Acting against the interests of His Majesty's forces, overseas. In breach of DORA, I shouldn't be surprised.'

That caught her attention. Even Martha must have heard of DORA – the Defence of the Realm Act.

'Dear Lord alive! Toby won't be happy when he hears! Won't want our girls going down there, to mix with criminals. And it would be, wouldn't it? Pru said you thought it was a member of the staff!'

'We will catch him Martha,' Will said soberly. 'Whoever it is won't have the chance to contaminate your girls.'

'Sounds as if you already have suspicions, who it is?'

'Not exactly,' Will said ruefully. 'There are several lines of enquiry I'm intending to pursue,' he added – trying to sound confident, but privately wondering what steps he could possibly take next. 'And when this fellow's caught he'll have an awful time in clink. Even jailbirds don't like people who work against the interests of the war.'

'Be a feather in your cap, if you do capture him,' she said, picking up the heater with a pair of tongs and slipping it into the iron as she spoke. 'There's not that many serious incidents round here. Course, there was that cart accident last year, when that poor soul was killed, and that rick fire over to Nanclere. That was a five days wonder at the time, when people thought that somebody had done it purposely, but it turned out it was only lightning!'

Will sighed. She was only saying what he'd thought himself, though he didn't welcome hearing it. Even with the war, most police work locally was disappointingly routine: looking for missing animals, pacifying warring neighbours, or catching up with children who were minching school. None of it the sort of thing that made for headline news. Even the scuffles outside the Tinner's Arms were rarer nowadays, what with the shorter hours, the government directive to water down the beer – and fewer men around to drink it anyway.

Martha had obviously heard the sigh. She flashed him a brief smile. 'Well I'm sorry, Will, I'd love to set the kettle on and stop and have a chat, but if there's nothing special that you want me for, I'd best get on with this. Should have got the ironing finished yesterday, but we've had a bit of excitement in the house. Might as well tell you – they're publishing the banns so it will be common knowledge round the village very soon. Ephraim Tull has asked for Pattie's hand, and she's agreed to have him.'

'Ephraim Tull!' Will could not keep the astonishment from his voice. 'Near old enough to be her father, isn't he?'

Martha turned away to test the iron by spitting on the base. 'He's a Strict Adherent, and that matters to her pa. Ephraim's a decent man and she won't be in want. It didn't seem to suit her down the factory anyway, she came home feeling cheevy yesterday and she's worse today – in fact Pru's taken a note to them today, asking permission for Patience to resign.'

Will could think of nothing sensible to say, except, 'They won't be very pleased. Your girls are all good workers – Mr Grey was telling me.'

Martha shook her head. 'Once she's better they'll want her back to work out the fortnight, I expect, but t'isnt sensible. You can't be too careful when it comes to food, though no doubt they'll hold back her last week's pay in lieu. Won't matter much to Pattie, any road – they're going to wed as soon as Ephraim gets a licence through.' She began to iron a pillowcase with ferocity, re-damping it by flicking water from a cup.

Will said, 'Bit sudden isn't it?' He then wondered if he should. Any other girl you would have questioned it – getting married in a hurry – but not this one of course.

Toby was more likely to disown a girl who got herself in trouble, than try to hide her shame. And as for Ephraim, he was stricter still! 'Him being interested in getting wed again,' he added hastily.

Martha was paying close attention to her task. 'Nothing new about it. Ephraim's offered for her several times. Only this time she's said yes. Just as well. He's not getting any younger and Patience don't want to end up a spinster, after all. As Ephraim says – so many young men are being killed these days, there's going to be a lack of husbands, by and by. Lack of everything, in fact. There's a question now where we're going to get the extra bread, even to make a sandwich for the witnesses. Man like Ephraim will expect a wedding tea. So, excuse me for not stopping to offer you some crowst, but there's things to plan and Toby will be home.'

The Sergeant nodded, but still he didn't leave. He hovered at the door. 'I'll call again, perhaps! Let you know how the enquiry's getting on?'

'You do that, Will,' she smiled. But she did not say it with her usual warmth and as he free-wheeled down the hill he couldn't shift the feeling that she wished he hadn't come.

So it was quite a pleasure to see Effie Dawes waving and smiling from outside her cottage gate. Looking pretty as a picture and dressed up to the nines.

–

Effie had put on gloves and hat, of course, as she was going to town – though she'd decided on her second-best coat and old-fashioned button boots instead of modern shoes. Crowdie had promised yesterday to give her a ride into Penzance, and that would mean his cart.

'Course I will my 'andsome – it's market day, I'm going in any case. Bring you back again, as well – save you the horse-bus fare – just so long as you don't mind budging up a bit! I already promised someone else that I would fetch them home.' And when she nodded gratefully, he said, 'Pick you up outside your cottage, then – round about five past tennish, if that suits?'

And here it was already ten o'clock. It was a chilly day, and she was grateful for the gloves, but it wouldn't do to keep Crowdie waiting when he'd been so kind. Then she saw Sergeant Jeffries cycling down the hill – and she'd been specially wanting to have a word with him! It was not the most convenient of times, but she smiled and waved and he drew up beside the wall.

'Marning, Mrs Dawes!'

'Ah Sergeant Jeffries. Here's a happy chance. I was thinking of coming to find you in the police-house later on. I can't stop long now – I'm going into Penzance – but there's a little matter on which I'd value your advice.'

He was absurdly flattered, you could see that in his face. 'Pleased to be of any help I can!'

'It isn't a matter of great consequence,' she went on hastily. 'It was only, I was wondering – with this war and everything – do you know where one could obtain a bicycle, and how much it would cost? One suitable for a lady bicyclist, I mean? Would they have one in Penzance do you suppose? I know it's difficult to get things nowadays. I wouldn't need a permit or anything like that?'

The Sergeant was staring at her as though she were completely mad. 'Who would that be for, then? Surely not yourself?'

'Why ever not?' She forced herself to smile. 'Lots of ladies ride bicycles these days. I was reading about it in a magazine.'

Sergeant Jeffries pushed his helmet back and smoothed his long moustache. 'Lots of men get drunk down at the Tinner's Arms,' he said. 'Doesn't follow that it's respectable. And no more's a bicycle – not for a decent married lady like yourself. Whatever put such an idea into your head? I don't know what your Alex would say if he found out!'

He sounded so certain that she wished she'd held her tongue. 'I suppose you're right,' she said, contritely. 'Perhaps it's not appropriate for me. Only I saw a vicar's daughter riding round the lanes the other day...' She trailed off.

'And you thought you'd like to try?'

'I merely thought how convenient it would be for me to go and visit my relatives that way, since I don't have a horse available!' And would not ride it if I did, she added privately, but she didn't say that to Sergeant Jeffries of course. But unaccompanied matrons rode horses nowadays, or even drove themselves in little traps, and no-one seemed to think that it was unsuitable at all! She sighed. 'But I wouldn't want to vex my husband for the world – if you think he wouldn't like it...'

'I'm quite sure he wouldn't!' The policeman's face had softened to an indulgent smile. 'It's one thing for a single girl to ride around, perhaps – though I aren't so certain even about that – but a lady of your station, that is something else. Now if you were looking for something for your maid...'

She shook her head. It still surprised her that she had a maid at all. She had never really wanted household staff

– after all, she'd been in service once herself – but Alex (and his mother) had expected it. He'd arranged it all the moment they were wed. So now there was young Amy who came in to cook and clean each day, just for the mornings, though there wasn't really much for her to do. (Effie had thought of urging her to put her name down on the Women's Register, to be available for war work – but Amy, at fifteen, proved not quite old enough.)

'I don't think Amy needs a bicycle,' she said. 'She hardly even leaves Rosvene. But I do – in fact I'm just about to now. Look, here is Crowdie, coming down the road!' Even as she spoke the cart came lurching down the hill and came to a gentle halt beside the gate.

She permitted Sergeant Jeffries to help her up, and she took her place by Crowdie as he flicked the reins and urged his ancient horse into a shambling walk again. 'Not the fastest transport, my 'andsome, I'm afraid,' the farmer said. 'But the blessed army's took my younger 'orses months ago. Still – if it helps our boys in France, I can't begrudge that, I suppose. Speaking of which, what news of Major Dawes?'

So she told him, happily, all the way to town and he listened – as he always did – as if her story was the most important in the world. It seemed no time at all before they reached Penzance.

Crowdie drew up at the cattle market at the top of Causeway Head. 'This is where I'm stopping, my 'andsome,' he said, jumping from the seat and coming round to help her down. 'Due to see a man about a bull. And there he is. Now, s'pose you meet me here again at four o'clock or so? Gets dark so early we should be setting off by then. That give you time to do everything you need?'

Effie thanked him and assured him that it would. Then, conscious he was watching, she hurried down the hill into the town. In fact, she knew her business would not take long at all, but she was looking forward to a little time at leisure in Penzance.

It was a treat she didn't often manage nowadays. Lunch in a tea shop somewhere, possibly? Married ladies hardly ever ate out anywhere alone, but tea shops were respectable enough. But things were scarce and in the first two places that she looked there were notices declaring that there was no meat today.

In the end she settled for some soup followed by a plate of fried flatfish with swede and chips, which – together with a pot of tea – cost her an eye-watering one and ten (though she declined the permitted two ounces of grey National bread). It made her feel a little sad, and very profligate – she could remember when sixpence would have seemed too much to spend on luxuries.

Perhaps it was the thought of luxuries that led her to the shop, Westons' Haberdashery, where she had briefly worked before she wed. She had not had occasion to come back ever since and it was sad to see how much the place had changed. Even the window looked dull and dreary now – rolls of bias binding and cards of hooks and eyes, instead of the former colourful displays of ribbons, lace and gloves – and the only millinery on display was black. The sole decoration was a swathe of draped black mourning 'crape', priced 2/6d (and spelt that way, as usual, to distinguish it from crepe material in more attractive hues.) The whole effect was more depressing than she could have dreamt.

Of course Miss Pearl had never had the flair – that had been Miss Blanche, and she had married and left

– but surely the change was not entirely the result of that? It must be partly the effect of war – there were obviously shortages, she thought, and so many people were in mourning nowadays, that perhaps the sombre colours were easiest to sell.

She let herself quietly into the shop, smiling at the familiar 'ting' of the little bell that rang when the door was opened. But looking round inside, she shook her head. The whole place – which had always seemed a treasure cave of jewel-like colours – was as bleak inside as the window goods had been. The shelves were half-empty, the colourful racks of silks and trimmings had all gone and (worst of all) the rear portion of the shop – which had once been a lending-library, and Effie's special joy – was turned over to a display of dismal hosiery. The books had disappeared.

So too, had the assistants, apparently – for there was no-one in the shop. Effie went out again and – by opening the door – 'ting-ed' the bell more firmly, and a moment later Miss Pearl herself came bustling from the storeroom at the back, wiping her lips discreetly in a hanky as she came.

'Can I be of service, Madam?'

'Miss Pearl!' Effie was surprised not to be recognized at once. 'Don't you remember me?' But even as she spoke she realized that – in any other place – she might not have known Miss Pearl. There was the same long black dress and apron, naturally, (that was expected if you were serving in a shop), the stout form was just as firmly corseted, and the hair was still pulled back in its uncompromising bun. But the stern face was sagging and the shoulders stooped. It used to be said of the elder Weston sister, once, that she might have been handsome if her habitual expression had not been so severe – but she looked worried, old and shrunken suddenly. Even the eyes which peered at Effie now, were pale and anxious behind their wire-rimmed spectacles.

'Why, if it isn't Effie Pengelly!' Miss Pearl sounded almost pleased. 'Or Mrs Dawes, as I suppose I should say now. Well, this is unexpected – and no mistake!' This was as near to a compliment as Miss Pearl ever paid.

Effie realized that. 'I don't get to town as much as I would like,' she answered, with a smile. 'But I got a lift today. I was hoping to pick up a bit of lace,' she added – though it wasn't strictly true. 'But perhaps that isn't possible?' she looked around. 'I hadn't realized that things had got so scarce.'

She gestured to the shelf above her head – where only a few rolls of ticking were displayed. There was a handwritten notice pinned to the lower edge, saying – in neat but shaky capitals – 'The management regrets that buttons (all sizes, shirt and fancy) are in short supply and the limited range of sewing thread in stock is likely to be the last available. Regular customers only need apply.'

Effie made a sympathetic face. 'Things are clearly difficult to get?'

Miss Pearl compressed her lips. 'You can buy some things, Blanche tells me, if you know where to look, but prices are twice what they were before the war. People can't afford it, things being what they are, so I don't have the turnover we used to have – and suppliers won't give you credit any more. So I couldn't get the stock, if there was any to be had.' She gave a disapproving sniff. 'But it's possible that I might have a bit of lace put by, that I might see my way to parting with – seeing how it's you. But don't you go telling anybody else, or they'll all be in here asking for the same.' She looked around as though there might be hordes of listening customers hidden in the shop, instead of it being as empty as the tomb. 'Come out the back and I will see what I can do. How much were you after?' She led the way into the little store and office at the back.

To Effie's surprise, given the empty shelves outside, the storeroom was as crowded as it had always been, with piles of wooden boxes everywhere, leaving just room for a table and two chairs beside the fire. It was a meagre fire – Miss Pearl had always been the careful one – and the woman had clearly been huddled over it. There was a kettle on the hearth, and a teacup and half-eaten sandwich on the table showed that she'd been eating when the shop-bell rang.

'Oh, I've interrupted your bit of lunch!' Effie exclaimed.

Miss Pearl put on her long-suffering face. 'It doesn't signify. The customer is always more important than the staff. My meal will have to wait,' she added in a martyred tone, as if the 'meal' in question was a hot cooked lunch. But Effie did not smile.

'But haven't you got an assistant in the shop? What happened to that girl who came to help you when I left?'

The thin lips pursed again. 'Left to get married when the war broke out – all in a hurry when her young man volunteered!' She sounded so bitter that Effie gazed at her, and realized suddenly that Miss Pearl was close to tears. That compression of the lips was to hide their trembling. 'But you are managing?' she said, with genuine concern.

The other woman drew herself upright, and then – as if defeated – let out a sigh. 'Tell you the truth, Effie... Mrs Dawes, I mean, I sometimes wonder how I will carry on.

What with the shortages, and these heavy boxes that want storing somewhere else...' She waved a hand towards the crates and Effie realized what she should have guessed at once. 'The books?' she murmured.

Miss Pearl nodded. 'No call for a subscription library any more – people can't afford it, they use the public library in Morrab Road or – if they don't care for charity – they go to Boots. For 10/6 you can sign up for a year, that entitles you to borrow any book – or you can pay extra and have more than one. And they've got hundreds more titles than we ever had. Who'd pay sixpence these days to subscribe to us – with food the price it is?'

She was clearly expecting Effie to say something comforting, but Effie's thoughts were running on a different track. 'Your books, though, aren't they? I mean you paid for them? Or, any rate, they are the property of the shop?'

The other woman stared at her. 'Well, course they are! I'd have returned them else, not have them cluttering up the place and getting in the way. I've even thought of throwing them away, and one or two I've torn the covers off and used to light the fire, but it goes against my nature. My father tied up a lot of money on those books, and I don't want them to waste, though I can't see how there'll ever be a library here again.'

'So, how don't you sell them?' Effie was so intent on her idea that for a moment her carefully acquired policeman's wife grammar had deserted her.

Miss Pearl went on staring. 'But how could I sell them? You can see they've all been read. Tea-stains and everything. And most of them are old. Battered corners to the covers.' She shook her head. 'It isn't possible! Let's stop talking nonsense. How much lace did you require?' She pushed aside a heavy carton full of books and pulled out a little cardboard box containing several ends of lace, wound onto little cards. 'This is all I've got. Would any of it suit?' But she was thinking about her visitor's proposition, anyone could see.

Effie went on urging: 'Course you couldn't sell the books full price – that would be fanciful. But people gave you sixpence just to borrow them – in that condition, exactly as they are. And there was a fine if they returned them late. Suppose that same sixpence bought you one or two? Don't you think subscribers mightn't jump at that?'

Miss Pearl had stopped fidgeting with the bits of lace. She shook her head. 'But they've got our stamp on them. People wouldn't care for that. Look like they'd been stolen, wouldn't they?'

'Then put another stamp in, saying something like "withdrawn due to the war". You've got that stamp where you can move the letters round – make it say any word you like – or you had, when I was here.'

'It would take hours…' Miss Pearl almost wailed, but she was warming to the project, you could almost see. 'You'd have to change the stamp each time – it only does one word – and every book would need stamping twice, at least!'

'Better than sitting shivering in here by yourself. And you don't have to do them all at once. Just a carton every week would do – make yourself a bit of space. And earn at the same time. Even a few pence a time would soon mount up. Put a notice in the window, too. People who used the library before might come in to buy a book they specially liked.'

Miss Pearl looked disbelieving. 'Who d'you suppose would do a thing like that? Most of my subscribers could easily buy new.'

That was true, of course, as Effie realized. Perhaps she'd let her notion run away with her. But she said stoutly, 'I would have done, for one! And I'm can't be the only person who likes a bargain, I'm sure. Specially now – when prices for everything are rising all the time and affordable little treats are getting hard to find.'

The shopkeeper said slowly, 'Well, perhaps you're right, at that. Couldn't do me any harm to try, I don't suppose. But there's so many of the dratted things, where d'you think that I should start?'

'I should start with this one,' Effie said firmly, indicating the carton which had been moved to reach the lace. 'Then, at least, it won't be in the way. In fact, if you'd like to serve me with that lace, I'll stop and help you set the stamp up and do a few of them. At least until another customer arrives.'

And that is exactly what she did, though it was another hour before the doorbell rang again and someone came in wanting darning wool. Effie watched from the storeroom – just in case – but the woman did not even glance towards the little pile of books with the sign: 'Withdrawn from the subscription library. Any two for sixpence' on the counter at the back.

'Just needs displaying a bit more,' she murmured as she left.

'I'll put a notice in the window when we close,' Miss Pearl agreed. But clearly it would take more than that to save the shop.

Four

Peter was waiting at the top of Causewayhead, wishing that he'd settled for the horse-bus after all. There was no sign of Crowdie or the cart and standing here, dressed up like Sunday tea, he felt conspicuous.

The cattle-market was over for the day, but there were lots of farmers still around the pens, engaged in private hagglings of their own and casting looks at him. They, of course, were all in going-to-market clothes – most with battered caps pushed back upon their heads, leather aprons tied around their waists, and their thumbs hooked round their braces or the pockets of their coats, though a few still wore old-fashioned floppy hats and working smocks. He felt already out of place in his best jacket, shirt and tie – as if 'I don't belong here any more' was written in large letters and hung around his neck.

But here was Crowdie and the cart at last, making its way from further up the hill. The farmer caught Peter's eye and gave a friendly wave. 'Had to leave this blamety thing up to Trevarnon farm,' he called. 'Took me longer than I thought to bring it down.' He drew up beside Peter. 'How d'you get on then? Still wanting a lift back?'

Peter nodded. 'But they've signed me on.' He put his hand onto the cart to clamber up.

'I should damty think so,' Crowdie said. 'Half bit your hand off, I shouldn't be surprised...' He broke off and gestured with his hand. 'But here's my other passenger. Help her up, there's a good fellow, and we'll be on our way.'

Peter turned to look, and almost fled. Coming towards them was Effie Dawes herself, looking a picture as she always did. He tried to say, 'Good evening,' but his mouth went dry.

She looked as shocked to see him as he was himself, and he realized that she hadn't known that he'd be there.

'Heard there was someone else to come. Never dreamt that it was you!' he muttered, mortified – and knew that his cheeks were turning that vivid shade of red which made the colour of his hair look worse than usual. How could Effie's chestnut locks look so becoming when she blushed – as she was doing now?

'Crowdie mentioned that he had a passenger,' she replied, putting only the faintest pressure on his hand as she climbed up into the seat. 'But he didn't mention who it was…' She tailed off. But there was no help for it – he had no money for the horse-bus now, so he had to climb up beside her on the seat, and hold himself against the side to stop from touching her.

'Sorry, my doves,' the farmer said, obviously surprised, as he urged the aging horse into a walk. 'Never supposed there would be awkwardness. I thought you two were friends.'

Effie laughed, that strained little laugh which she seemed to have adopted recently. Part of her being a fancy policeman's wife, perhaps – instead of the natural Cornish girl he'd known at school. 'Of course there is no awkwardness, Crowdie,' she said. Her voice had got all la-di-dah as well, 'proper elocution' as her pa had proudly said, but it was still as sweet to Peter as it had ever been.

'Peter and I have known each other years. It's just that we were both a little bit surprised.'

It wasn't true, of course, though Crowdie couldn't know. There was an awkwardness. Bound to be, when he had loved her all his life and she hardly noticed these days that he was there. She was happy with that policeman and he was glad of that – if she hadn't been, he'd have found the man and punched his eyes out, constable or not – but it wasn't what he'd hoped for. Even now he woke up, now and then, dreaming that they were six years old and back at school, kissing at the gate with the teacher scolding them. But it was no good mooning over what was past. She had made her choice and, from now on, so had he. He shook his head. She was saying something to him.

'You're dressed up like nine pence. Very smart you look. Come in to town for something special?'

Crowdie laughed and gave him a proud look. 'I should think so, too. Tell her, then, boy – it won't be secret long.'

Peter was too flustered to find his tongue at first, but then he shook his head. 'They sent a high-up general round the mines last year. Wanted men who'd handled dynamite. Special duties. I came to volunteer.'

'Volunteer?' she sounded shocked. 'You're going to join the army after all? I thought you had abandoned that idea. They need the tungsten, don't they? Or that is what I heard.' Why did it please him that she seemed alarmed?

He forced himself to smile. 'Well, I got a second chance and I have decided that I'll go. I don't like being stopped by dreadful old women in the street, waving white feathers in my face and calling me a coward. And anyhow—' he refused to look at her – 'I aren't very happy being where I am. But what Crowdie says is right – when they knew that I handled dynamite and was going to evening classes

123

on engineering work, they signed me up at once. Half-expected to be on the train to London before you could say "knife" – but turned out I had time to go home and let them know. I report tomorrow.'

'And after that there will be training, I expect,' Effie said, almost as if she welcomed the idea.

He shook his head. 'Not for the tunnellers, apparently. You don't need training for working underground, that's what the fellow said – not when you have done it all your life. And they're desperate for men to do this special job. I'll be off to France as soon as there's a ship. Told me a bit about it, but I'm not allowed to say.'

Effie said nothing, and he said nothing back. There was an awkward silence and then Crowdie said to her, 'You do everything you wanted in the town?' and Effie started on about the haberdashers shop, how it was close to fading, and she had ideas for it. Lucidly, since there was no need for Peter to join the talk at all till they got back to Nancarrow and Crowdie stopped to let him off.

'You all right for getting to the train?' the farmer said, as Peter jumped lightly down onto the road.

Peter nodded. 'I'll get the early horse-bus, they've given me a chitty for a railway pass. And one for uniform. I'll get kitted out when I get there, it appears. So I'll see you – sometime, if everything goes well. Goodbye Crowdie. Good evening, Mrs Dawes.' He took his cap off to them and nodded her a bow.

'You take care of yourself, Peter,' she said, with unexpected warmth. 'I'll be thinking of you.'

Of course she wouldn't, but it was nice to hear! He watched her sadly till the cart was out of sight, then put his cap on and went home to face his folks. It was going to be a tearful evening, he could see.

Sunday was a rather unhappy day, all round.

The problem started the night before, because Vee and Pru were on late shift for once. The factory was working round the clock and seven days a week, and everybody had to do one 'unsociable' a month, but of course the Tregorran girls, as Strict Adherents, would not do Sunday work. This meant they, together with others like the Bible Christian girls, had to do an occasional evening shift – which up to recently had been reserved for men, because of going home in the dark. It wasn't as bad as you might think, in fact – there were a whole group of people walking back, most of whom had lanterns, and the girls were escorted right up to the gate.

The trouble started when they got inside. It was almost midnight and the girls were ravenous but the pot of stew that Ma had left beside the hearth was getting cold. Vee made the mistake of poking up the fire, to give a bit of light, and putting the stew back on to warm a bit.

It smelt delicious, but the fragrance must have drifted through the house, because no sooner were they sitting down to eat – huddling on stools beside the flickering flames – than Pa came storming down the stairs, in his flannel nightshirt and the matching cap, carrying a night-light in his hand.

'What do you two think you're doing? It's the Sabbath day! Thou shalt do no labour! Don't you know the Word!' He seized Pru's bowl of soup and threw it on the fire. He might have done the same with Vee's as well, if she hadn't snatched it instantly aside.

'It's a sin to waste good food when there are children starving!' she declared, daringly tipping a portion of the contents down her throat. 'Aren't you always saying that?' It was something that he often declared at mealtimes, though she'd never found a Bible text supporting it. She realized that he would be furious, but she did not care. If she got a hiding, at least she'd had some food.

Pa, however, was too astonished to respond, so she gulped another mouthful – never mind the spoon – and passed the bowl to Pru. Her sister, though, was too afraid to follow suit and simply sat there weeping tears of hunger, shame and fright.

Pa found his voice. 'Are you defying me?' He sounded threatening.

Vee shook her head. 'No, Pa, of course not. We didn't mean to break the Sabbath.' It was true, *but* she tried to sound appropriately penitent. 'We didn't realize it had got so late. It was an accident – by firelight you can hardly see the clock. And didn't Jesus say, "Forgive them, for they know not what they do?" And even He picked corn on the seventh day, and rubbed the husk off so that He could eat. And when Pharisees grumbled, you know what he said—'

'"The Sabbath was made for man, not man for the Sabbath",' Pa supplied reluctantly, adding something about the devil quoting scripture for his purposes. However, he didn't seize the other bowl or throw away the stew and Vee knew that they'd escaped a row, if not a leathering. He put the night-light down. 'Too much like your mother, you are, Verity!'

'Besides, Pa,' Pru said, suddenly more daring through her tears, 'I think we'd heated it before the clock showed twelve. And blessed it to our use. So it should be sanctified. Besides, "it isn't what goes into a man that defiles him" – doesn't Mark say that?'

'No, he doesn't,' Pa retorted. 'You're misquoting Gospel, now find the text and learn it right before you go to bed. Let that be your penance, both of you. And Pru, stop snivelling. You're older, you should take the lead. However, you may finish what Vee has given you. She at least has shown the gift of generosity, that her "abundance should supply your want", and perhaps we should not be ungrateful to your ma, who lovingly prepared the stew for you. And you may light a candle to see your way upstairs – can't have you falling over in the dark – but don't go stirring that fire up again! Just ask the Lord for mercy when you say your prayers!'

And up he went again, the stair-boards creaking at every step.

'My heaven,' Vee whispered, when silence fell again. 'That was a near thing and no mistake! I thought we'd feel his belt across our backs for sure. Pa's been in some funny mood these last few days. Teasy as an adder one minute and soft as dough the next.'

She looked to Pru for sympathy, but all her sister said was, 'Not surprising, p'raps, with everything going on. Now come on to bed or we shall get no sleep at all. Chapel in the morning.'

But chapel was no better. You'd think there might have been a bit of joy, for once, when Ephraim announced he was applying for the banns and where they would be posted – as he was bound to do – but Patience looked so dismal and upset, you'd think it was a notice about her funeral. And Ma was just as bad. When Ephraim led the usual (interminable) prayers, and asked the congregation to 'pray specially for the woman who is to become my wife, that she may put all sin behind her' – which was just the sort of thing he always said – Ma looked furious and did not say 'Amen!'

The only person who seemed pleased at all, was Grandfather, who came grim-faced and solemn, to shake Pa by the hand, though even he was tetchy 'cause he'd not been told before. Vee was more than usually glad when the fellowship was over and it was time to leave.

Though lunch wasn't much to speak of, when they came to it. Pa's gesture with the soup had put the fire right out last night, instead of leaving embers to burn slowly down, so the house was more than usually chill – and the tongue and cold potatoes, washed down with watered milk, made for a particularly cheerless meal.

Then in the afternoon, there was another fuss. You could not read or play games on Sunday, of course, but Vee had devised a scheme for getting out by taking a walk across to see her aunt again. She knew that Pa would not approve, of course, but she had a reason ready, as she explained to him.

'I got to go,' she told him, when he opposed the plan. 'I left my woollen shawl there, when I went the other day – caught it on a bramble and made a hole in it. Aunt Dorcas said she'd unravel it and knit it up again. Before tomorrow too – you know how quick she is with things like that. It would have took me hours, and it's the only one I've got!'

Pa looked for all the world as if he might refuse, but Ma said quickly, 'No, Toby, she had better. I'll write a note to Dorcas to tell her Pattie's news and she can take it with her. Better that she hears from me, and not from other folks.' She turned to Verity. 'But don't be very long. And don't be going alone. Take young Mercy with you for a bit of exercise. Your pa's decided – for reasons which we won't go into now – that from here on, none of you girls is to go walking on the cliffs, without there's someone with you. Do you understand?'

Seven baffled faces answered that they did, but Vee saw Pru and Patience exchange a rueful look. Those two understood why this new rule had been imposed, though Vee had no idea, and no amount of private pleading would make Pru say a word, even when they went upstairs to get Mercy dressed to go. It was no good asking Patience, naturally, she never told Vee anything at all!

So Ma wrote her letter. She didn't write things often and it took her quite a time, licking her pencil between every word, though Ma and her sister had both learned when they were young. So the afternoon was well advanced before Vee got away.

It was not quite the pleasure that Verity had hoped. For one thing, it was very cold without her shawl, and for another she had Mercy with her – which was itself a trial. Mercy was 'more top than child' as mother always said – never still a minute and forever rushing round. Walking on the cliffs with her was not a restful thing: Mercy was never where you thought that she would be, insisting on running down every little track they passed. You had to watch she didn't rush out on the road and be run down by some passing cart, or go the other way and fall into the sea.

Auntie Dorcas's house was welcoming and warm. She had turned Methodist these days of course, so things were not too strict. Verity could drink hot tea beside the fire while Mercy sat on Uncle Terence's lap to 'read' her favourite book – a picture one, with Eskimos and bears, which Uncle Terence had won at Sunday school. 'For good attendance', it said inside, which always made Vee smile. The Strict Adherents didn't give you prizes for just being there each week! That was expected – there were questions if you weren't!

Out in the scullery, she gave her aunt the note. Dorcas couldn't read it – she didn't have her spectacles, she said – so Vee did it for her. 'Going to be married as soon as possible.'

'My dear life!' Aunt Dorcas said, putting down her cloth. (It was all right to dry dishes on Sunday, in this house.) 'I always thought your Pattie was a wayward one, but I don't envy the poor girl, and that's a fact. Though I suppose it's a mercy. Ephraim Tull! Whoever heard the like! Man's got more charity than I supposed. It isn't his – it can't be?' She looked across at Vee.

'What isn't?' Verity was genuinely perplexed.

Aunt Dorcas looked at her surprised, then smiled and shook her head. 'Never you mind, my handsome. I'm just being foolish, I shouldn't be surprised. Forget I ever said it – but you tell your ma I'll come and see her sometime in the week.'

If Vee had been surprised before, she was astonished now! It was one thing for the nieces to call here now and then – though even that was not approved of very much. It was quite another matter for Dorcas to call on them – Verity could not remember such a thing. Grandfather would have apoplexy at the very thought and Pa would side with him. There'd be no end of row.

Dorcas laughed. 'Verity Tregorran, you should see your face! I know what you're thinking, but I meant what I just said. With a wedding coming she'll want a bit of a hand. And someone to talk to, I shouldn't be surprised. Woman needs her sister, at a time like this. So you tell your ma I'll come, and never mind the men – without she sends word to say she'd sooner I stayed home!'

Vee promised that she would, although it spoiled the afternoon – she felt like Sam Chegwidden at the forge, carrying a heated iron in the tongs, as if inevitable disaster was about to fall. She was almost glad to rescue Mercy from her post and claim the mended shawl.

Her aunt had made a lovely job of mending it, as usual – Dorcas was clever with her needles and you could hardly see the join – and Vee thanked her with a hug. But that message weighed upon her like a ton of bricks as she set off across the cliffs again.

And then, to crown it all, she saw that man again. She was certain – almost certain – that it was the one she'd seen before. Same thin build and beaky face, and battered bowler-hat, but with a bicycle this time. She and Mercy were walking on the path that led up to the stile, and there he was ahead – with someone stocky, in another bowler hat – having some sort of heated argument. Seemed there'd nearly been an accident.

'Can't you learn when to stop? Coming careering round the cliffs – it's downright dangerous! You'll run into someone, next thing, if you don't look out. Other people want to use this lane, you know!' This other fellow seemed to have a pony and trap; he looked somehow familiar, but his back was to Verity and she could not see his face. She strained on tip-toe from behind a bush to see a little more, without drawing attention to the fact that she was there, when a cry behind made her wheel around.

Mercy was up to her little tricks again, and was (naturally) nowhere to be seen. Vee went back to look and found her down a side path to the sea; tripped over on a stone and fallen into a furze bush by the path, screaming like a weasel because it hurt to move.

'You little varmint!' Vee seized her sister's two arms and extracted her, then crossly mopped her bleeding knees and picked most of the prickles out of her. She was impatient to get back to the stile and get a better look, but by the time that Mercy had limped her tearful way back to the vantage place, there was no sign of anyone. The pony-trap had vanished and the men had gone.

Here was a dilemma. Should she tell the police? Sergeant Jeffries had suggested that she did, if she saw the man again. But what could she tell him? Nothing new at all. He'd only laugh and call her fanciful again. Then, the answer came to her. Of course! Tomorrow, after work, she'd call and confide in Mrs Dawes. She was kind, she was a policeman's wife arid she'd know what to do.

But there was still the problem of the message from Aunt Dorcas. Vee clenched her teeth and dragged a protesting Mercy home to deliver it. It was not as bad as Verity had feared – only a brief outburst from her pa – but there was an atmosphere at supper, and an outbreak of fierce, whispered arguing downstairs when she had gone to bed.

And the visit to see Mrs Dawes next day was even less what she had hoped.

–

Effie was entertaining her new step-mother to tea when the knock came on the door.

Before that, the afternoon had not been entirely a success, though Amy (bless her) had conjured up the butter, flour and eggs to make a sponge, which – with the war – was a rare and splendid treat. The atmosphere was friendly, but without Pa there it was a little stiff. The problem was with names.

Effie could not bring herself to call his new wife 'Mother' as he would have liked, 'Mrs Pengelly' was too stuffy, and 'step-mother' sounded like a villain from a fairy tale! But one couldn't go on calling her 'Mrs Richards' now – though Effie accidentally occasionally did – and things were awkward till they settled upon 'Jillian', which solved the problem, for the most part anyway.

Not that Jillian was difficult to like; quite the opposite, in fact. She was a small, thin, cheerful woman with a care-worn face and a heart, as Pa said, 'bigger than outdoors'. Many another woman might have borne a grudge, seeing that her son was blinded in the mine in that same accident which had crippled Pa, and for which – as leader of the team – Pa felt responsible. But Mrs Richards – Jillian! – took a different view.

'Nobody knows mining like your pa – Capt'n Maddern told me that hisself – so if he didn't see that rock-fall coming, no-one would have done. And I've got him to thank that I've a son at all. Hadn't been for throwing himself over Jimmy when he did, the boy would have died, for sure. And Walter's been so good to us, these last few years. Treated Jimmy as though he was his own. Lad couldn't have had a better father if his own had lived, or me a better 'usband. Did I tell you that he's arranged a course, now, learning Jimmy how to re-cane chairs?'

It was the first that Effie had heard of such a thing and she was grateful for the opportunity to talk about the boy. She'd always found it awkward to enquire after him. 'Where is that to then?'

'Has to go up Bodmin every week, Monday to Friday,' his mother said, trying to sound proud but sounding rueful too. 'Class is run by the society for the blind, so Walter and me have only got to find his keep, and that's in a special hostel so it isn't dear.' She fumbled in the drawstring purse that dangled from her waist. 'I've brought his first report to let you see – he's doing well, apparently and "showing aptitude".' She took out a crumpled sheet and smoothed it flat.

Effie understood at once. Jillian wanted to hear it read aloud again – she wasn't very good at ciphering, herself. She obliged, with pleasure, then gave the paper back. 'All the same, you'll miss him dreadfully, I expect. Though if it means that you can come and visit me sometimes, I shall selfishly be pleased.'

The woman laughed. 'Perhaps I can arrange to come again, at that!'

This visit was not a usual event. Jillian could not normally leave the house without the boy, and it was not easy to take him anywhere. In any case, she had rheumatic knees so it was hard for her to walk, and the horse-bus times in this direction weren't convenient, so up to recently Effie had always called on them. But Jillian was finding the house too empty now, with Jimmy gone, when Pa was at the mine.

So Pa worked out a scheme. He'd heard that the waggoner who served the tally-shop down at Penvarris mine came to the dairy factory now and then, to pick up new supplies, so he'd had a little word, and – for a consideration – the man had agreed that next time he was this way, he'd give Jillian a lift.

He had delivered her today at two o'clock. 'I should be back by five. Let's just hope that nothing holds me up, or it will get too dark and we risk getting overturned by hitting something in the road,' was his lugubrious farewell.

No wonder Jillian had been a little tense at first. But she'd relaxed by now, enough to put the paper back into her purse and say, quite innocently, 'There's someone else your father's going to miss. That Peter Kellow from next door, you must remember him? Gone to be a soldier – all of a sudden rush. Only left on Friday, went up London on the train, and his family had word from him today – he's off to France before the week is out. Don't know what got into him, he didn't have to go, but when he makes his mind up there's no changing him. Walt says there's some girl he's sweet on – 'e won't tell me who – but apparently she's upped and married someone else. Anyhow, your pa'll miss him. They've got to be good pals. But there you are, the world goes on I suppose...'

Effie made some indistinct response and got up to pour another cup of tea she didn't want, but it hid her blushes as she turned away. 'Speaking of which,' she said, 'I had a letter yesterday. Alex is...' She broke off as there was a rapping on the door. 'I wonder who that is?' She went to answer it.

It was Sergeant Jeffries. He was looking grim. There was a boy on a bicycle behind him at the gate.

'Effie. Mrs Dawes... something's come for you. Came to the police-house. I said I'd bring it down, but he insisted that he had to deliver it himself.'

Effie looked at him, uncomprehendingly, and then at the boy who was walking up the path, holding something towards her in his hand. A telegram. Of course, she should have recognized the uniform! Even then she did not take in the significance.

Only when she opened it and read the words: 'It is my painful duty to inform you... died on escort duty...' The world seemed to have stopped. There was a dreadful howling. She wished that it would stop. But she was doing it.

She was aware that Sergeant Jeffries had taken her by the arm and was leading her inside. 'No,' she said, 'I can't go in. Alex won't be there. He's…' She had stopped screaming, but she couldn't cry. Nothing was real.

Mrs Richards had appeared from somewhere and was offering her some tea. As if she would ever want tea any more! She shook her head and sat down on the chair. Sergeant Jeffries came back – she had not noticed that he'd gone – and tucked a rug around her and poured something down her throat. It tasted horrible and hot and stung her throat, but it must have done her good because the shivering slowly stopped.

'She'll sleep now for a little,' she heard the policeman say. 'Best thing for her, too.'

She wanted to deny it – who could sleep with Alex dead? – but her eyes were closing and the voices were becoming far away.

'I'll stay with her,' said Mrs Richards, or was that a dream? 'I'll send a message back to Walter with the cart. Better if Effie isn't left alone.'

And she must have stayed because the next time Effie woke, it was getting dark. The oil lamp was lighted and the fire was banked, and there were unfamiliar voices at the door.

'No!' That was Mrs Richards! What was she doing here? 'You'll do no such thing. Mrs Dawes is in no state to talk to anyone. No, not tomorrow either. She's had bad news and there's an end of it. I'm sorry, but that's that. Yes, her husband. Thrown when his horse was frightened by a shell. She's shocked half to death herself. Now go away and let the poor soul get a bit of sleep.'

But the 'poor soul' had remembered – there was no more sleep that night.

Part Three

February 1916

One

Alex's funeral was held at Falmouth, at his parent's home, or rather at the little church nearby which he'd attended as a boy. His father, the Major, had arranged it all, from bringing the coffin back from overseas to the choice of hymns, the date of the service and the location of the grave.

'Laid to rest among his ancestors,' he said to Effie on that dreadful day, as he handed her into the carriage – pulled by the family's one remaining horse – in which she and the older Mrs Dawes were to be conducted back towards the house. There, the best war-time funeral tea available had been laid on for the select mourners who had been invited to remain 'for refreshment afterwards'.

The Borough Police Commissioner was among them, and several other former colleagues from the Penzance Police Station, who had formed an arch of honour outside of the church. They were following with the other men on foot behind the coach, as they had done on the journey to the church. But there was no one from Penvarris, Nancarrow or Rosvene – even at the funeral itself – other than Sergeant Jeffries and Effie herself. Pa had volunteered to come, of course, but Mrs Dawes senior had made very clear that – though he'd had an invitation card – he wasn't really expected to accept.

'It's very good of you, Mr Pengelly,' she had said, on one of the rare duty visits she had paid since Alex died. 'Of course you are a relative by marriage and all that. But you'd hardly know a soul and it must be very difficult for you to get away. Besides, wherever would you stay? I'd offer you a bed myself, of course, but we shall have a houseful, with my family. Scores of cousins – to say nothing of my aunts. And of course we'd understand if you decide that it's too far! You wouldn't be the only person unable to attend – even my other sons are serving overseas and won't be there. We're grateful for your willingness, of course, and we'll see that you are mentioned in the press report. And don't go to the expense of sending flowers up – we have a greenhouse full of blooms, the gardener's brought white lilies on especially.'

It hadn't occurred to her father to send flowers anywhere, he had only thought of paying his respects and supporting Effie on the day, but he could take a hint. 'I'd just be in the way,' he told his daughter, when the woman had gone home and he and Jillian were sipping tea in Effie's sitting room again.

'Bossy besom!' Jillian exclaimed, clearly insulted on poor Pa's behalf. 'It isn't their place to plan the funeral like this, all single-handedly. Effie should have been consulted from the start.'

'Perhaps it's for the best, though, Jilly,' Pa murmured peaceably, filling his pipe again before the fire. 'I expect the Major knew what strings to pull. Otherwise the army might have buried him out there. That's happened to a lot of poor fellows recently, I know. Cornish boys lying forever under foreign soil.'

Jillian clucked her tongue impatiently. 'But that Mrs Dawes wrote all the bereavement letters to acquaintances and sent out all the invitations to the funeral – on black-edged stationary showing *their* address. You know she did, you had a card yourself! You'd never think that Alex had a wife.'

Effie listened vaguely, but in truth she hardly cared. Nothing had seemed real since she got that telegram. She'd gone on living only in a kind of dream. She could not rouse herself to anything – scarcely had the energy to wash and dress, and probably wouldn't have bothered about eating anything, if it hadn't been for Amy, who made little treats for her (though they tasted like sawdust, like everything these days). And without Jillian, who had more or less moved in, and Pa who came whenever possible, she might not even have been ready for the day itself.

Jillian had helped her pick out a black dress and coat – off the shelf, since Effie wasn't up to sewing anything. Alex's mother had offered to send her own dressmaker by train, but Effie had turned that down so flatly it was almost rude. Instead she'd suffered herself to be taken into town to purchase a crape-trimmed mourning outfit from Westons' shop – so with her best black boots, black gloves and hat, and one of the long crape veils that she'd been so scornful of, she looked respectably widow-like today. And thanks to Sergeant Jeffries, who arranged a trap to take her to the train and came with her all the way, she had managed to attend this funeral without absently missing her connection on the way.

The senior Mrs Dawes had not approved at all. Quite early on she had written to confide that: 'I confess I was alarmed when I learned that you propose to come by train – I'm of a generation which would privately prefer that the tender sex did not go to funerals at all (such things may be too much for their sensitivities) and that new widows should not go about in public – but I learn that, with the war, even the best families are doing these things now.'

That was the only opposition Effie met. 'Very brave,' the awful cousins murmured as they squeezed her hand outside the church (or, if they were female, made imitation kissing motions at her cheek).

But there was nothing brave about it. Effie could not cry – partly because she still did not believe that this was happening. How could it be Alex in that horrid wooden box? Any day, surely, there would be a letter from the regiment telling her that it was all a terrible mistake? In the meantime she would have to live and breathe and somehow manage to do what was expected at the grave.

But at last it was all over and the coffin laid to rest. Her mother-in-law leaned back against the cushions of the coach. She, of course, was in deepest mourning too, but contrived to look quite dashing in the latest style with black guipure lace insets at her neck, and trimming of jet-black beads round the edges everywhere.

'Well, that went off as well as possible, I think!' She wore a veil, of course, though just across her face, and throughout the service she had kept lifting it to dab her eyes with a special black lace-edged handkerchief. 'Just remember, Ethel,' – her in-laws always called her 'Ethel', which was properly her name, although Effie hated it – 'there's room for you here too, you know, whenever the time comes.'

'Oh no, I couldn't!' Effie cried, appalled.

'It's customary in our family for women to be buried beside their husbands,' Mrs Dawes said stiffly, obviously stung. 'Though it may be different among your people, I suppose. Unless you have plans to marry someone else?'

'Oh, course, not.' Effie was embarrassed and confused. 'I'm sorry, Mrs Dawes. I thought for a moment...' She tailed off, blushing. 'I thought for a stupid moment you meant coming here to live.'

'Oh my dear.' It was the other woman's turn to be embarrassed, now. 'Of course there would always be a home for you with us. We could do no less for our son's widow, if you needed it. But of course you have a family of your own back in Penwith, and we would not wish to press you to come here against your wish. And you'll have money from Alex, so you won't be in want. You could find a little cottage that might suit you, I am sure.'

Effie nodded. There would be a pension from the army – they'd already been in touch – and a little from the police. More than enough to rent a little place.

Though it occurred to her suddenly that she would have to think of doing so – she could not go on living as she was, expecting to move back into the police house at Rosvene, after the war. The Borough would have to send a replacement policeman now, and Sergeant Jeffries would want his cottage back. For the first time the realization came to her that, from here on, life was different. Alex was dead and he wasn't coming back, and the future that they'd hoped and planned for was not a future, but a shattered dream.

Somehow she got through the tea party (or the 'funeral reception' as her mother-in-law insisted it was called), enduring sympathy from people that she hardly knew, until at last the guests had gone and it was time to catch the train. The Major – who had scarcely said a word to her throughout – came across, quite warmly, to bid farewell to her, and to Sergeant Jeffries, who had stayed behind, because he was escorting her of course.

'My coachman will be waiting, just outside the door. Have the servants brought your wrap? Then allow me to offer you my arm.' Major Dawes (not Alex, she thought bitterly, but a different Major Dawes), extended an elbow and she took it gingerly.

He led her quite swiftly to the entrance hall, leaving Sergeant Jeffries to plod on behind. A moment later, the reason became clear. 'Wanted to mention,' he murmured, quietly, 'there'll be a little sum. Put it in trust for Alex when he married you, for heirs and dependents. Haven't told his mater, but I thought you ought to know. Meant it for my grandchildren, but it will come to you. It isn't a great deal – if he'd outlived me he'd have had a share of this estate – but enough to give you a little something to fall back upon. Now, here we are!' They were at the door by this time and he signalled to the coachman, who brought the carriage up. The Major helped her into it, but as she took a seat, instead of letting go he squeezed her fingers tight.

'I did not approve the marriage, I'm ashamed to say, but you made him happy while he was alive. Thank you for that, Ethel. I only wish we'd contrived to do the same a little more.' It was the briefest of gruff murmurs but coming from that man, so stern and unbending, it was a special compliment.

Those were the words that acted as a balm all the way back to White Cottage at Rosvene. Perhaps it was that which gave her strength to remark to Sergeant Jeffries, when he left her at the gate, that she understood that he might require the place again – and even to smile wryly at his evident relief.

'Hadn't wanted to worry you, my dear Mrs Dawes, but I'm glad you brought it up. I would have had to speak to you sometime. The Borough Commissioner told me, when I spoke to him today, that they'd found a replacement now that…' He broke off and fingered his moustache. 'Since there's now a vacancy,' he corrected hastily and then was so embarrassed he could hardly wait to say goodnight.

The house seemed very empty when she let herself inside. Jillian or Pa had been there earlier and banked up the fire for her – so it was warm at least – but already it did not feel like home.

She spent the evening wondering where she ought to look. Not here, there were too many memories. Penzance, perhaps, or would that be too dear? Or over at Nancarrow, where she'd be close to Pa – but no, that wouldn't do, Peter Kellow's family lived further down the street. She fell asleep still sitting in the chair and woke next morning stiff and chill, still in her funeral clothes – and only then when Amy came tapping at the door.

'Oh, my dear life, madam! You'll catch your death of cold. Here, let me make a cup of tea for 'ee, and 'elp you out of that long veil and take your coat, at least. You'll have to wear the rest, from 'ere on, all the time, I suppose, and a widow's cap indoors. Though you'll have to get a change so you can launder them.'

That was another disconcerting truth. Effie could hardly manage to give her a wan smile and sip the tasteless tea that was prepared for her.

–

It was awkward going into the dairy factory these days. There were rumours flying round – concerning Patience, you could tell – though people didn't generally say so to your face. What they did was huddle into groups and whisper to each other when your back was turned.

It was worst at crowst time. Groups of girls were sitting on the wall, eating the bits of bread and scrape they'd brought, or a little pasty (if they were lucky, and there were enough scraps left over from their pa's). But no one spoke to the Tregorran girls.

Prudence came and found Vee, who was sitting on her own, toying with the crust and cheese that Ma had given her. 'Not hungry?' Pru enquired.

Vee shook her head. 'Not with all they staring!'

Pru was never happy just ignoring things. She called out to a little knot of girls, some of whom worked on the packing-line with them. 'What's going on then, Gloria Tresize? What are you staring at?'

Gloria, who was a sort of friend, turned pink but she left the others and came over to the pair.

'Here Vee.' She dropped her voice. 'I hardly like to say, but is it true your Patience was caught out stealing things and that's why she's left?' She made a little face. 'I didn't think it likely, you being Strict Adherent girls and all, but that's what folks are saying, and perhaps you ought to know.'

Verity felt her heart sink to her boots. So it was true, then, what she'd thought? Gloria was looking at her enquiringly but Vee said nothing. What answer could she make?

Pru, though, was on her feet and clearly hopping mad. 'I don't know what this factory is like. If it isn't one daft rumour going about, it's an even dafter one. Of course our Pattie did nothing of the kind. She went off home 'cause she was feeling sick. She's not been quite well lately – you might have noticed that! And the reason she's not coming back is that she's getting wed.'

'Wed?' the girl called Gloria echoed, looking mystified. 'You hear that?' she called out to her friends. 'Patience is getting married!' She turned back to Pru. 'Who to, then? Anyone we know?'

'It's Ephraim Tull, the farmer,' Pru said, defiantly. 'If any of you went to chapel you might have heard by now. Banns are being published and they'll be married very soon.'

One of the other girls had drifted over now. 'Bit sudden, isn't it?'

'Nothing of the sort. He's wanted her for years. So don't go jumping to conclusions about that!' Pru added, as people crowded round.

One of the listeners gave a knowing laugh. 'Only one reason I know why people rush to wed!'

Gloria whirled round, unexpectedly. 'Well, not this time, stupid. Prudence is quite right. If you knew Ephraim Tull, you'd realize. Drier than an old stick. And a Strict Adherent, too. More moral than a month of Sunday schools. He wouldn't get a girl in trouble, if he was able to – or take a girl to wife who wasn't what she ought to be.'

'And that includes a thief. So let that be an end to gossip,' Pru said, sitting down and opening her crowst bag with a flourish. 'I wonder you lot don't apologize.'

'You're right. I'm very sorry, Vee.' Gloria was a nice girl, and she sounded quite contrite. She raised her voice. 'It obviously wasn't Patience who was stealing things! I don't know how I ever thought it was!'

'Nor do I,' Pru told her. 'And that goes for all of you. So stop your wicked lies. And ask yourself who started the stories anyway, cause if it wasn't Pattie stealing, it must be one of you!'

People began to drift sullenly away, and Gloria turned to Verity again. 'Sorry to hear that Pattie's really sick – though now I can see the sense of why she's getting married, quick. Man like Ephraim would hurry things along – doing her a Christian favour before it gets too late.' She flashed Vee a friendly smile. 'Well, tell her that I wish her well and hope she gets better – even if she don't. And send my best wishes for her wedding too. Though – Ephraim Tull! I'm glad it isn't me!' She went off, shaking her head, to join her friends.

Vee, who had been sitting silent through all this, tried to take a bite of crust but found her hands were shaking. She dropped them to her lap.

'Well?' Pru said crossly, 'crow got your tongue, or something? Couldn't you speak up for Pattie, too, a bit?'

Vee shook her head. 'You're so much better at it. You know just what to say. Besides,' she confided, taking a deep breath, 'I wasn't certain that the story wasn't true. I thought perhaps she had been... you know... taking things...'

Pru turned her head so sharply that she almost shook her clean white work-cap off her head. 'Pattie, stealing? You must be mad – or blind! Of course that's not the trouble!' She paused, and took a bite. 'Mind you, I suppose the truth is just as bad.'

'And what's that?' Vee persisted.

'Oh, you are a baby? Don't you really know?' Pru jumped down from the wall abruptly and brushed imaginary breadcrumbs from her skirt.

'Not unless you tell me...' But the whistle went and Vee didn't get an answer. She had to stuff the whole crust in her mouth, or she wouldn't have managed any lunch at all. Then, of course, there was no chance of hearing anything. On the packing-line you weren't allowed to talk – unless it was about some problem with the goods, or you were showing some new arrival what to do.

She would ask Pru later, when they got back home, Vee told herself, but by that time there were other things for her to think about.

–

After the initial excitement of enlisting as a tunneller, Peter was beginning to wonder if he'd made a bad mistake.

It had been all right at first. He had accepted the humiliating tests which they called a 'medical', because they were supposed to prove that you were fit to serve (though he could not work out how) and was moved by the solemnity of taking the sworn oath. The train ride to London was an adventure in itself. Peter had never been further than Penzance in his life and he had no idea that England was so big – while the pride of a travel warrant and a brand-new uniform had given army life a splendid start.

But 'joining his company' in London was not quite as he'd hoped. He had expected a lot of fellow Cornishmen, but most of his companions came from what they called 'oop nawrth' and talked about coal pits or 'kicking claay', in dialects so broad he could hardly understand, though they seemed to find his honest Cornish quite as difficult. 'Hast thee 'eard this?' one muttered. 'Says nowt but arr—arr—arr!' It made him feel like a foreigner, himself.

Then, far from being part of the brand-new unit being formed, he found that he – with only a dozen others – was to be posted to an existing squad, as 'urgent replacements'. The solitary fellow Cornishman among them, Tremean, a lugubrious stocky lad who'd worked down Wheal Jane mine, raised his brows at this.

'Urgent replacements? What do they mean by that? That when we get to France we'll be like kiddly-boys – the least experienced people in the company – and yet be on active service straight away! You wait and see if I'm not right!'

There was not long to wait. Forty-eight hours later they were on the ship to France: two days and nights of total misery, retching and heaving in an airless berth, while a February gale tossed the vessel like a toy.

Peter could not even stagger up and take the air, which Tremean did constantly – on the recommendation of the older hands, who'd made the trip before. It seemed to do him good, but Peter's one attempt to step out on the deck nearly resulted in him pitching overboard, and he was embarrassingly and comprehensively sick in any case, so after that he simply lay down in his allotted space and wished to die.

Dry land, when it finally appeared, did not offer much opportunity to rest. He'd barely had time to grow accustomed to the fact that the world was no longer lurching under him, than his contingent were whisked away again and he and Tremean found themselves herded into a railway carriage, together with a lot of men from somewhere else, and rattled down the line.

The troops that they were travelling with were seasoned warriors; they'd been in the trenches just two weeks ago, and were returning from a period of 'rest and relaxation' back from the line. Their talk was loud and raucous and they smelt overpoweringly of sweat, cigarettes and beer. Tremean got into conversation with one or two of them, boasting about the girls that he had known, while Peter pressed himself into the corner, uncomfortable and cramped on the unforgiving wooden seat, wishing this would end. But the train seemed to get slower as the day progressed, and by late afternoon they were running through abandoned towns and ruined farms. It was noticeable that the rowdy conversation had hushed, while increasingly a sort of intermittent thudding could be heard – remote at first, but growing louder all the time.

'Fritz is busy,' someone muttered, as the ground shook underneath the tracks and the sky ahead turned red. 'FI3 Howitzers, by the sound of it. Won't get much sleep tonight.'

Peter had been prepared for hearing gun-fire and was careful not to flinch. But he couldn't help it when John Tremean dug him in the ribs, and said, 'What load of old rigmarole is that, then?' – pointing out that a village they were passing through (or what remained of it) had signs and shop-fronts that he couldn't understand.

Peter should have been prepared for that, as well, perhaps – he had watched his mother buy from the Breton onion-sellers, years ago, with much gesticulation and holding up of fingers to display the price. But somehow he had not anticipated that, in France, you wouldn't find English generally written or spoken anywhere. Here, he really was a foreigner – and every second took him further from the coast, and home.

So it was almost a comfort, when they finally rattled to a stop (at a sort of deserted platform in the rain) to have a Sergeant Major march along the train, tapping each door frame sharply with his stick and roaring commands in a language you could understand.

'Everybody out! Tunnelling contingent, form up – single file – by the wall. The rest of you, fall in, in ranks of three. Come on, come on, what are you waiting for?' The new recruits, a little mystified, went shambling over to the indicated point – while the returning unit transformed itself into three long, tidy files, at a speed which to Peter seemed miraculous.

The Sergeant Major, however, did not seem impressed. 'Call that a line?' he bellowed. 'Get yourselves properly fell in. Never mind the puddles. Bit of rain won't hurt.' Then – as the line became so straight you might have run a ruler down its length – 'That's a little better! Don't let me find you straggling again. You're back with me, you lucky devils, you! Now, wait for the command. D Company… right… turn! By the left, quick march. Left, right, left, right.'

And he harried his contingent out onto the road.

Peter and Tremean's little group were still standing sheepishly about, trying to shelter from the rain against the wall, when another officer appeared from a motorcar which had just drawn up outside. This time it was a proper major with a peaked cap and all, who tucked his baton underneath his arm and came in to shout at them. 'Mining squad… in two ranks, fall in. *Atten-shun*. By the right dress!'

Peter did his best, trying to remember the drill they'd had at school, and – like the others – shuffled to align himself, stretching out his arm to touch the shoulder of the fellow next to him. Compared to 'D company' it was a hopeless mess, but the officer in charge just sighed and marched them off – or rather stood in his slow-moving vehicle and watched as they trudged behind it down a lane. It was growing dark and sleeting gently now, and in the gaps between high hedges there was nothing to be seen except dark fields on either side. The road underfoot was unmade and full of slush and the new boots rubbed his toes and ankles painfully. It seemed a long, cold thirsty tramp before they reached their goal – which appeared to be some sort of disused factory.

The officer got down and dismissed them just outside the gate. 'Find yourself some billets, then get to the canteen. Lance Corporal Smith will show you. Report in the morning. Eight sharp at this gate.' And he was gone.

The billet proved to be an area of floor with a small pile of hay to place your blanket on. The room was a massive space, open to the roof. Work-benches and disused machinery still stood around the walls, though the area had been divided by makeshift blanket screens. The newcomers were together in a section of their own, and Peter found himself beside Tremean again, which – at least – was mildly comforting.

The Lance Corporal, a wiry lad who looked no older than his charges, saw the doubtful looks and laughed. 'Count yourself lucky you're not infantry. You could be in a trench, up to your knees in muddy water and dead rats. You've got a roof to keep the rain out – most of it, at least – plus, you get decent rations and clean underwear each week. No wonder some of the lads are bloody envious – even without you earning six times what they do!' He grinned. 'Still, I'm not complaining. I wouldn't want to work in a damp dark hole for hours, waiting for a ton of rock to fall on me.'

'Not a tunneller yourself?' Peter found himself asking, though he'd not intended to.

'"Not a tunneller yourself," Lance Corporal!' the youth retorted. 'You're in the army now, and you don't talk unless you're spoken to. But no, I'm not a tunneller.' He pointed to his sleeve, which had a chevron stripe but not the pick-and-shovel badge. 'I'm just on attachment – mostly moving soil, so the Bosch can't work out where the mining is – which means, at least, I get to share your benefits. So, if you've finished admiring your luxurious beds, come and have some delicious army stew, before it gets cold and coagulates.'

He led the way, between the hanging screens, to where a smaller room led off the back. Several men, all with the tunneller's flash upon their sleeves were sitting at a trestle table, eating something hot and steaming from enamel plates. They glanced up as the new recruits came in, though without much interest. They all looked deathly tired.

'Replacements for Sam Golders' team,' Lance Corporal Smith announced. 'Only arrived in France today, and no idea what's what. Is there a bit of stew that they can have?'

One of the men pointed to a saucepan with his fork. 'Plenty left in there. Field kitchen's closed, but they kept that hot for us. Bread in that metal box,' he said and nodded at Peter who had gone to open it. 'Any left over, make sure you put it back, else the rats'll have it. Miners all of you?'

There was a general murmur of agreement.

'Welcome to the secret war, then. Met the Lieutenant yet? If not you will do!' He put on a mocking voice. 'First lesson, learn what silence means!'

It was obviously a quotation because everybody laughed. 'Old Judd has got a point, though,' one of the others said. 'This lot are only here because Sam Golders never learned.' He mopped his plate with a small crust of bread. 'Thought he was immortal, but Fritz proved otherwise. Must have heard them working. Sammy and his men – set off a mine and blew them all to smithereens. And destroyed the tunnel we'd been working on for weeks. So you learn that first lesson if you know what's good for you.' He gulped the bread and took a swig of something from his mug.

'And second lesson,' said the man who'd spoken first. 'Though Old Judd won't tell you this – if you're captured, don't tell Gerry what you do. Tell them you blow up bridges, anything – but they hate us tunnellers. Give you a bad time if you fall into their hands. Better a clean shot between the eyes.'

This was not an encouraging beginning, Peter thought. He had obtained his plate of food by now (the mess tin he'd been issued with had been curtly waved aside) and sat down at the table, thoughtfully. There were a thousand things that he'd have liked to ask – not least how you could mine without making any noise – but he was too embarrassed to say anything at all, so he ate his food in silence.

It tasted horrible, but it was warm and he ate it gratefully, washed down with great gulps of sugared tea. When he looked up the previous diners had all left the room.

But just as he was about to ask Tremean what on earth he thought they were supposed to do next, Lance Corporal Smith returned. 'Right then, if you've finished! Wash your plates and eating irons and turn in for the night. Move then. At the double, you lazy sons of—'

Peter had never been so harassed in his life. In fact the day had given him so much to think about that, despite his

weariness, he was sure he would not sleep, but – notwith-
standing the unaccustomed hardness of the 'bed' and the
thousand worries about what the dawn would bring – he
had no sooner put his head down than he was slumbering
like a child.

If Private Tremean had not shaken him awake, he
might not have stirred even when the morning bugle
blew.

Two

'Old Judd' made an appearance at the parade next day, after a swift roll call and inspection of the ranks. To Peter's surprise he was not really old at all – hardly any older than the rest of them, though he was sporting lieutenant's epaulettes and had an important barking voice.

'As you were, squad! I want a word with you!'

There was a Cornish accent in the snapped command – and something about it made Peter look more sharply at the man. The face seemed half-familiar, though that seemed improbable and, if so, he could not think from where.

'All of you miners in civilian life?'

There was a general murmur of assent.

'The answer is "yes, sir"!'

'Yes, sir!' came a ragged chorus. Tremean caught Peter's eye.

'Think he was a general, not a bally double-pip!' he muttered, out of the corner of his mouth.

'No talking in the ranks!' The Lieutenant gave an unexpected smile. 'Do things the proper way, and we shall get along. You've been picked to come here, because you were the brightest of the bunch. So I'll be training you myself and I expect a lot of you. Don't disappoint me. Any Cornish here?'

'Yes!' Peter and Tremean replied in unison, and managing to add, 'sir!' only just in time.

Judd nodded. 'Land round here is not dissimilar to what we get back home, though there's more clay than granite. Any clay-kickers?' he added.

Peter knew what that meant now – they were northern men, who'd found a way to shift wet clay more quickly by working a special shovel with their feet, rather than by hacking at it with a pickaxe, like you did with rock. Along the line a few more hands went up and Judd went to have a word, absently rubbing his left ear as he went.

It was that little quirk that did it. Of course! Surely this was a boy he'd faintly known at school – one of his eldest brothers friends, who had gone on to work down Dolcoath Mine? Peter shook his head. Hard to imagine that he could be here. But Judd – that sounded right!

Caleb Judd – it was coming back to him. That was the fellows name. And he'd never been much good at anything but sums, though he'd won the school prize for running once or twice. Years older now, of course – in fact, Peter might not have been sure that it was really the same Judd, except for that crooked scar across the Lieutenant's cheek, where he'd fallen off the chapel wall and gashed himself, trying to get birds' eggs off the tree nearby.

Peter could hardly listen to the pep talk afterwards, how there would be a day or two of training now with Judd and then they'd be 'straight at it' – he was too busy looking at that scar.

The sight of it was cheering, though it was hard to say quite why – suddenly Peter felt better than he had felt for days. Not that there was anything special to rejoice about, perhaps, remembering what the diners had said the night before. It was no advantage to have known the Lieutenant slightly years ago.

'Any questions?' Caleb Judd was asking now, in a tone which suggested that there ought not to be.

But Tremean was already wading in. 'Yes... sir,' he ventured. 'About this mining school. If we re supposed to be here because we know the type of ground...?'

'Fair question, Private!' said the Lieutenant. 'But if you thought you knew mining, you'll have to think again. All sorts of things you've never come across. Listening devices – any of you ever heard of a geophone before? New techniques of tunnelling and setting dynamite – you might have set charges to bring down a bit of rock, but we're looking to blow a bloody great crater underneath the Huns. And then there's other things, first aid, resuscitation, what to do if you encounter gas, how to use a gas mask or – come to that – a gun. Answer your question, Private?'

Tremean, abashed, murmured that it did.

Judd rocked back on his heels. 'But there's one thing in particular you'll have to learn. The first lesson in warfare tunnelling, I always say. Know what that is, do you?'

'First lesson of tunnelling – learn what silence is,' Peter heard himself reply, to his considerable dismay, quoting the diners of the night before. His mind had still been half-thinking of the bird's nest and the scar, or he would never have dreamed of piping up like that. The whole group, he realized, had turned to stare at him, and then quickly turned their attention to their boots. 'Sir!' he added hastily, and decided that he had only made it worse. It sounded insolent. 'That is...' he faltered.

But Caleb Judd was nodding. 'Quite right, sapper. Work in silence – don't talk unless you have to, and only

159

whisper then. Don't cough, if it kills you. Tiptoe down the tunnels and make sure your boots are wrapped in rags before you start. Don't let so much as a matchbox drop onto the floor. Silence is more than golden, it's life or death to you and − if you've been used to working with others underground, chattering and singing − it's the hardest thing to learn. But you won't last long round here unless you do.'

Peter was chastened, as he was meant to be, and he said nothing further till they were all dismissed and ambling back towards the 'training room' so-called, which turned out to be a draughty, disused shed out at the back.

As he was wandering in to find himself a seat, Caleb Judd came up to him. 'Well done, sapper. It's Kellow, isn't it?' He gave that unexpected grin again. 'Saw the name and recognized the hair. Think I knew your brother − many years ago.' He nodded briefly. 'You've clearly got his brains. This is nasty work we're doing here, and very dangerous − often less than six feet from the Kraut we're trying to blow up, and who is trying to do the same to us − but our work could turn the war if the miner knows his stuff. And generally they do. So I expect a lot of them − especially Cornish ones. Yet they seem to do all right. Charmed lives, I do believe. And look at me, promoted in the field, and given a commission, like a gentleman. So stick with me, Kellow, and we'll see this war through yet.'

A moment later he was an important man again − standing out in front, drawing diagrams on a blackboard with a piece of chalk and looking 'more general than double-pip' again. But ever after, Peter felt, Judd kept an eye on him − even a few days later when the proper work began and he started for the first time to tunnel through the ground.

'I'm starting you on clay – it's easier to work on without making any row,' Judd said at the briefing. 'You'll be joining an established team – just do as you see done – but keep your mouths firm shut. We're laying listening pipes to hear what Fritz is up to overhead and we don't want him hearing us instead. Form a human chain to send back the spoil, the infantry is standing by to bury it elsewhere – don't want to advertise the entrance from the air. And keep the caged mouse with you, in case there's any gas – it's better than a bird, if it escapes it doesn't tell the Kraut we're there.'

It was wet, cold, lonely work, working in water that came half-way up your legs – but it used Peter's skills. Even knowing that he was only feet from death, it was good to feel that he was being useful to the war and part of a proper mining team again.

–

There is always a deal to do, with a husband and nine girls to look after, and with a wedding day in view there were a thousand extra things to see about. Flour bags to wash and hem and turn into soft new knickers for the bride, knitted vests to launder and petticoats to trim with little bows of ribbon or tiny scraps of lace. That was the task that Martha had set herself today. A bride – even a Strict Adherent bride – must have a bottom drawer of decent underwear, though she wouldn't have a special outfit for the wedding.

'Vanity,' Ephraim had called the fashion for special wedding clothes, in one of his more thundering sermons a month or two ago, and perhaps he was right – though it would have been nice to think of Patience in a good new coat, at least, instead of her usual going-to-chapel best.

And that might have been managed, she thought ruefully. Mrs Chegwidden, next door, had a lovely one she couldn't use, blue wool (sent to her by her sister in America who had tired of it) but it was far too tight – it wouldn't meet and there was not enough material for letting out to fit. She would gladly have swapped it for one of Toby's pails, and with a bit of nip and tuck it would have done Pattie fine.

But Toby had put his foot down. 'I'm not spending time and effort making pails for Pattie's sake. Better off making one that I can sell, earn a bit of money for a pair of boots for Hope, she's only got Mercy's pass-me-downs and she hasn't done anything to deserve rubbed feet. Besides,' he went on bitterly, 'darn coat wouldn't fit Patience more'n a week or two and there's no telling she'd ever be that size again.' Strong words from Toby, but he had a point, of course. Patience would be needing bigger, baggy clothes quite soon.

The important thing was to get her wed before that happened and there was anything to see. Only three more weeks now – Ephraim had managed to get the license organized and the banns published (at the Methodists) in time, so the marriage could take place before the start of Lent. No Strict Adherent would ever wed during the Remembrance of Christ in the Wilderness, so otherwise it would have been delayed after Easter – and that was far too late.

Martha put down her stitching with a sigh. If only she knew exactly how far on Pattie was. Three or four months? It was hard to tell. The girl didn't seem to have the least idea, herself (though it was important to keep that from Toby, and from Ephraim most of all. They both thought there had only been the once!) And, if the mother didn't know, there was no way of finding out.

Her thoughts were interrupted by the girl herself, coming downstairs in that listless way she had developed recently, carrying a long pink flannel nightdress in her hand. 'This the one you mean? I found it where you said, in your bedroom under-drawer.'

Martha nodded. 'It's the one I had when I was wed myself. I'd like for you to have it.' She took it in her hands and looked it over carefully. 'It's got the moth in it a bit, here just above the hem, but if you look in that pewter jug up on the mantelpiece, you'll find a piece of ribbon I've been saving purposely. Take a bit of thread and sew that right around the gown, an inch above the edge. That will cover it, nobody will notice and it will look a treat. I believe there's even a bit of sewing-silk to match.'

There was, in among the darning needles and the cards of mending wool. Pattie fetched it, then suddenly bent down and kissed her mother's hair. 'Ma, you're some good, you were saving that nightdress specially, I know. Are you sure?'

Martha was embarrassed. 'My dear, I haven't worn the thing in years. Really kept it to be buried in – but I'd ten times sooner you had use of it. If I come to need it, you can give it back!'

Pattie actually smiled (the first time Martha had seen her do so since the day this all began) and went to sit beside the window – in the light – to sew.

Martha cast an appraising glance at her outline as she moved. The girl looked quite normal – at the moment, anyway – and once she was married it would not matter quite so much. When she was in seclusion (you couldn't go out in public once the bump began to show) she'd be living in that farmhouse, miles away from town, so no one would be looking at her and calculating things. Then when the child arrived, you could hint that it was early (as both Hope and Mercy had genuinely been) – though without actually saying so, of course. That would be telling lies and lying was a sin.

She sighed. There were so many not-quite-truths already, she would be anxious for her soul – if she had the time to think about such things. She'd just have to go on praying that things would be all right and the reputation of the family – and of the Strict Adherents – would be safe. In a little village like Rosvene, rumours spread like furze-fire if the slightest hint got out.

She was in the act of picking up the petticoat again, and rethreading the needle which she had allowed to fall, when a rattle at the latch on the door made her pause. The sound was followed by a gentle tap and – in the same instant – the door was pushed open and Edna Cheg-widden from next door came in.

She was a stout, plain, cheery woman, dressed without vanity in a shapeless frock with a clean apron over it. Her hair was pulled back in a no-nonsense bun, and her plump face was wrinkled with perpetual smiles. 'Mornin' Martha,' she was saying heartily, but her eye fell on Patience and she stopped, confused. 'Oh, I'm some sorry, my lovers. Didn't realize there was illness in the house. Your Patience poorly and stopping home today?'

Martha put her sewing down, got slowly to her feet and hung the kettle on the fire to boil. Act naturally, she told herself. 'No, Edna, you're quite welcome. And you needn't fear for germs. Pattie was peaky a week or two ago, but she's recovered now. Though she isn't going back down that factory again – it don't agree with her.

Besides, there's news. She's getting wed quite soon.' It was encouraging to see her neighbour look surprised. If there were rumours they clearly hadn't reached next door.

'Well, my dear life! How didn't you come in and tell me straight away!'

Martha shook her head. 'Ephraim Tull came up here to ask for her again – and this time she said yes. We haven't said a lot to anyone as yet, but I'd sooner that you heard the news from me.' It was no real answer to the question, but it was the best that she could do.

Edna could have been affronted, but she was a friendly soul and she turned to Patience with a beaming smile. 'Well, I'm delighted for you, Patience – though folks will say Ephraim don't deserve his luck. But you won't regret it. He's a decent man at heart and he'll never give you a minute's worry all your life' She glanced at the sewing task. 'That's pretty, what you're doing. For your bottom drawer, I suppose?'

There was an awkward silence, then Pattie forced a smile and managed to say, 'Yes. And thank you for your good wishes, Mrs Chegwidden,' with a semblance of good grace.

Martha got new tea leaves and put them in the pot, as a token of special friendliness. (The used ones that were drying would do for supper, later on.) 'Sit down, Edna, and have a cup of tea and a bite of something, do. I made some jam tarts earlier, will you try one of those?'

Edna shook her head. 'You've got your hands full, by the sound of it and you made those tarts for your family, not me. But I won't say no to a cup of tea, if you are making one.'

Martha nodded, fetching down the cups and saucers from the shelf. 'Anyway, what brought you here today?

Just come to say hello, or were you wanting Sam? I'm afraid he's gone out with Toby, somewhere, fetching back a cart.'

Edna Chegwidden shook her head. 'No. Truth is, I wanted somebody to have a look at this. Had a postcard letter this morning from our Ned.' She produced the missive, smiling now so broadly it seemed her face would burst. 'He's coming back to England. I'm sure that's what it says – though I'm no great hand at reading, specially when the handwriting's not clear. I wondered maybe if you could read it out to me, just to make quite sure I got it right – or perhaps your Vee could come and do it, when she gets home from work?'

Martha was puzzled. Edna was no great scholar, but she could cipher well enough – unless it was some official letter full of great long words. But perhaps she just wanted an excuse to share her news.

So she took the card and flattened it – it had only come that day but it was already creased with constant reading – and took it to the other window, to the light, to see. '"I should be in England in a day or two, though I won't be back to see you straight away. I've got to go to a convalescent place, but when the board decides I'm fit enough to go back to my unit, I should be able to come home for a few days before I leave."' She folded up the card and gave it back. 'I think that's what it says – except he sends his love, of course.' She didn't add what Edna clearly knew, and did not want to say aloud with Patience sitting there, that the last words that he'd written were: 'Tell Verity for me.'

Which she would do, she decided – whatever Toby thought. In fact, on second thoughts, why should he ever know? If Pattie did not go blurting it out in front of him, that is. She was still wondering about this, when a knock came on the door – and this time the caller did not come in until Martha answered it.

–

It wasn't Pattie stealing from the factory. Verity was finally convinced of that, because – despite security – occasional losses had begun again, though on a smaller scale, and one 'dishthreepency' had been reported just this week. So it wasn't her. But whatever it was that Patience had actually done, it had certainly altered the atmosphere at home.

Take today, for instance. When Vee and Pru got home from work, it was to find another full-scale argument going on. This time it was Aunt Dorcas's fault, apparently. She had done as she proposed and called this afternoon – about the wedding, to know was there anything she could do to help – and Pa was livid. The other girls were sitting round the kitchen table, cowed, while he thumped his fist and roared. He paid no attention as the working pair came in.

'Turn my back for half an hour and what happens?' he was demanding, of no one in particular. 'Comes uninvited and you ask her in. You know my views about what she has done! Has a man no say at all about who comes into his house?'

And Ma, for once, was standing up to him. 'She's my sister Toby, and she came to offer help – trying to save me trouble, not creating it. And Edna from next door was here, besides – what would she have thought if I had slammed the door on my own flesh and blood? In any case, what has Dorcas done so much? Married a good man who loved her. Is that such a sin? I can think of worse ones.'

Pa looked more annoyed than ever, but the barb went home. He humphed and sat down on the stool beside the fire to take off his working boots, turning his back on everybody else. (It was an indication of how cross he was, that he'd come in with them – normally he removed them at the door.)

Ma went up behind him and put her hands on his shoulders. 'Not everyone can be so fortunate as we two, Toby.'

The soft words calmed him – as Ma generally could. He shrugged her off, but put his stockinged feet against the hearth and wiggled his ten toes – a sure sign that the worst was over now. 'Well, what's past is past, I suppose,' he grumbled, 'so there's nothing to be done. But she needn't think she's coming to this wedding, all the same – your father would walk out, never mind if we were in chapel at the time. He's a man of principle, even if I'm weak.'

'You mean he's stubborn – "proud and stiff-necked", I think the Bible says,' Martha said with feeling. 'While you are prepared to forgive those who trespass against you.'

Vee lingered at the doorway, pretending to hang her bonnet on the hook behind the door, but watching Pa's expression carefully. He could clearly find no answer to what Ma had said, so he changed the subject. 'What did Ma Chegwidden want, in any case? Come to borrow sugar, or something, I suppose?'

Ma looked at Pattie, but she was pretending to be busy with some sewing on her lap, so Ma said quickly, 'Wanted to share some news about her Ned, I think. He's going to be transferred again to some other hospital – which means he's making better progress now. I only got the gist of it, cause just then Dorcas came – and Edna, not wanting to be in the way, just said hello a minute, then hurried off, claiming that she'd left baking on the griddle iron. I didn't even remember to give her back that bowl she left behind, when she came here Christmas with those nuts for us – Vee, would you do that for me? It's there on the corner of the shelf. I was going to give it back to Sam to take to her – but now I've missed him and she might be wanting it.'

Vee was astonished. For one thing her parents didn't generally like her going next door, and for another Ma Chegwidden clearly wouldn't need that bowl. It was a big one, and there were only the three of them these days – (and Ned had said his father did not have much appetite – something to do with working on the calciners at the mine). But she knew when she was lucky. She seized the bowl, and without even pausing to put her cape back on, was out of the door before Pa had a chance to say, 'Why Verity? And what's the sudden rush? Constance can slip round with it, when we have had our tea!'

But if he did say something of the kind, by then it was too late. She was already down the path and opening the gate and running the few steps along to where Ned used to live.

It was a tiny cottage, much smaller than their own but, with fewer people in it, it seemed very spick and span. No pots of salted beans underneath the chairs, or piles of mending on the windowsills – Mr Chegwidden, a wizened little man with an appalling cough, had been very handy in his day and there were lots of hooks and shelves around the walls, with a place for everything.

All the same, it was always welcoming. It was Sam who came to answer her uncertain knock today – still holding a piece of bread and butter in his hand – and the room was full of the delicious smell of rabbit stew. Mrs Chegwidden rushed over to shepherd her inside, while her husband looked up from his plate to smile and say, 'We're having supper, but there's a bit to spare? Want a bit, do'ee?'

Verity had been raised to know that to accept such offers was to make the family go short. 'I dursn't!' she replied. 'Pa wouldn't like it. It's a wonder that he let me come at all. I've just come to bring your bowl.' She put it on the table. 'But I hear that you've had word from Ned?'

'Here, my lover, read it for yourself.' Mrs Chegwidden was already getting down the card from its pride of place above the mantle clock. 'Some good news, id'na?'

Verity nodded, her heart too full for speech. Ned, back in England. Maybe coming home. How could she get to see him? 'Let's just hope he doesn't come the week of Pattie's wedding!' she exclaimed.

Mrs Chegwidden nodded. She glanced around the room, then motioned Verity towards the door. 'Thank you for the bowl. I'd clean forgotten where I'd left 'un to.' She ushered Vee outside and said, in a low voice. 'Tell me, my lover, is everything all right? With your Pattie, that is? She don't seem glad to me. Wouldn't have Sam and Freddie hear this for the world, but… it isn't a case of having to get married, I suppose?'

Vee looked at her, perplexed. 'Well, she had to marry a Strict Adherent, I suppose – or that's what Pa would say. But she didn't have to have him – she'd said no before.'

Ma Chegwidden shook her head. 'That isn't what I meant. I just wondered… Not that I suppose it can be, since it's Ephraim Tull?'

'Wondered what?' The woman was talking in riddles – like Pru the other day.

Ned's mother shook her head again. 'Never you mind, my lover. I should not have said.'

'But I do mind,' Verity burst out. 'People keep asking questions and not saying what they mean – and make me feel a fool cause I don't understand.'

'It isn't that you're foolish, it's that you're innocent – and that's a fine thing, my 'andsome.'

'But I'm not a child!' Vee protested, 'I'm nearly seventeen. I can see there's something up. But Pru won't tell me, she said to talk to Ma – and when I tried to, Ma got flustered and said "another time". And Pattie's no help – she just keeps bursting into tears. Though I still don't know what I said to make her cry.'

Mrs Chegwidden looked long and hard at her. 'You're right, my 'andsome. Perhaps you ought to know. There's no great mystery. People are bound to wonder – I was wondering myself – if poor Pattie was in the family way. Though, as I say, it isn't likely – not with Ephraim Tull.'

'But how could she be in the family way, in any case?' Vee was more perplexed than ever, now. 'She isn't married yet.' You had to be married to have children, everyone knew that (and it was difficult and painful, she knew that too, because she'd seen them born) though quite how it came about, she was not exactly sure. Something to do with kissing, Constance thought, because you weren't allowed to do that 'in case it led to things' – though Vee was more inclined to put it down to miracles.

Ma Chegwidden was looking amiably at her. 'Oh, my dear lamb. No, of course you're right. But if your ma don't tell you more than that before you wed, yourself – even if you don't get married to our Ned, as of course we hope you do – you come and see me. Will you promise that?'

Vee heard herself say, 'Course I will,' but she hardly paid attention to the words. Marry Ned? And the Chegwiddens hoped she would! She almost floated back to

Blacksmith's Cottage, and though Pa grumbled, 'Took your time! What were you up to, with your supper getting cold?' she accepted the scolding meekly and didn't mind a bit.

Three

It was Sergeant Jeffries who found the cottage in the end. Effie had genuinely meant to ask around, but the one enquiry she'd made – to the postmistress who had a notice up about a 'pleasant small house and garden in Penzance' – had quoted a rent of full ten pounds a year. Costs seemed to have skyrocketed since before the war and even Alex's pension (which she'd received at last) would leave her little spare if she paid as much as that. The experience had discouraged her, and – not wanting her step-mother to feel obliged to offer her a room, and lacking the energy to take further interest – she had mentally resigned herself to going to Falmouth after all, and hadn't really said anything more to anyone.

So she was surprised to see the policeman ushered in.

'Sergeant Jeffries, madam, should I make some tea?' Amy said and busied herself with making it, just as if the kettle wasn't on the hearth three feet from where Effie was sitting on the chair.

As a grieving widow she was not bound to rise, but she did so anyway, smoothing her black skirts down nervously. 'Sergeant!' She hadn't seen him since the funeral. Was that really just a few short weeks ago? Already it felt as though a lifetime must have passed since then. 'What errand brings you here?' It must be something serious for him to call on her – a widow on her own. She could not help remembering the last time he had called – but no, she would not think about that awful telegram.

'Good news, at least I hope you'll think so, Mrs Dawes,' he said. 'You mentioned you were thinking of starting somewhere new. Well, I've heard a little rumour.' He tapped his nose, and sat down – uninvited – on the other chair. 'There's a cottage coming vacant, out Penvarris way. Belongs to a farmer, used to have it for a man who'd been with him for years – an older fellow with a family and not wanted for the war. But now that chap has died – a granite post that he was moving fell down and crushed him flat; their boy went for a soldier at the beginning of the war and the widow's going to move in with her married daughter down St Just – so the cottage is coming up for rent.'

He paused, but she said nothing.

'Thought it might just suit you,' he went on, 'it's quite a modern place. Got a Cornish stove to cook on, and flagstones on the floor, a proper privy and a pump outside the door. And the furniture is in it – so that there won't be that to find, which might have been difficult, things having got so short. It might not be exactly to your taste, of course, but there's enough for you to manage, in the meantime anyway.'

He looked quizzically at her, but she could make no reply. She wanted to shout, 'Please let me be! I can't think about such things!' but her brain was not connected to her tongue. Just as well, perhaps, since this was kindly meant and he did have a right to be interested. This was his cottage and he'd soon be wanting it himself.

Her silence might have led to awkwardness but Amy chose that moment to pour out the tea, and the Sergeant was occupied with selecting sugar lumps, and declining the last of Jillian's potato-flour buns. By that time Effie had regained her wits enough to say, 'It's very good of you to think of me.' She sounded like an automaton, even to herself, but she'd managed at least a semblance of civility.

He stirred his tea – two whole lumps of sugar, when they were so scarce! – and sipped it gingerly. 'Glad if it turns out any use to you. Only trouble is, this cottage – almost a house, I suppose you'd say – is outside the village, half a mile or so. Might be a bit lonely, if you're not used to it. You'd want a live-in maidservant, at least – I wouldn't be happy to think of you out there alone at night. Mind, it's on my beat and I'll be passing every evening, round six o'clock or so – long as I'm still a policeman, anyway.'

Perhaps it was the idea of being on her own that made her take a sudden interest – being away from people and well-meaning sympathy. 'Oh, I'm sure I could manage, Sergeant.'

'Pardon me for interrupting, ma'am…' Amy paused in the act of refilling the pot. 'But I couldn't help overhearing what was said. If you do decide to go and you want live-in help, I'd be happy to oblige you, for a year or so at least. Me mam is always saying how I ought to get another place, something full-time where I get my keep – make more space round the table and less work for her at home. I was wondering how to tell you.' She glanced guiltily at Effie. 'I hadn't wanted you to think that I might let you down, but maybe this would suit the both of us? And I'm sure the Sergeant's right. You wouldn't want to be out there in the dark all on your own. You never know who might be wandering about – drunk men and all sorts, out there on the cliffs.'

'And you don't think that would frighten you?' Effie said gently.

Amy shook her head. She said stoutly, 'Oh madam, don't you worry about me. I've got five brothers, and I'm used to it. I can stand up for meself – and you besides, if it came to such a thing.'

The idea of Amy – all of five foot two – as a protection against marauders, almost made Effie smile.

Sergeant Jeffries, however, pulled at his moustache. 'In fact, perhaps, on second thoughts, it isn't suitable. Ideally you'd want a man about the place. There's quite a garden too.'

That did it, Effie thought. Pa would love to have a bit of allotment of his own again, where he could grow a few vegetables like he used to do, but there was no space for that where he was living now. She put her cup down and sat bolt upright. 'Well, Sergeant Jeffries, however much I need a man around the place I haven't got one now. Amy and I will simply have to manage as we are. I presume the rent they're asking is affordable?'

'Does that mean, madam…?' Amy interrupted eagerly, but the Sergeant silenced her.

'I believe the farmer wants four guineas for the place – with payments quarterly. That's quite a lot, I know – rents have been rising like bread-dough every month – but it should not go up again. The government has put a lid on things. From now on if a place comes vacant and you let to someone else, you can't put up the price. Often that means it's pegged at what it was before the war. People try to get around it, naturally – I've been called in to investigate the problem more than once.'

Effie was hardly listening. Four guineas. Less than half the Penzance house. Of course, out here, there would be no gas for lights, either in the house or in the street, and no night-cart to clear the privy every month. But the same was true of this cottage they were in, and until she'd had that telegram she'd been quite happy here.

'Can you give me directions, Sergeant?' she enquired. 'It may not do at all, but I will, at least, go out and have a look.' He had thought of that already, it appeared. 'I've spoken to the man who owns the place,' he said. 'I've had dealings with him once or twice about the farm – all the regulations about feeding animals – and I told him about you. I spoke very highly of you – as of course I would – and he said, if you would like to go and take a look, he'd come here in his cart and take you over there.'

Sergeant Jeffries put his teacup down. 'I'm not suggesting you go unchaperoned. You could take your step-ma too.'

But Effie was reluctant. She'd have to take somebody, for form's sake, naturally, but suddenly she wanted to do this on her own. 'Better I take my maid with me if she'll be coming there.' Jeffries nodded. 'On Friday,' he suggested, around noon if that would suit? He's got to come in to the blacksmith anyway, get the carthorse shoed that day.'

And so it happened that on Friday afternoon she and Amy went out to the house. The farmer – a thickset, melancholy man, as unlike Crowdie as it was possible to get – drove in virtual silence for a quarter of an hour, then drew up by an entry and motioned with his whip.

'There 'tis. Nawthin special, but I've had un painted up and put a new 'inge on the door that creaked. Yours if you want'n. B'lieve you knaw the terms. I'll sell 'ee milk and eggs and curdled cheese, if you would like, but don't 'ee come calling at my house otherwise. My wife's a blimming termangent – I'd never hear the end. Bad enough my letting the place to a widow as it is. Only that she heard you were a p'licemen's wife.' He waved the whip again. 'What d'you think, then?'

Effie looked, and knew at once it was the place. It was a strange little cottage, with crooked whitewashed walls and tiny window-panes, and a little stable-type front door that opened in two halves. The small tiled porch above it looked like a moustache above an open mouth, while the tiles came down like eyebrows over the upstairs casements, and gave the whole house an expression of amused surprise. The garden was a riot of blackberries and weeds, and a gravelled path meandered to the door between scruffy bushes that leaned sideways in the wind.

She had enough wit to demand to see inside: a kitchen-cum-scullery with a flagstone floor and Cornish stove (exactly as the Sergeant had promised there would be), two little sitting rooms with an enormous fireplace each, and a staircase steep as Jacob's ladder leading to three further tiny rooms upstairs. There were gloomy pictures on the walls and the place was full of gloomy furniture, but it hardly mattered – the thick walls seemed to put their arms round her, and she felt at once that she had found a haven and a home. If Alex was looking down on her, she thought, he would have liked it too.

'Wash house and privy out the back,' the farmer said, as they came out into the wind again. 'And that there used to be a pigs' crow, years ago.' He gestured to a tumbled shed against the further wall. 'No key to 'un, but you could store things there, if you can fight your way to it. Though mind if you go in. Don't believe that it's been used for years – there's bound to be spiders and there might be snakes.'

But this did not deter her. She'd been bred a country girl, and she didn't really want the shed in any case – though pa might like it if he came gardening.

'I'll take it,' she told the farmer, and – when he looked surprised – she added quickly, 'when I've shown it to my family and providing they agree.'

Pa was more measured, when he came to have a look. 'I can see you like it, Effie – and it's nearer us, so we aren't likely to object, I don't suppose. And an allotment might be useful for the lot of us – few extra leeks and that – supposing I have to time to come and work at it. But it's a big decision for a woman on her own. Don't rush into anything you might regret.'

'I won't!' she told him. And she never did.

–

Patience's wedding was a disappointing one – not at all what Martha would have wanted for her girls. It had to take place at the Methodists, of course, since the Strict Adherent chapel was too small to have a register itself, and arranging a special license would have taken far too long. So it wasn't very homely, anyway – and Ephraim seemed to have set out to make it worse.

First, he had discovered, just a few days earlier, that the lady 'organist' who had agreed to play the harmonium for the two chosen hymns, had attended the Adherents' Sunday school when she was young – before she went and joined the Wesleyans. That made her a 'back-slider' in Ephraim's eyes and he refused to have her play, which offended everyone, with the result that there was no music or accompaniment at all. Even 'God bless this holy union' sounded thin and flat, and not even Grandfather's booming tenor could disguise the fact.

Then he'd chosen to preach on self-denial just the week before, a homily on how mortification of the flesh was not reserved for Lent, and how greed and show were always signs of sin. So the True Adherents who had come to see him wed, had not dared bring any contributions to the wedding 'tea' – as people were doing more and more, with luxuries so scarce. If it hadn't been for Dorcas looking out some pre-war jam and making some potato scones to spread it on, and Crowdie – bless him – sending round a piece of tongue, there would have been nothing for Martha to hand round afterwards except a dozen marrow jam-and-ginger tarts and fish-paste sandwiches made with horrid national bread. And she'd had problems getting even that – extras were so hard to come by nowadays.

So it was fortunate perhaps that so few people came – only a half-dozen of their Strict Adherent friends and the borrowed minister conducting the affair. And of course, there was the family – ten Tregorrans took up lots of space (the little ones had taken the day off school to attend) – and Grandfather was there, appearing to fill up an entire pew himself, though Dorcas and her husband politely stayed away. Methodists – like Edna Chegwidden – who might otherwise have come, had mostly sided with the affronted organist: 'Nothing against you or Pattie, Martha,' one of them had said, 'it's just I wouldn't feel easy coming, after what he said to her!' Though Martha had kept hoping that Edna might forgive and was secretly disappointed not to see her there.

It didn't help either that Patience looked so glum throughout, more like a mourner at a funeral than a bride – while Ephraim's high old-fashioned collar, his old black suit and usual solemn air, made him look like the officiating undertaker, standing at her side. But Pattie made her responses audibly enough, and looked respectable – if her Sunday outfit was still a little tight around the waist (though Martha had let it out as far as it would go) it was not enough to be conspicuous.

And so the thing was done. Pattie Tregorran became Mrs Patience Tull. Potato scones and pieces of sliced tongue – together with the tarts and sandwiches – were offered on trestles in the church hall afterwards and (with the young ones instructed not to eat too much) there was food enough to spare.

Ephraim himself had brought some cordial – made by his wife, while she was still alive, and none the better for being stored for years – so after the speeches (a short one from Toby and a much longer, earnest exhortation from the groom) the couple's health was duly toasted in blackcurrant drink and tea. Then everyone went home – everyone but Martha and her older girls that is, who stopped to tidy up the hall and wash the borrowed cups and plates, while Constance and Toby walked the little ones back home. Toby was especially anxious to get back and change and hurry to the forge, praying that Sam had managed to keep the furnace hot. It was Wednesday and he could not afford to take the whole day off.

Ephraim and Patience set off on foot, as well. Ephraim would have thought it 'vanity' to have brought the cart – let alone have decorated it with wedding bows – so it was a longish walk for them across the fields. And in their best clothes too! Martha watched them, with a sigh.

At least she'd managed to arrange to take Verity and Prudence out there to the farmhouse yesterday and between them they had scrubbed the kitchen clean. They hadn't been permitted to do anything upstairs, but the place would be a bit more welcoming for Pattie, anyway.

She shook her head. She had been the one to urge this wedding day – and now it was over and the problem of the baby had effectively been solved. Exactly as she'd asked the Lord to let it be. So why did she feel so gloomy? Ingratitude for blessings was a mortal sin. She'd have to pray about it – quite a lot – when she had time to think. But that would have to wait until tonight, when everyone was fed and all the children were asleep. In the meantime there was this hall to tidy and the dishes to be done.

–

Ned was sitting in the courtyard, playing draughts. It was chilly, but he was muffled up against the cold – the matron of the convalescent home was keen on her patients getting plenty of fresh air – and, after the stuffy hospitals and crowded trains – it was surprisingly pleasant to be out. His companion was another gas-gangrene sufferer, Fred Wills, who'd lost a leg through it and who'd travelled down with Ned from the London hospital – crammed into a carriage with a lot of badly wounded men. Most of them were officers on their way down to Penzance, where there was a different convalescent hospital – in what had apparently once been a manor house.

However, Ned and Fred ('the terrible duo' the matron had christened them at once) were only 'other ranks' and their destination was not a smart, converted, private resid-ence, but this grim stone building surrounded by high walls.

'It was the local asylum before the war broke out,' Matron had informed them, as she showed them in and they were helped upstairs, 'But they've moved the lunatics and turned the building over for wounded soldiery. And it has proved ideal in many ways: big dormitory wards with lots of room for beds, as you can see.'

She gestured to a pair of empty ones, right in the middle of the row. They were fairly basic, but they were neat and clean and after the jolting journey in the train, the fresh sheets and pillows looked inviting. One or two fellows were sitting propped up in their beds, or on chairs beside the window in their dressing gowns, and one called out cheerfully, 'Come to join us, have you? Welcome to Ward Three. People in your beds left us yesterday – both of them off home.'

That sounded promising and Ned was about to say so, but Matron (a plump bouncy woman with a breezy air) had not finished with her explanations yet and waved them quickly on.

'Through here—' she thrust open an adjoining door – 'you'll find proper sinks and sanitation close nearby – though the baths are made of granite and not really suitable. If you need a bath we'll bring you a tin tub of water up. Once a week is usual, unless the doctor advises otherwise. Now if you'd like to leave your kitbags in your lockers there, I'll show you round downstairs. I'll get a nurse to help you down, of course – but try to use your sticks as much as possible.'

It was a mighty struggle, even for Ned who still had both his legs, but with assistance the two lads managed it though they were almost too exhausted to get more than the most general idea. There was a dining hall – a little like a mess, with trestle tables and forms on either side – an office for the doctor and a 'surgery', and another larger room, in which more men, all in convalescent blue, looked up from writing letters, reading books or playing cards.

'This is the recreation room, where you can find a comfortable chair when you are well enough – though I hope to have you sitting out before so long, and even doing a little exercise. Strengthen those muscles, and with good food and rest, you'll soon be right as rain.'

Fred made a face at Ned behind her back – which Ned understood at once. 'Right as rain' did not seem probable, with only two and half good legs between the pair of them.

But Matron was oblivious. 'Now I'll have a pot of tea sent through to you, this once – since you have missed the urn. It comes around at three o'clock – starting with the bed-bound cases in Wards One and Two. I've put you in Ward Three, with the semi-ambulants. Most of the men there will improve enough to leave, barring new infections – and so should both of you – but only if you're prepared to work at getting strong. Now are there any questions? I think I've shown you everything and there is work to do.'

There were a lot of questions – naturally there were – but Fred and Ned had both been soldiers at the front and knew that the best information did not come from those in charge but from other fellows in the same predicament as yourself. But, when they were finally permitted to undress and get to bed and rest, their ward companions did not have much critical to say.

'Grim old place, of course,' the fellow in the next bed told them cheerfully, between deep puffs on an aromatic pipe. 'And that's the first thing that always strikes your visitors, supposing you have any. But when you've been knee-deep in mud and blood for weeks, like most of us – it's more like heaven than your family would believe. Matron's not so bad, though she can be sharp – quite a dragon if she thinks that you're not trying hard enough.

But the nurses...!' He sketched a curvy shape with his remaining hand – his right arm and shoulder had been blown off by a shell. 'Next best thing to angels—'

'Especially one or two who are devils underneath!' one of the other men put in, unexpectedly. He had a bandage over both his eyes and could not move at all without a guide, but he gave a bray of laughter, and the rest joined in.

It was more encouraging than the other places he had been; people here believed that they were getting well, though they weren't in such a hurry to improve that they wanted to get back and find themselves fighting in the mud again, as apparently had happened to one or two who'd gone. But there was improvement, almost instantly. The very fact that one could go outside, or sit and make an entry in the 'effort book', where patients were encouraged to draw or paint or write – instead of lying helplessly in bed, while people did things to you – made you feel that you were coming slowly back to life. Ned was even learning to play draughts, though Fred was far too good at it and beat him absolutely hollow every time.

Ned had just made a move, now – inadvisedly – and Fred was wreaking havoc on the board by hopping over several of Ned's draughts to capture them and claim himself a queen, when Ned looked up and saw a figure coming through the gate.

'Mother!' He was so astonished that he tried to stand and sent the board and all the pieces spinning to the floor. 'Ma!' He even permitted her a kiss. 'They only let me write you yesterday, to say that I was well enough for visitors. I can't believe that you have come so soon.'

His mother bent to pick the pieces up. 'Came the minute that I got your letter. Course I did – what else would you expect! Mind, I had been hoping that they'd send you to Penzance! But there are trains to Truro several times a day, and it wasn't hard to manage once I'd put my mind to it.' She was panting with exertion, but she'd got the board and plonked it on the table with the draughts. She turned to Fred. 'How d'y do? Sorry to have spoiled your bit of game.'

'Fred Wills – my mother,' Ned said hastily. 'Fred's been teaching me.'

Fred nodded. 'Pleased to meet you, Mrs Chegwidden!' But he was already reaching for his sticks. 'No offence, but I've done enough for now – so I'll hobble off inside. In any case you've come to see your son.'

He said it ruefully. Poor old Fred, he came from Manchester, which Ned had learned was many miles up north. (He blushed to remember that he'd once exclaimed, 'Isn't that in Scotland?' which made Fred laugh a lot, and caused Ned to wish he'd paid more attention to Geography at school. The teacher had a roller-stamp which made a map, and you had to write the names of places in – cities and towns and rivers – but Ned had always copied from the board without attending much to what was where.)

'Seems a nice fellow,' Ma remarked. 'But never mind all that. How are you in yourself?' She said it with a smile, but Ned noticed that her eyes were bright with tears. It quite surprised him. He was accustomed to thinking that he was doing well, and was feeling smart in his bright blue uniform. He knew, of course, that he had lost a lot of weight, and his leg looked all peculiar and wasted at the top, but it had not occurred to him that she'd be shocked at what she saw.

He reached across and gave her arm a squeeze. 'All the better for seeing you,' he said. And then, because it mattered very much, he added, 'You didn't bring a message from Verity, I suppose?'

Ma made a rueful face. 'No, poor girl. I haven't seen her since your letter came. She'd be here like a shot herself, if she only could, I know – but it's no good you thinking that she might arrive. More chance of her going to Greenland, the way things are just now. Her father wouldn't let her, in any case, of course – and Vee is far too well-behaved to go behind his back. Couldn't if she wanted to – let alone the cost. That factory is working round the clock, now, seven days a week – and of course she won't work Sundays, so that's her one day off. And you know how much hope there is of her escaping, on the Sabbath day!'

'She knows I'm here though?'

His mother shook her head. 'Haven't had chance to tell her – though I wanted to. Haven't had a minute to see her since your letter came. I did pop round, in hopes of seeing her today, but that aunt of hers was in there – and that's always awkward when Toby is about. Come about this wedding, I suppose...'

'Wedding?' Ned was instantly alarmed.

'Oh, of course, I forgot you didn't know. I didn't know where to write you, when I knew that you'd moved, until I got your letter giving this address It's that eldest sister, Patience – she's getting wed today. Funny sort of business – she's married Ephraim Tull.' She shook her head. 'I'd sooner marry a Chinaman, or nobody at all.'

Ned smiled. His mother had never seen a Chinaman, he knew – only as an illustration in a book – so to her it seemed the most unlikely thing on earth. 'I met a

Chinaman,' he said, to her surprise. 'He was in the hospital in France – he'd volunteered to join the army from Hong Kong.'

His mother gazed at him. 'You've been in some rum places, Ned lad, haven't you? I suppose you've seen a lot of foreigners?'

'Shot at a few of them, as well!' he grinned, and that seemed to break the ice. She wanted to hear what France was like – did they have houses like we had at home? And was it true they only dined on frogs and snails? So he told her, not about the mud and ruins, but about the churches and the estaminets and the places that he'd seen, when his brigade once had a fortnight's respite back behind the lines.

They were still talking when the matron came and made him go inside ('Now, Chegwidden! Before you catch your death') and Mother had to leave to catch her train.

Four

It took all the energy that she could summon up to move into the cottage – or An Dyji, as it was called on official documents, to distinguish it from the farmhouse proper, though there was no sign anywhere on the property itself. The name meant 'Little Cottage' the land agent explained, and it fitted perfectly, so Effie thought of the place that way for ever afterwards.

It was surprising to discover how many items she possessed, though of course there was stuff stored upstairs in the police-house still, as well as the clothes and photographs and things she'd taken to White Cottage when she had moved in there. Even in crates, it was a wonder how she'd ever get it all across, without it costing pounds – even supposing she could find a waggoner. (With so many horses taken for the war, there were not the carts for hire.) But up popped Crowdie, his usual helpful self, offering to transport all her boxes on his cart and refusing to take even a shilling in return. Without him it would have been a much worse headache than it was.

Jillian had volunteered to come over on the day and lend a hand to help her to unpack. 'And perhaps your Auntie Madge could spare an hour or two – although Samuel's poorly and I know she's pushed.'

'That's kind of you – you've been so good to me, all through – but Amy has insisted it's her job to see to that,'

Effie said. 'She's so proud of being a "proper" live-in maid, as she calls it, that I didn't have the heart to disagree!' She did not add that there was a certain pleasure, too, in the idea of arranging things herself, in her own way. 'Don't be offended.'

'Course not, silly thing,' Jillian laughed in her easy-going way. 'We'll come to tea when you are settled in. See if there is anything we can help with then. I'm glad your Amy's coming with you, she's a lively little thing. I was talking to her, just before she left today, and she's so excited by the idea of a bedroom of her own – you'd think it was a palace you were offering her!'

It was scarcely that. There was hardly room for the single bed, small chest of drawers and washstand it contained, but Amy had never had a bed all to herself, let alone a bedroom, and was happy as a puppy unpacking her few things and arranging them around.

Effie had instructed her to do that first, thinking it would permit her a moment to draw breath, but it didn't take five minutes – the girl owned hardly anything – and then she was downstairs again unpacking 'madam's clothes', and finding homes on surfaces and shelves for Effie's wedding gifts. Even Peter Kellow's wooden bowl was taken out and filled with rosehips from the straggling bushes near the gate. Amy was keen to prove her cooking skills: 'no need to bring in a woman specially', and was promising to turn this bounty into a pudding by-and-by – a sugarless wartime one made with potato starch – but they looked so pretty that Effie told her to leave them where they were, on the middle-room table, as an ornament, meanwhile.

It had taken hours to crate up everything to move, and it was clearly going to take as long to take it out again, even with two people doing it. So Effie decided they should concentrate on making just a few rooms habitable first – the kitchen, middle room and a bedroom each – and leave the rest for later, and that is what they did. Even so, by the time they'd finished, the night was drawing in and they had to find a box of candles, matches and a lamp to get the last few necessary items unpacked and put away.

But the place looked much less gloomy with her own few bits around, especially the 'parlour' with a bright rug on the floor and her knitted blanket on the easy chair. And once a cheerful fire was lit and Effie could sit down to a nice hot cup of tea and a reheated portion of the swede-and-onion stew that Jillian had sent round yesterday, An Dyji was already beginning to feel as if it might one day be home.

Effie finished eating, pushed the plate away, and moved the few inches from the table to the armchair by the fire. It was an ugly, old-fashioned piece of furniture, but surprisingly comfy when you got into it and let yourself lean back against the cushions.

She didn't close her eyes; they did it by themselves. It troubled her vaguely that Amy was in the scullery, still busy washing up – it made her feel like Alex's mama, spoiled, rich and indolent! But the girl seemed happy, she was singing as she worked, and tonight her mistress was too weary to protest. Once or twice, in fact, she almost drifted off.

She really had not slept much since that telegram arrived – except for that evening of the funeral, when she'd been exhausted in body and in mind. This was a different kind of tiredness. Of course she had been working hard today, in unaccustomed ways, but there was something more – a feeling of arrival, of something like content. Even in this semi-dream she knew exactly why. This place was not full of painful memories of Alex, he'd not sat on these chairs or walked down the path outside – so it was not full of his absence as Rosvene had always been. Even in White Cottage she could not escape the past – he'd visited it with her several times before he went away. But here she was alone and he was simply in her mind, and there was only sweetness in the thought and not sharp regret. Perhaps people were right when they urged you to 'move on'.

And with that thought she fell properly asleep – so soundly that Amy had to come and shake her arm. 'Mrs Dawes, ma'am, it's a shame to wake you up, but it's nigh on ten thirty and you ought to be in bed. I've put a hot pan in there, warmed up the sheets for you, and taken some hot water up for you to wash yourself.' She paused. 'Want for me to come and help you get undressed? Lots of maids do that for their mistresses, I know – I might not be much help at first, but I'd be glad to learn.'

Effie shook her head. 'Only when the mistress keeps other staff as well – it's generally a lady's maid that does that sort of thing. I'll manage nicely, thank you Amy, I'm quite used to it.'

Amy was not so easily dismissed. 'I wish you'd let me come and help you all the same. Never know. Might come in handy for me one day, knowing what to do, when you move along and I am looking for another post somewhere.'

'I'm not planning to move on anywhere.' Effie was amused. 'And there is nothing much to learn – I used to have to do it for my own mistress once – just brush her hair and put her nightclothes out on the bed. Oh, and hang her dayclothes up and brush the hems. The rest of it

– fetching washing water and heating up the room – you seem to have already done in any case. But there really is no need to bother, I can see to things myself.'

Amy shook her head, defiantly. 'I aren't here to be an ornament,' she said. 'I'm supposed to be a maid. It's awkward for me, if you won't let me do the things a maid should do. And what do you think that Mr Dawes would say? It was him that wanted you to have me, wasn't it?'

That was quite true of course. 'I'm too tired to talk about it,' Effie said, sounding a little ungracious, even to herself. 'Though I suppose that you can come and help me, just this once – I own that I'd be grateful for a bit of help tonight.'

'There you are then,' Amy said, delightedly. 'Now, I've lit a candle for you, should I take it up? And I tried to light a fire in the fireplace up there, but I couldn't make it draw. Something up the chimney, I shouldn't be surprised. Have to get a man to see to it.'

Effie nodded. 'We'll get the sweep around. Supposed to be good luck.' Ridiculous to feel a sense of pride, that she – a woman – was taking charge of things, and planning to get workmen in to sort a problem out. She'd have to ask Pa, though, how much it ought to cost. It would be very easy for the man to overcharge. She gave a rueful smile. 'Though I hope there aren't going to be too many more unlooked-for costs.'

Amy had picked up the candlestick and was already blowing out the lamp. 'Well, there is just one thing, madam. I hardly like to say, but could you arrange for me to have a uniform? Don't feel right, somehow, me wearing normal clothes – and if you had callers, I don't know what they'd think! It's different from me coming in an hour or two a day. I'd like to feel I was a proper maid.'

Effie remembered – all too clearly – how proud she had felt herself the first time she'd been given a servant's uniform 'like a grown-up person rather than a child'. She was not aware that she'd said the words aloud.

But she must have done, for Amy said at once, 'Exactly, madam. My ma said not to ask you, but I knew you'd understand.'

'We'll see to it as soon as possible.' Effie was deliberately brisk. 'We'll go to town and buy material – I know just the place – always supposing that they've got any in stock. If not, and it would make a stopgap anyhow, I believe I've still got the uniform I used to have myself – in one of those boxes that we haven't yet unpacked. We could alter that to fit you: it was done before, when it was passed to me – or rather I did it. I was good at things like that.'

'No "was" about it, madam, excuse me saying so. I saw that black bombazine you made over for yourself,' Amy said referring to an outfit that Jillian had looked out and handed on, from when she was mourning her first husband years ago. 'Beautiful it is. I wish I had the skill. I'm a fair hand in the kitchen and with a scrubbing brush, but I'm all thumbs instead of fingers if I try to sew. But if you really mean it, I'll hunt out that uniform. That would do me lovely – if you'll help to alter it.'

Effie nodded, but before she managed to say another word, Amy was leading the way out to the hall, holding the candle to light their way upstairs.

She held it high so Effie could see to climb the narrow stair. 'I'll look for it, first thing,' she murmured, almost to herself. 'There aren't so many boxes left unpacked, where it could be. Though I'll have to do something with all the empty ones. One or two of them would do again, I suppose, but a lot of them have spoiled where the nails have split the wood.' They had reached the landing by this time, and she stepped ahead to show her mistress to the bedroom door. 'I thought we might be able to put them on the fire – if I can find anywhere to store them where they'll still be dry. They're all right where they are for now, just overnight – but do you know if there's a coal-hole or a woodpile anywhere?'

Effie shook her head. 'Haven't seen one.'

'Pity. Though there's that old pig's-crow shed outside. Perhaps we could put them there. I'll have to get them moved before we do the room. That will be the front room and you'll want it looking something like before it's Sunday and your family arrive. Now, if you're ready madam…?' She pushed the door ajar.

Effie allowed herself to be led into her room – it did look welcoming with the clean sheets turned back, the patchwork quilt she'd made herself (and never had a chance to use before today) and her warm flannel nightie laid out on the top. She did not even protest as Amy helped her to undress and wash – and as for having someone brush her hair, it almost made her weep. No one had done that since her mother died, when Effie was a child. Not even Alex – though he'd offered to. She wished now that she'd let him, but it was too late for regrets. Better to be grateful for the blessings that she had.

'Thank you, Amy,' she murmured as she snuggled into bed – the bedclothes were still slightly warm from where the pan had been. She meant to tell the girl how comforting that felt, but she was asleep before the words had reached her lips.

–

Peter was in the tunnel under no-man's-land. It turned your blood to ice sometimes to realize where you were – moving ever closer to the enemy, like moles beneath the earth, while the ground above you trembled with the shock of shells and distant thuds sent showers of small stones down from the roof.

Those listening tubes had been installed for weeks, with excellent results. The enemy's position had been identified and now the company was involved in what Judd called 'proper war'. Peter's team had spent the last few weeks between the 'geo-phone' – he had proved to be rather good at listening – and occasional short bursts of working at the face, scooping out the narrow passage down which, this very day, a huge charge was to be set – as close to Fritz's front-line trench as possible.

Short bursts, because it was exhausting work; they'd now run into rock and getting through that silently was difficult and slow. You could not use a back-swing, because that made a noise, and noise was a killer this close to the Bosch. Plus there was the constant dust – sometimes you could hardly see the others on your team – though that was a change from a little further back, when they had been working in wet clay above their boots.

Between these duties, you joined the bucket-gang that shifted the spoil back from the tunnel-face. Wooden buckets here, because they made less noise. These were passed – as silently as possible – from man to man towards the entranceway, where members of the poor old infantry were awaiting it. It was their job to move it outside – under constant fire – so that no trace was visible even from the air. Enemy observers flew over constantly and heaps of newly evacuated rock would have alerted them at once to what was happening.

Because today – though nobody knew it but themselves, and headquarters of course – was blasting day. The company was making one last forward drive, the explosives were to hand and the plan was to set them before the hour was out, seal off the cavity (to direct the force upwards as much as possible) then withdraw the miners and set off the fuse. So all hands were on the buckets, no respite today. Peter was working in the second team – which meant the miners in the blast chamber were out of sight ahead, and the tunnel entrance was out of sight behind. Visibility was sometimes poor in any case, not merely from the rock-dust in the air; the narrow hewn-out passages were only lit by candles on ledges on the walls.

He took another pail of spoil and, in total silence, passed it back – though every load seemed heavier than the last. He was also slightly hampered by a loop of rope he wore around one arm, though that was his own fault, he acknowledged ruefully.

It was a system of his own invention, born of something that they used to do as boys, gathering seagulls eggs down on Penvarris cliff. The person climbing down would tie a line around his waist and tug it to warn the others when he needed them – one tug to haul the basket up when it was full of eggs, and two to signal that he wanted pulling up himself.

Peter had suggested such a thing to Judd, as a means of communicating in emergencies, and Judd – who had no doubt collected eggs himself – had surprisingly agreed. He not only ordered that the team should try it out, but added an adaptation of his own. So each man had a slender line clipped on his right to the belt round his waist. He carried a loop of slack around one arm, and the other end was fastened to the man ahead, but on the left-hand side, so that a tug from either direction would be felt at once and the recipient could swiftly pass it on. There was even a code for how many tugs meant what.

It had taken some practise to perfect the use of this – there were grumbles that it limited free movement under-ground, and there were false alarms when it was trodden on or caught on some projecting lump of rock – but it had already proved its worth. Only a day or two into the trial, Tremean, who was working as the lead man, boring-in, had hit a natural pocket filled with unseen gas and been overcome by swift unconsciousness. Gas like that could kill in minutes, and it often did, but the weight of his falling was communicated back and he was rescued quickly and brought out alive – for which he was embarrassingly grateful afterwards. The system was soon adopted by everybody else – even by those who muttered about 'bloody bits of rope'.

Peter grinned grimly and turned to grab another pail. It was worth the unremitting effort, Old Judd often said. 'Underground charges put the fear of God up Fritz like nothing else.' He was very likely right – the Tommies on detachment here all said they felt the same; even in the trenches the most frightening idea was to be blown up silently from underneath – worse than cannon, which at least you knew were there.

Another pail of rubble to pass back. No tubs on tracks to help you here – they were too far forward, the rumble might be heard. It was very tiring. He paused to rub his hand across his brow. As he did so he leaned back against the wall – and felt his blood run cold.

Against the silence there was suddenly a noise. Not from the tunnel, but from overhead. Not the thump of an exploding shell, you got quite used to those. This was different – a soft, insistent tap. Muffled – you could only hear it if you strained – and intermittent.

For a moment Peter wondered if he was hearing his own heart – however many times you did this job it still thumped painfully – but no, there was no doubt, there it was again. He recognized it from his recent listening stint. A tapping that caused a fearful pricking of the skin and the sudden, never-to-be forgotten taste of mortal fear.

Jerry! It had to be. Underground himself, and not too far away. Had our boys been heard, in spite of everything? Was that sound the enemy laying booby traps? Or trying to get through to where the British trenches were? Either way the Bosch was clearly mining on his own account. Mining, in the soldier's sense of setting mines – explosive charges that would blow the earth apart and blast all human life around to smithereens. And Peter and his team were directly underneath.

The first temptation was to shout aloud – scream a warning, call his comrades back – but Old Judd had done his training well. Instead of shouting, Peter tugged the cord. He gave the 'imminent danger' signal – three sharp tugs, a pause, and then three more, and got the reassurance of an answering two, each way.

The system now demanded that the team evacuate, using the line to guide them if the candles failed. You were supposed to undo your right-hand rope at once, so the man behind could reel it in, then wait for fifteen seconds, for the man ahead to do the same. If the cord went taut and nobody appeared, after that time you'd drop the line and make your own escape. This would be a signal for a general alarm – the likelihood being either that there'd been a fall of rock, and men were trapped, or that Jerry had broken through into the shaft and people were in there fighting hand to hand: both things had happened several times elsewhere.

That was the theory. Reality, however, was rather different. Fifteen seconds is an eternity when there's an enemy, probably with dynamite, just through the ceiling overhead. Peter had forced himself to get to ten – he was attempting to count the seconds down – but he never reached eleven. Ahead of him the line went slack all right, but before he could begin to coil it in, down the tunnel came a clatter and a roar of running men. Pails and buckets scattered, men came bursting past – the rush of their passage blew the candles out.

'Run! Run!' one shouted. 'You've got two minutes. Run, for pity's sake!'

After the tiptoeing silence of the last two weeks, the sudden commotion was a shock, so violent it was almost physical. Peter was so startled that he stepped back against the wall and the trailing line got caught around his legs and almost brought him down. He had just the wit to shake it free – if he had fallen at that moment he might well have died, trampled underfoot as still more men came crashing past.

Tremean was one of them. He took one look at Peter and grabbed him by the arm. 'Come on, man! Judd's set the charge. Get out before it blows!'

And Peter joined him, groping in the gloom towards the entranceway. Feet, muffled in rags to save the clang of boots, bounced against pails and scuffed on scattered spoil. But the men around him had been miners all their lives – there were helping hands to push and pull, and soon there was a gleam of daylight up ahead and Peter and Tremean both stumbled into it.

As they did so there was a massive roar. The ground behind them seemed to rise up like a wave and – somewhere out in no-man's-land – a monstrous fountain made of rock and smoke burst through and scattered everything – dead men, guns, mud, legs, bits of twisted iron. Peter was thrown forward with the blast of it, and the last thing he remembered as he hit the ground was the taste of earth and the sensation of gravel in his mouth.

-

'Af'noon, Martha!' Will Jeffries drew up beside her on his bicycle and slid off so that he could walk with her. 'A chilly bit of wind! Where you been off to? Don't often see you out walking at this time of day. Leastways, not in this direction. Everything all right?' Obviously it wasn't. It looked as if she'd been having a little private cry.

Martha gave him an anguished look that touched his heart. 'Been out to see my married daughter...' She broke off and said no more.

'That's your Patience? I heard that she'd got wed, but—'

'Couldn't have asked you, Will, if I'd have wanted to. Special service down the Methodists – only the Strict Adherents there, and just as well, perhaps. Joyless old business – no music for the hymns – but a wedding all the same. I don't know if I was right to hope for it so much.'

'How so, Martha? He's never harsh to her? Not a man like Ephraim?'

She shook her head. 'It nothing that he's done, so far as I can see, 'cepting that he's prayed her half to death. And of course a girl has always got to learn to be a wife. But it isn't suiting her. I never did see a girl so changed in all my life. Like as if the life has all gone out of her. Mind, that old farmhouse would make anybody glum. I've been down helping her to get the copper lit, and do a bit of mangling so she could get the washing out – this bit of breeze will get it nicely dried, supposing that it doesn't come to rain.'

Will could think of nothing very sensible to say, but she seemed to have cheered up a little now, so he ventured, 'Glad of a bit of a hand with all of that, I'm sure.'

She gave him another of those looks. 'I should think so, too! You never saw the like.' She stopped at the corner of the hedge and fixed tearful eyes on him. 'Eight years that Ephraim's lived there on his own, and I don't believe he's ever washed a rag in all that time – 'cept perhaps his underwear and an odd Sunday shirt. Certainly that boiler hadn't worked in years: took us half the morning to get the thing to light – birds' nests in the flue and I don't know what, and as for cleaning out the spiders' webs and verdigris inside! And then you had to boil the sheets for half an hour before you could begin to see that they were white!' There was angry exasperation in her tone as she turned away and began to walk on, down the hill again.

'And Ephraim?' he asked, keeping step with her.

She made scornful noise. 'Too busy writing his address – next Sunday's homily – to be any use, though he did chop up the kindling and fetch the water, I suppose. Wonder he gets any farming done at all. Still, it's a sin to grumble at what the Lord provides. Fortunate they've got a wash house copper and a well – I'd pity Patience washing otherwise.'

They had reached the stile at the bottom of the hill by now. That was Martha's quick way home, but Will was reluctant to see her go so soon. 'Lucky she's got you for a ma, that's certain,' he said, with feeling, and was rewarded with a smile.

'Kind of you to say that, Will, but I'm not so sure. I let our Toby make too much of her, I think – being the firstborn girl and all that sort of thing. "Withhold not correction from the child", the Good Book says, but perhaps that's what we did.' He couldn't answer that. Toby had never been one to 'spare the rod and spoil the child' – more likely to be the other way about, they'd been brought up so strictly that they wanted to rebel. But she was waiting for an answer, so he said, 'You don't think she's content?'

Martha sighed. 'Stuck up there in that great shambling place where nothing's been cleaned or put away for years? There's stuff in the back room upstairs that's not been used for years – hanks of wool and lengths of cloths and the dear what besides, all heaped up anyhow – worth a fortune, these days, if it was only clean – though who knows what moths and things might have got into it. I shall have to go and help her sort it out, though what we're going to put it into I have no idea. There isn't enough cupboards and drawer space in Rosvene!'

She said it with such vigour that it made Will laugh aloud, but then an idea struck him. He was always anxious to be of service to Martha if he could. 'So happens, Martha, I might just be able help you there. Effie – you remember Mrs Dawes, the wife of that young constable that died?'

Martha nodded, yes.

'Well, she was living in White Cottage – the place my mother had – but it's likely that I'll be retiring from the police force very soon and I'll be wanting to move in there myself. She's moved now, to another place, out Penvarris way, where she is nearer to her folks – nice little cottage, which I found for her. Point is, I know she bought a lot of wooden crates – had them to pack her stuff and move it over there, and I'm fairly sure she won't be wanting them again. Glad to let you have them for a few pennies, I should think – if that would be any use to you? Very likely, she'll only burn them else. I'm going out that way, later on so – if you like – I'll call on her and ask her what she wants to do with them.'

Martha was no youngster now, but she still had a lovely smile. 'Oh, Will – would you? It would be such a help! Pattie'd be delighted. You're very good to us!' She held out a hand for him to shake and he used the opportunity to help her cross the stile.

'Bye then, Martha,' and he got onto his bike and pedalled out as fast as possible to call on Mrs Dawes. The area had not actually been on his intended rounds today, but he'd meant to call in soon in any case – to see if she was settling in all right – and was glad to have found a legitimate excuse.

She was in the garden when he reached the house, to his surprise, watching Amy lopping back the weeds beside the path. It was rather shocking to see her standing openly outside, dressed in black and with her widow's cap on, naturally, but no cape or mourning veil. She waved in greeting when she saw him at the gate.

'I'd forgotten what hard work this is,' she said, as he came up to her. 'Used to help my pa do this when I was young – this is his patch-hook that Amy's using now. She volunteered to do it, she's keen to clear a path to that old pigsty there, that we want to use for storage. But it's new for her – she's been working for ten minutes and she's hardly made a start. Wish I could do it for her, but of course I can't. AH right Amy, that's enough for now!'

The maid dropped the implement – with gratitude, he thought. 'You and the Sergeant would like a pot of tea?'

Effie nodded and then turned to Will again. 'Want to come inside and see what we have done? Haven't finished by a long way, but it's coming on.'

It was. The sitting room looked bright and cosy now. 'Makes a difference, don't it, Mrs Dawes, having a bit of fire and few nice rugs about?'

'Especially since I pulled those curtains back and let the sunshine in.' She saw his disapproving look. 'There's no disrespect to Alex, his corpse was never here. And little Amy's done such a splendid job, cleaning the windows – she was up at daybreak, washing down the panes – it would have been a shame to muffle them. She wanted to do it before I was down myself. Says I would have stopped her, and probably that's true, it doesn't seem right to sit about while others work, to me.'

'That's why you were standing in the garden, watching, I suppose? Though what your mother-in-law would say, I hate to think.' He smiled to make this seem a little less of a rebuke.

She gave him a wry look. 'Oh, I think we could guess exactly what she'd say! She writes me little homilies, on black-edged notepaper, almost every week, telling me how a member of their family should behave. No balls or public dinners for at least a year, and general seclusion from society!' She gave a bitter laugh. 'How many balls and dinners does she suppose that I attend?'

'And what about "seclusion from society"?'

'It only proves what I have always known – my world and her world are a universe apart. Take poor old Jilly

Richards, before she wed my pa. She mourned her husband, yes of course she did – this dress I'm wearing was one of hers, in fact – she did not go out seeking jollity and she wore decent black for several years. But how would she have done if she'd stayed prettily at home? She had a boy to care for, and household bills to pay. She had to shop and cook and clean the way she always had – and take in boarders now, as well, to help to pay the bills. And better for it – as she said the other day. That's been half my trouble, Sergeant, I believe. I'm not like her – with jobs to do, to keep me busy and occupy my mind, or like my mother-in-law with lots of wealthy friends who've nothing else to do but call on her, to offer sympathy and keep her company, without her having to go anywhere herself.'

She spoke with so much passion that he could only say, 'So you decided to take an interest in the gardening? Nobody to see you out here, I suppose?'

'I haven't seen a soul, except yourself,' she said. 'And it wasn't gardening. I was only explaining to Amy what to do, so we could put a few of those old crates in the shed – they're piled up in the other sitting room and there isn't room to move until they're gone. I wasn't intending to stay out very long. But you know, Sergeant Jeffries, I was quite enjoying it.' It was obviously true. She looked at him, her eyes and cheeks aglow – more alive than he had seen her since her husband's death. A breath of fresh air and an aim to think about had done a bit of good – 'taken her out of herself' as Ivy would have said.

'Tell you what, my han'some,' he said heartily, 'I'll have this bit of tea, and if you like I'll stop and give a hand. I'm out on general patrol, keeping a lookout on the cliffs, so I'm not expected anywhere particular – though I can't be long, of course. But let me have that billhook and a stone to sharpen it, and I'll clear a path for you before you can say "knife".'

He thought for a moment that Effie would refuse, but she gave a rueful smile. 'I expect you've got the trick to it,' she said. 'I used to have it, but I can't explain to Amy how to hold the hook. I was deciding I would have to wait for Pa – he's coming here the weekend, when he's got a half-day free, and hopes to make a proper garden by and by. But I'd be glad if you would help – just enough so we can move the crates. We can't finish the unpacking till we've got rid of some.'

'Those crates, now—' Will was saying, when Amy interrupted by bringing in the tea – not bad tea either for a brand-new pot – and she even remembered that he liked two sugar lumps. No one offered anything to eat. Unfortunately people often didn't, these days, with the war. But the tea was very nice. 'Now, Mrs Dawes,' he ventured, when he'd taken a long sip, 'as I was saying, funny thing about those crates...' And he outlined his suggestion.

Effie was even more enthusiastic than he'd hoped. 'If she can find some way of fetching them, she's welcome to them free. Nothing but a nuisance, in a tiny place like this. Some of them are rather spoiled and split, I was going to get Pa to chop those up for kindling wood – but there's at least a half a dozen that are good as new.'

'Martha – Mrs Tregorran – will be delighted, I am sure,' he said, finishing his tea. 'She'll send the older girls to pick them up, I expect. Now, if you'd like to show me where you want these weeds took down...?' He lumbered to his feet.

'Amy will show you,' Mrs Dawes replied, rather to his disappointment. 'I'd better change my skirts. Got my hems all wet and grassy and they need sponging clean, though I wasn't there five minutes – and serve me right, I suppose. I'll see you in a moment!' And she went off upstairs – every inch the mistress of the house.

'Done her good to come here,' he said the words aloud and was rather surprised to be answered by the maid.

'Worlds of good. More like she used to be when she first took me on. But I'm glad you're going to come and clear those weeds a bit. Man's job that is, and I nearly told her so – but she wouldn't have harkened and it's not my place to say. Now – want me to show you where this path is supposed to be?' She was already leading him outside. 'There!' she pointed with her finger, sketching out a line. 'Funny thing, they can't have used that shed for years – but there's a path that leads right to it, over through that field. I went round to have a peek and you can see inside.'

'Anything in there?' he said, in policeman mode.

She shook her head. 'Not a chibble. It's all swept and clean. But someone's been using it for something, by the looks. Wonder who would want to come there, wouldn't you? Smelly old pigsty – what would be the use?'

Will Jeffries gave a thoughtful tug at his moustache, but he had been a policeman far too long not to think how it would make a trysting place, out of the weather and out of public sight. For unfortunates like Pattie Tull, perhaps?

But he did not say that to Amy. He took off his jacket, whetted the billhook, and set about the weeds. After all, as Effie Dawes had said, there was nobody to see. There were lots of thorns and brambles and it took longer than he thought, but by the time that Effie Dawes came down again (prettier than ever – in black cashmere this time) he'd managed to hack a narrow pathway to the shed.

'Better be off then. Be in touch about the crates,' he muttered as she tried to thank him fulsomely. That was two lovely ladies helped today, he thought. He put his helmet and his jacket on and rode off whistling.

Part Four

April – August 1916

One

Life at An Dyji had begun to settle into order now. Amy had moved the empty crates out to the shed, and most of the rest had been unpacked and put away. Not quite all, there was some stuff of Alex's which she could not bear to touch. She would have to deal with it sometime, but she was not ready yet – she just left it in the boxes and put it out to store.

The parlour (if the tiny front room deserved the name) looked a little better with some photographs and embroidery on the walls, Effie's pretty antimacassars on the chairs, and the mantle clock that Pa had given them installed above the fire – though that had not been lit. That chimney too needed the attentions of a sweep. The third tiny bedroom, which to start with had a truckle bed in it, had become what Amy grandly called 'the writing room'. Effie had moved the truckle to underneath her own bed in the room next door, pushed the chair and washstand table into the space this left behind – underneath the window where it got the light – and filled the two sloping shelves with her books and sewing things. The whole house felt a lot less crowded suddenly.

The Sunday visit was a great success. It was mostly conducted in Effie's crowded middle room, because of the problems with the parlour fire, but Pa and Jillian both declared An Dyji – and the rosehip pudding, too – to be 'simply wonderful – and in no time 't all!'

After that Amy was finally induced to take her half-day off, though she insisted on keeping on her uniform – Effie's old one, duly taken in to fit. That had been the first achievement of the 'writing room' – and Amy was so delighted that she wouldn't take it off (though she had consented to remove the apron and the cap before she went).

'Want to show it off to Mother,' she declared, twirling to display it as she brought in Effie's lunch. But, though the garment had been partially unpicked and all the darts resewn, to Effie's eyes it still didn't look quite right – there was too much fullness in the cut for Amy's skinny form.

'It will do,' she said to Amy, who was now itching to be off. 'But that material is faded and the alterations show. Next time I go into Penzance I'll try and get some more and we'll make you a uniform of your very own – supposing there's the gingham to be had.'

Amy put down the basket she was carrying (rosehips, for her mother) and gave a little cry. 'Oh, madam. I like this one.'

Effie smiled. 'You'll want another one in any case while this is in the wash. No steam laundry out here that we can send it to, to get it clean and ready while you have your free half-day! Now!' She spread a little of Jillian's pre-war bramble jam onto her National bread (no butter – that was almost impossible to get!) 'You hurry off, or you won't catch your bus. I'll see you this evening.'

'Yes, madam,' Amy said. 'I'll be back to make your tea. You'll be all right, while I'm gone – out here all on your own?' She was enjoying her new responsibilities so much, sometimes she seemed to think she was not a servant, but a sort of mother hen.

Effie managed to suppress a smile. 'Perfectly, thank you. There are letters I must answer, and I've a book to read.' It was a treat she was promising herself. There was a story about sisters, called *Pride and Prejudice* which Alex (knowing how she loved to read) had sent her as a Christmas gift the year he went away. She had begun it, and liked it very much – but she had not read a word of it since she got that telegram. But she had come across it, in the move, and told herself that – as with everything else – it was time to start again.

But she had hardly settled in the 'writing room', with a comfy cushion at her back and her feet on an embroidered footstool from downstairs, when – through the window – she saw a horse and cart draw up outside. This room did not directly overlook the road, so she could not see the person who got out – from this angle they were hidden by the hedge – but it was clearly someone coming to the house. And a woman – she was almost certain she had glimpsed a skirt.

Effie was puzzled for a moment. Who'd be calling here? The landlord's wife perhaps? She craned a little further, but she couldn't see, and the visitor by this time was knocking at the door. Effie sighed, put her book away and went to answer it.

There was a young woman on the doorstep whom she did not recognize. 'Is Mrs Dawes at home?'

The question was so bald that it was almost rude – not even a conventional 'good afternoon'! Effie was about to make some curt reply, but there was something about the woman that made her think again. Thin to the point of skinniness and very plainly dressed, with pale cheeks, a drawn expression and a pair of anguished eyes – yet oddly familiar, she could not think why. 'Should I know you?' she heard herself enquire.

'Oh, I'm some sorry, madam. You must be Mrs Dawes! I didn't realize. I thought you were the housekeeper, at first. But of course you are in mourning – that's why you're in black. My sympathy, of course.' She'd embarrassed herself, clearly, and she hurried on: 'No, I don't believe you know me, but you've met my sister Vee.'

Vee? It took Effie a moment to work out who she meant. And then she remembered. 'The Tregorran girl?' There was a faint resemblance, when you came to look – though this girl was a waxwork ghost compared to Verity. 'Of course! You've come about those boxes? Sergeant Jeffries told me you might come – though I wasn't expecting horses!'

A faint smile lit the bloodless lips. 'I'm not rightly a Tregorran – not any more at least. I'm Patience Tull these days and that's my husband Ephraim on the cart. He had it harnessed up to take some produce to the town, and thought while we were passing with an empty cart…'

Effie said, 'Of course. Now, shall I show you where they are? Or would you like to come inside? A cup of tea, perhaps?' The woman looked as if a rest would do her good.

But Patience Tull was shaking her head emphatically. 'Oh, no thank you, Mrs Dawes, that wouldn't do at all. Ephraim wouldn't like it, he doesn't care for company – not without they're Strict Adherents like himself… or like ourselves, I suppose that I should say.'

Effie nodded. 'I recall your sister saying you were members of the sect. How is she? I haven't seen her for a little while.' She began to lead the way towards the pigsty shed.

Mrs Tull came trailing after her. 'I wanted for her to be the one to ask you for the crates, being as she knew you – but she wouldn't come. Said she called to see you once when you were down Rosvene, but you'd just lost your husband and she got sent away. After that she didn't like to bother you again. Anyhow, she couldn't have carried many crates – better for me and Ephraim to do it with the cart.'

'Of course,' said Effie, and led the way into the shed. 'There they are – you can see the empty ones. Help yourself to as many as you like.'

The woman looked hunted. 'How much would they be?'

'I don't want money. They are no use to me. I was planning to put them on the fire.'

Verity's sister shook her head again. 'Ephraim wouldn't like if we didn't pay. "I will surely buy it from you for a price", the Bible says.'

'And "God loveth a cheerful giver", it says that as well.' The devil might quote scripture for his purposes, but so did Uncle Joe, and Effie had heard him say this many times – usually when he wanted something! 'Your husband would not deny me that blessing, would he now? Anyway, I owe your family something as an apology. I did invite your sister to come and talk to me – but she chose a dreadful moment, and I must have seemed unkind. Please tell her to come and visit me again.'

'I'll be sure and do that,' Mrs Tull replied.

She had assembled up four crates into a pile and would have bent to lift them if Effie had not said, 'Surely, your husband...?' She had suddenly realized that the woman

217

was with child. 'You'll do yourself a mischief, lifting things like that!'

The visitor flashed her a bleak smile. 'Oh, Ephraim offered, but I said I'd fetch the crates myself. Tisn't fitty a strange man should call on you – a widow on your own. It's not as if there's any weight in them.' She seized up the pile of crates, refusing Effie's help. 'In any case,' she added, over her shoulder as she went back down the path, 'I'd sooner Ephraim stayed there with the horse. I'd have had to hold it otherwise – and it's a wilful thing.'

It looked about as wilful as a hedgehog, Effie thought, as she accompanied her visitor out to the road again. A sour-faced man was sitting on the cart, holding the reins and scowling, but he tipped his hat to her. 'Marning, missus. Very good of you. Hope she paid you decent – I gave her money to.'

'You're doing me a favour by taking them away,' Effie told him, and then wished she'd held her tongue. A look of such anguish crossed the woman's face, that Effie realized she'd been hoping to keep those few pence for herself. Very likely her husband kept her short.

But there was no time for regret. The woman had hoisted the crates onto the cart and clambered up beside her husband on the seat in front. He tipped his hat again, then flicked the reins, urging the 'wilful' horse to a reluctant walk and the cart went lurching down the road and out of sight.

Effie went back to the shed and shut the door. Funny thing, she hadn't been in here before today but she could see what Amy meant about it being clean and swept. It was completely empty, other than her crates – but something else had clearly been stored here recently: there were fresh marks in the dust where something had been dragged across the floor. Clearly not the crates – there was an indentation where the weight had been – and it was an entirely different size and shape. Maybe the previous tenant had used it after all.

She shrugged and went back to *Pride and Prejudice*. Those letters would have to wait until another day.

–

When Peter woke up he was lying on a bed, with a splitting headache and a sensation of swelling and stiffness in his face. Something seemed to have happened to his eyes – he could hardly open them – and when he did so, everything looked blurred. He did make out a figure – some sort of medical orderly – who was bending over him.

'All right, sapper? Back with us, I see? You were knocked unconscious by the blast. Broken nose and a couple of lovely shiners, but otherwise unharmed. Might spoil your beauty, and you mustn't exert yourself or blow your nose for a little while – so you'll be excused duties for a day or two, at least – but after that you should be right as rain.'

Peter blinked at him. 'What blast? Where am I?' But even as he asked, strange confused impressions began to come to him – being in a tunnel, people rushing past, being pushed into the daylight. 'What's happened to Tremean? He saved my life, I think.'

The fellow picked up a water bottle from the cabinet and poured some into a sort of drinking cup. 'Less fortunate than you. Hit a rock and broke an arm and shoulder in the fall. You're in the first-aid bay – still with the company, while we have room for you. They've sent him off to a Base Hospital to patch him up again. Though you two were lucky. Several men were killed. Now, have a drink of this. Now you're conscious, we'll get you on your feet. The Major wants to see you, when you're fit enough.'

Peter tried to raise his head and take a sip, but he seemed to have a thousand hammers where his brain should be. He sank back on the pillow and waved the cup away. But the orderly persisted. 'You've been out cold for hours. You have to make the effort.' So at last he did.

And that was the pattern of the next few days – being required to do things through a mental fog and a splintering headache, though that was very slowly wearing off and the bruising round his eyes was no longer quite so black. The doctors had diagnosed 'commotion of the brain', and treated him quite kindly – though they were less impressed with one poor fellow from the infantry who'd come in a quaking wreck, following a spell of being caught in no-man's-land. (He hadn't been unconscious, though, at any stage, and that made it 'shell shock' which it seemed was different.)

No-man's-land. That struck a chord somehow. Of course, that's where the tunnel was, when he had heard that noise.

At the recollection he felt his spine go cold and he shivered, physically shivered, at the very thought – a fact that was noted by the orderly, who was assisting him to take a few steps of exercise outside. 'Feeling feverish, sapper?'

Peter shook his head. 'It's just that the memories are starting to return and I realize that I'd never been so frightened in my life. But I suppose that it is progress. And

I noticed this morning that my sense of taste and smell are coming back.'

'Are they now?' the fellow said, and rushed off to report.

After that, things moved with a surprising speed. The doctor came to see him and pronounced him largely cured (though he couldn't blow his nose for weeks without his right eye swelling up, and it never returned to its proper shape again). 'You can return to quarters, with immediate effect – though come back to see us if you suffer dizzy spells. Two days light duties only while you recuperate – I'll give you a chitty to that effect, of course – then you should be fit for proper service, with no permanent effects. You can tell the Major so when you report to him – he wants to see you anyway, as I believe you know.'

Peter had forgotten – those early hours now all seemed like a dream – but the summons troubled him. Did the Major blame him for the panic underground – could it really be less than a week ago? He took a deep breath. There was one way to find out. Next day reported to the company 'office' – actually a disused storeroom at the factory.

The Major – who was 'acting officer in charge', though Peter had scarcely seen him since the introductory day – was sitting at a table, signing things. He looked up at Peter and acknowledged his salute.

'Ah, Kellow. Pleased to see you fit and well again.'

He seemed to want an answer so Peter murmured, 'Sir!' – though, under the cool scrutiny, he was painfully aware that the skin around his eyes was still greenish–purple with the fading bruise, and his nose was swollen and a peculiar shape.

'I expect you guess why I have sent for you.'

Peter had not the least idea, and said as much.

The Major leaned back in his chair and laced his fingers in a pyramid. 'Judd spoke most highly of you. You were aware of that?'

Peter mumbled that – with due respect to Judd – 'That might be just because he knew my brother, sir. We're fellow Cornishmen and went to the same school.'

'You think it might be simply favouritism, eh?' The Major riffled papers. 'Says here you "showed unusual intelligence and initiative. Quick grasp of theory and outstanding listening skills. Invented a system of communicating silently, to minimize the danger of alerting the enemy to where mining operations were taking place." Does that sound like you? Or was it your brother?' He gave Peter a wry look.

Peter felt the flush rise to his cheeks, and feared for a moment that his nose was going to bleed. 'Yes, sir. That is – it was my system, sir – though it was Lieutenant Judd who altered it and made it work. Though it didn't really, did it? When there was danger people simply dropped the ropes and ran – I nearly fell over a trading end myself.'

'And why were they running? Ah yes, I recall. Somebody employed the system, I believe, and signalled "danger" to the miners at the face. In fact, my enquiries suggest that it was you.'

Peter was not used to this kind of mocking praise, and did not quite know how to answer. He said, simply, 'I heard the Germans tapping, making a hole to set their charge, I suppose. They must have heard us working – and arranged a counterblast. Well, I have to hand it to their engineers. Destroyed our whole tunnel, most effectively – and killed several people, so I'm told.' He stopped. The

Major had stopped looking quizzical and was staring in surprise.

'I don't know who told you that! It was nothing of the kind. Our offensive was a great success. It was the German tunnel which was utterly destroyed. Judd received your message, recognized the threat and set our charge off at once. Sent his team to safety and lit the fuse himself, I understand, though he must have known what that would mean for him.'

It was Peter's turn to stare in disbelief. 'Lieutenant Judd is dead?' It seemed impossible to comprehend.

The officer said, quite soberly, 'Blown to kingdom come and Lance Corporal Smith as well. He defied the order, so the men declare, refused to abandon Judd and stayed there to assist – but they took a lot of Germans with them when they went, and probably saved the lives of many of our men. I've recommended both of them for bravery awards.' He folded his slim arms across his chest. 'But you see what that means for this company, of course.'

'You've lost a pair of first-class men?' Peter ventured.

The Major gave a snort. 'More to the point, I've lost a lieutenant and an NCO. We're not a big unit, but we're already under strength. They've been promising a replacement for the RSM for weeks – and then I lost Samson and now it's Judd and Smith. So I'm looking to make a temporary appointment in the field.' His face had taken on that mocking look again. 'Someone with a grasp of theory, proven mining skills and expertise with things like geophones, who might help to train up the replacement tunnellers. Can you think of any likely candidate?'

Peter racked his addled brain. 'I don't know many people well, so I can't really help you,' he replied, rather astonished to be confided in like this. 'Tremean is a good fellow – respected by the men – but I understand that he's in hospital.'

The Major leaned back in his chair to fold his arms again. 'Kellow, you are supposed to be intelligent! It's you, I mean, of course. Only acting, till the rank is ratified, but it does mean extra pay and a privilege or two. I'm sure that will be welcome. Do you have a girl at home?'

He felt himself go scarlet, and feared for his nose again. 'No, sir,' he mumbled. 'That is, not exactly.'

'What is "not exactly"?' The officer leaned forward and gave him a searching look. 'Not one of that sort, are you? Might have to think again.'

This time, Peter understood at once. 'No, sir, nothing of the kind. Did have a girl, once, but she married someone else.'

'Ah!' There was a long pause and then the Major said, 'So I may take it that you would accept? Promotion to Lance Corporal with immediate effect – assuming that the medicos are right, of course, and you are none the worse for your little episode. Have to stand you down at once, if there is any doubt.'

And Peter said, 'Yes, sir,' and the thing was sealed. A few days later he had a chevron on his sleeve. Something to write home about, at least – Mother would be thrilled. He only wished that Effie could have known.

–

Verity's Friday could hardly have been worse. It had started very early, with a thumping on the door even before the household was astir. Vee had thrown a cloak around herself and tiptoed down the stairs, just in time to see Pa – still in his flannel nightshirt – fling open the door, while Ma half-hid behind him to see who might be there.

'Why Brother Ephraim!' Pa said, and put the poker down. 'To what do we owe the…' He stood aside to let the caller in.

But Ephraim, who seemed to be in nightclothes underneath his coat, shook his head and didn't move. 'It's Mrs Tull!' he muttered. He was pale and looked distraught, not a bit his usual self. 'She's bleeding heavily. I think she may have started – or she's losing it. I tried to pray with her, but she's shouting for her mother and I think you'd better come.'

'I'll come straight over. You get back to her!' Ma was already halfway up the stairs, but as she pushed past Verity she said, 'You go get Prudence and tell her to go down, wake up Sergeant Jeffries and ask to use his phone – call the midwife over to St Just and tell her where to come.' She paused for a moment at her bedroom door. 'And when you've done that, you run down yourself and fetch your Auntie Dorcas over to the farm. Factory will have to do without you for an hour.'

Vee hesitated, waiting for Ephraim to object – he was worse than Grandfather for not wanting Dorcas round – but Tull was already rushing down the path and it was left to Pa to shut the door and mutter gloomily, 'I don't know why your mother wants that backslider sister of hers over there! T'isn't even as if she has got children of her own.' But his face had gone as white as chalk and there was not much venom left in the remark.

Ma had done miracles in throwing on her clothes – the ones that showed, in any case – and, already on her way downstairs again, she must have overheard. 'Because she'll be a bit of help to me, that's why.' She hurried to the door and flung her cloak around her shoulders, as she spoke. 'She's assisted at half-a-dozen births round here, as well

225

you know – including Sam Chegwidden – so at least she's got some notion what to do. More than anyone could say for Ephraim Tull, it seems – for all his sheep and cows!' She wriggled her bare feet into her boots and turned to Verity. 'Now are you going to stay there gawping on the stair all day, or are you going to get help for your sister when you're asked?'

Vee hurried off without another word. There was no need to waken Prudence, she was already wideawake – as Vee knew, since she had been promoted to Pattie's empty bed and now shared the room with Pru.

'Hear that?' she demanded, as she went in there now. 'You're to go and wake the Sergeant—'

'Yes, I know, I was listening on the landing!' Pru exclaimed. She was sitting on the bed, dressed in her petticoats, rolling on her knitted socks and putting garters round. 'How do you think I'd be half-dressed otherwise?' Her voice was shaking and she was obviously upset. 'You realize, do you, what this has to mean? If Pattie's really bleeding she could die of this.' She stood up and pulled her skirt and blouse on as she spoke Vee had known that it was something serious – that was obvious from how the adults had behaved – but the idea of Pattie dying had not occurred to her. 'No!'

'Wouldn't be paying for the midwife otherwise.' Pru was already rushing from the room and clattering like seven demons down the stairs. Vee had a hundred questions but there was nobody to ask. There was nothing for it but to quickly dress herself, and she had almost finished when Constance tapped the door.

'What is it, Vee, whatever's happening? Where's everybody off to, at this time of day.'

Vee gave her a very swift account. 'You want to do something – you mind the little ones. Give them a bit of breakfast and get the girls off to school in time. I don't know what Pa's planning doing – I doubt he'll work today. Pattie was his favourite, out of all of us. But get him to eat something if you can.' A moment later she was down the stairs, out of the gate and hastening down the hill.

It was funny to be out on private business at this time of day, instead of going into the factory, especially when she passed a group of workmates on the way. 'Me sister's taken bad,' she told them. 'Shan't be in today – or not till later on,' and hurried off before more questions could be asked.

Aunt Dorcas was eating breakfast by the kitchen hearth – toasted bread and dripping and a cup of tea – but when she heard Vee's errand she pushed the plate away. 'I'll just get my hat and shawl,' she said. 'And you pop out and tell Terry where I'm gone. He's outside chopping kindling for the fire.'

Verity did so, and when she came inside, found her aunt already in her bonnet and her shawl. She looked at Verity. 'You're looking famished, lover. Come out without a bit of breakfast, I'll be bound. Want to finish off that slice that's on my plate, a minute? There are a few things I need to fetch.' Vee was so embarrassed she almost wanted to refuse, but her stomach had been rumbling at the delicious smell – as her aunt had very likely heard. She muttered thanks – to both Dorcas and the Lord – and stuffed the tasty morsel in her mouth. She had hardly swallowed it before her aunt was back, carrying a covered basket on her arm.

'Now then, I'd best get over to Ephraim's farm and see what I can do. Never easy for a woman, first time round

227

– but it's the child I worry for. If it's much too early it won't survive the birth – but I've a suspicion there might be just a chance for it. But it will be very small. I've got some knitted clothes here that I made for Mercy's doll. I was going to give them to her, Christmas – but they'll be just the job – and I've put in an eye-dropper. Always carry one at a time like this, in case the baby isn't strong to suck. There's a bit of soft blanket I've looked out, as well – if this infant lives, it's going to be important to keep it very warm, Don't suppose that Pattie's got anything together for it, yet?'

Vee shook her head, not so much in answer as in astonishment. She knew that her aunt was really talking to herself, but it was shocking to realize that, within a day or so, there might really be a tiny baby needing all these things. When Faith and Hope and Mercy had been born, it was just a question of handing clothes and cradles down – and you were used to Ma having babies now and then. But this was different – imagine, any minute she could be Aunt Vee – and as for there being Aunty Faith! The thought was sobering.

Aunt Dorcas, (who might be Great-Aunt Dorcas, very soon!) was clearly anxious to be on her way. 'Take me some time to get there,' she declared. 'Good thing your mother's with her. Just pray I'm not too late!'

Verity had been doing little else, but she nodded. 'Want me to come with you? I wouldn't be much use, but I could fetch and carry and put the kettle on.' She knew from Mas confinements that hot water was required.

Dorcas shook her head. 'Too many hands already if the midwife's sent for too. Mind, she knows what she's about, and I'll be glad to see her if Pattie's struggling and losing lots of blood. No, my 'andsome – you've done all you can.

Best go to work, now – your ma's a bit more strapped now, with one earner less, though I know she wouldn't say so for the world.'

Verity hadn't really thought of that before, but of course it was likely to be true, and it gave her purpose as she parted company with Dorcas (whose quickest route lay 'over fields') and set off down the cliff road towards the dairy factory. It was late by this time – she had heard the school bell ring some time ago – and all her fellow workers would be well into their shift. She only hoped the couple that she'd met had explained to Mr Grey, otherwise there was likely to be trouble later on – she'd very likely be docked an hour or two in any case.

She was just rehearsing what she would say to him when – of all things – she saw the man himself, trotting past her in that pony trap of his. By the time she realized who it was, he was already twenty yards along the lane, and though she called and waved her arms, he did not notice her.

Drat! It was the strongest word she knew, but this seemed to call for it. He was travelling towards Penvarris, too, which meant that he would probably be gone some little time and Vee would have to give her apologies and explanations twice – Mr Radjel would insist on her seeing Mr Grey, and that would be half the morning's earnings gone.

Just as she was thinking that things could not get worse, she was almost run over by a bicycle – it whooshed up behind and rang its bell at her so that she leapt into the ditch, covering her skirts with strands of sticky weed. Her fault, no doubt, she hadn't been listening out or looking where she went, but surely the fellow did not have to ride so fast?

Because it was a fellow, and as he disappeared from sight she realized with a lurch which fellow it had been.

It was the man that she'd encountered out here twice before. He didn't have his bowler hat on, but she was almost sure of it. She hurried after him – she was going in that direction anyway, but she was suddenly anxious to see where he was going. And she was rewarded, as she came up to the bend, she saw him dismounting and going into a field – but a moment later he reappeared, jumped on his bicycle and pedalled back again, nearly knocking her over as he passed.

It was decidedly peculiar. She went up to the stile where he had crossed into the field, but there was nothing whatever to be seen, except a few broccoli waiting to be dug. She stood a moment, wondering if she dared follow him again, when all at once she heard a voice from across the hedge.

'Verity? Miss Tregorran? I thought that it was you. I saw you from the writing room upstairs. Have you come for crates? You'll need to come this way.' And there was Mrs Dawes, the policeman's widow, standing – all in black – at the gate of the little cottage right next door.

Two

Effie was answering those letters at long last, while Amy was out in the back garden beating mats. She was just writing the final paragraph, when – glancing up, she was startled to see a woman standing in the lane, apparently attempting to peer over her hedge. A second glance told her that it was Verity Tregorran – which surprised her even more. Had the girl come specially – either in answer to her invitation or perhaps on the excuse of picking up some crates – and then at the last minute had a loss of nerve? It would not be surprising, given the reception she'd received last time, but this was an opportunity to make amends.

She got up and hurried down to the front door. Verity was not walking up the path, she was still simply loitering outside in the lane. Plucking up courage to come and knock the door? Effie went out to the gate and called her name, 'Verity? Miss Tregorran? Verity?'

The girl seemed genuinely astonished to see Effie there – almost as surprised as Effie had been to see her – but she answered pleasantly enough. 'Mrs Dawes?'

'You've come to visit me?' Effie prompted, and then – with a little twinge of guilt – she added, with a smile, 'At least, I hope you have. I told your sister she should ask you to.' Verity shook her head. 'I just happened to be passing. Didn't even realize which your cottage was – though I suppose I should have done. I knew this one had recently been let.'

'Your sister found it – as I expect you know.'

'Asked Crowdie, I suppose. Said she was going to.' There was an awkward pause. 'She'd want me to say thank you for the crates.'

'How is she, by the way? She looked a little tired the day she came out here.' Effie chose her words with tactful care – one didn't comment that a woman was with child.

A stricken look crossed Vee Tregorran's face. 'Truth is, Mrs Dawes, she isn't well at all. That's how I'm here, this minute. Came to ask Aunt Dorcas to go and see to her.'

Effie nodded gravely. 'The aunt you went to visit when you saw that man on the cliffs that time?'

'So you remember that?' The girl gave her a sudden, sharp appraising glance. 'Funny you should mention it, in fact… I've just this minute seen him – out here in the lane.'

Effie frowned. The girl had a 'flighty' reputation after all. 'You're sure it's the same man?'

'I'm certain sure of it. And he's acting strange again. Went into that field next door to you, though he didn't stop there long. Just walked in, turned round and walked straight out again. I saw him from the road.'

'Lost?' Effie wondered.

'Not him. He had his bicycle out waiting by the stile. And it wasn't a call of nature or anything like that.' She shook her head. 'Up to something this time too, I'm almost sure of it – but I couldn't for the life of me make out what it was. Nothing but broccoli there that I could see.'

A startling idea occurred to Effie, suddenly. Amy had mentioned a trodden path across that field, leading to that shed! Was it possible that Sergeant Jeffries had been wrong and the girl had really seen something all along? Well, there was one way to find out. 'Come in for a moment, Miss Tregorran. We can speak in private then.' She stepped back to let the girl inside and ushered her into the middle room. As she did so, Amy came hurrying from the back, flustered and murmuring an apology.

'I'm sorry, madam, I didn't hear the door...' But Effie shook her head and placed a warning finger to her lips. Amy looked puzzled for a moment, shrugged and obediently disappeared again.

Effie followed her visitor into the middle room, but Verity hadn't noticed the presence of the maid. She was too busy gazing nervously around. Effie indicated one big easy chair, and settled herself in the other one. 'Do sit down, and welcome to my little cottage.'

Verity sat down awkwardly on the very edge. 'You got it looking lovely, Mrs Dawes. But I ought not to be here really – and I can't be long, I've got to go to work and I'm already awfully late.'

'All the same, I'd like you to repeat what you said outside. You saw that man again? The one you thought was acting suspiciously before?'

The younger woman nodded. 'It's not the first time either. That's why I tried to call on you before. I'd seen him on the cliffs – though he seemed quite normal then, apart from having an argument about a right of way. But he's acting suspicious this time. Or odd, in any case. Why would he ride like seven demons getting to a field, walk into it and out of it again, and ride away like seven demons back the way he'd come? Nearly knocked me over each time, too.'

'Was that deliberate?'

'I don't believe he even noticed me – though I was in full sight, I wasn't trying to hide or anything. I think he was just too busy with his thoughts! Not nice ones either by the look of it. He was scowling like the deuce!'

'He wasn't carrying anything, by any chance?' Effie asked, thinking about those drag-marks in the dust. 'Boxes, for example?'

Verity was shaking a decided head. 'Not even a lantern this time, Mrs Dawes.' She gave a rueful laugh. 'I suppose you'll think I'm daft – but it does seem peculiar, the way he carried on.'

'It isn't daft at all. I only wish that I'd pursued this earlier. I think it's possible your stranger is a smuggler, after all.'

'Never!' Verity was staring at her in disbelief.

'It's just a theory.' She explained about the pigsty and the drag-marks in the dust. 'What's more, there is a trodden path to it across the field – though the one this side was completely overgrown. The farmer who owns this cottage told me that the pigs-crow had been disused for years, but somebody's been storing things in it, and fairly recently. Suppose your suspect knew that it was there – it would make a perfect hiding place for contraband…?' She tailed off and shook her head. Even as she said it, it sounded ludicrous.

Verity, though, was seriously weighing the idea. 'It could be, I suppose. It was close to here I saw him, first time round – though it wasn't your cottage where I sheltered from the rain. It was the next one down the lane, just opposite the stile.' She shook her head. 'But that don't make much sense of what I saw today. Why would he start to go in there and then turn back again?'

Effie had already thought of that. 'Perhaps because my maid was in the garden beating mats, and he thought he might be seen?'

'And how would that be different from any other time? Place was being lived in before you rented it.'

'I don't think the woman who was here before went out there very much – certainly not for the last few months or so, after her husband died. The place was a proper tangle when I first arrived – though my father's made improvements since, with a little help from Sergeant Jeffries.' She looked at Verity. 'Speaking of Sergeant Jeffries, should we tell him, do you think?'

The girl made a disbelieving face. 'Tell him what? That I thought I saw a man I thought I saw before, walk into a field, do nothing, and disappear again? You can imagine what the Sergeant would have to say to that! He thinks I'm flighty anyway, I told you that before.'

It was so heartfelt that Effie had to laugh. 'When you put it that way, I suppose we'd better not. And of course I have no proof that the man's been in my little shed – today he didn't go near it and it's empty anyway, or it was until I put my crates in there. But I am quite serious – I really think that's where he meant to go, and if he has been using it without permission, I have a right to know. That would be trespass, if it's nothing else. I'll keep a watch for him in case he comes again.'

Verity looked doubtful. 'But how will you do that? You can't see the shed from here. Even from the back there'd be bushes in the way. One of the reasons that he might have used it, I suppose.'

'If I'm upstairs in the writing room, I can see – especially if I move my table to the right a bit. I am often up there, and from now on I'll keep an eye. Of course it may be wholly innocent – or something trivial like keeping his bicycle in there – but I'd like to know for certain what it was that caused those marks. Come into the garden and see for yourself. I feel I owe you that – for sending you away the last time that you called.'

The girl had got that hunted look again. 'I shouldn't really. I'm already hours late. They'll have stopped me a morning's wages as it is, I expect.'

'Then a few more minutes isn't going to make much difference!' Effie stood up and led the girl outside. 'This was your puzzle. I think you ought to see. Here's the shed,' she murmured, opening the door. 'And there's the...' She broke off in surprise. 'Good lord, I don't believe it! Miss Tregorran, look at this.'

–

Martha was upstairs trying to calm Patience when her sister Dorcas came. She glimpsed her through the window, and called down with relief. 'Up here, my handsome, quickly as you can. The girl's beside herself, carrying on and bleeding so I don't know what to do.' And that was all that she had time to say, because Patience gave another sobbing scream and clutched the bedclothes like a drowning man.

'Make it stop, Ma! Make it stop. How don't you make it stop?'

Martha dipped a cloth into the washbowl on the stand, then hurried over and mopped her brow again.

'Tell her I'm praying for her.' Ephraim had been hovering on the landing ever since she came, still in his nightshirt – though he'd taken off his coat – and now he put his head around the door, wringing his hands as though doing so might help.

Martha heard her sister's footstep on the stairs and a moment later Dorcas came into the room. Martha said, 'Thank the Lord, you're here. Never been so glad to see anyone in my life. Midwife's been sent for, but I think she'll be too late.' She shook her head. 'Wicked of me, Dorcas – but I'd rather it was me. Easier to do it, than watch your child in pain. And she won't let me near her, won't even let me look.'

'Well someone's going to have to,' Dorcas said, stripping off her cloak and bonnet while Patience screamed and twitched. 'Leave this to me a minute, lover. You look worn out yourself. You go and put the kettle on the hearth, get a bit of water to the boil. I'll call you when I need it – it might not be long – but she's better off without you for a little while. You're suffering with her, and that's no good at all. Go do something useful and, while you're at it, make a cup of tea.' She made a sympathetic face that was better than a hug, and started unpacking the basket she had brought.

Martha nodded and took a step towards the stairs but before she reached the doorway there was another shrieking groan and there was Ephraim, peering in again.

'Remind her of the scripture. This is the price of tempting Adam with the fruit. "In sorrow shall you bring forth children." But the Lord is merciful.'

Martha was so furious she could have pushed him down the stairs but her sister was made of sterner stuff. 'Then I pray He'll be as merciful to you. In the meantime, you've a farm to tend. A house in travail is no place for a man – not without he is a doctor – so get some clothes on and go and leave us be. If you must quote scripture go and quote it to the pigs, or the cows or the chickens, or anywhere but here!'

Ephraim was so astonished that he actually obeyed. He seized a pile of garments from a nearby chair and disappeared with them – and when Martha went out to fetch the water from the pump, she heard him clattering in the yard, scattering cooked scraps to the chickens (it was illegal to feed them corn or bran) and muttering darkly about backsliding infidels.

Martha filled the kettle and put it on the stove. It had cleaned up lovely, and was working handsome now. Proper Cornish stove, it proved to be – little oven where you could cook the meat and bread, or put in a pot of stew, and separate iron rings on top where things could stand to boil. She lifted one of them with the special hook, poked at the fire underneath (though it hardly needed it) then set the kettle back – amazed at how quickly it began to sing. Perhaps all her girls would have a stove like this one day – hard to imagine, but it was the twentieth century after all!

Her thoughts were interrupted by another sobbing scream upstairs, and then Dorcas shouting down, 'We'll have that water now!'

Martha looked around her for a cloth – the handle was too hot to carry as it was – and found a knitted kettle-holder hanging from a nail. She was in the act of disengaging it, when the back door flew open and Ephraim sidled in, accompanied by a large stout lady in a button coat. Martha had never had a midwife attend her in her life, but she knew at once that she had met one now.

'Where is the patient?' The woman sounded urgent, crisp, but not unkind. A shriek from upstairs answered her. Ephraim gave an anguished look and hurried out again.

'Go on up,' said Martha. 'Her aunt is there with her. I'm her mother. I've just boiled the kettle – I was going to take it up.'

'I'll do that,' said the woman, and put out her hand for it. Martha gave it to her and meekly stood aside while the woman went upstairs. She sat down at the table, wishing she had taken Dorcas's advice and made a cup of tea. Waiting was dreadful. Was this how fathers felt? There was a sudden shriek, another, and then a sobbing moan. Then there was silence.

Martha went to the bottom of the stairs, hoping to hear the crying of a child. But there was nothing. The bedroom door was shut and there was no noise from within. Silence was far worse than all the screams had been.

She could bear it no longer. She hurried up the stairs – just as the woman came out of the room, bearing a bowl of something with a towel over it. Martha looked enquiringly at her, but the midwife shook her head.

'You can go in now, she is weak – she's lost a lot of blood – but give her plenty of beef tea for a day or two and see she stays in bed, and she should recover, well enough. Whether she'll ever have another child is quite another thing.' She gestured to the washstand bowl that she was carrying and Martha realized, with a lurch, what it contained.

'Poor Pattie!' she murmured, though now that there wasn't any urgency she led the way downstairs to show the midwife out. 'Poor Ephraim, come to that.'

The woman surprised her. 'I'm not sure the girl is going to mind,' she said, turning in the kitchen to look Martha in the eye. 'Says she lost it falling down these steps, but there's no bruising on her like there would have been if she'd gone over stairs. I think she might have lifted something heavy, on purpose, possibly.'

'To bring it on?' Martha was horrified. 'Never!' Pattie had already given way to sin, she thought, but interfering with God's plans for human souls would be mortal wickedness.

The woman shrugged. 'Otherwise, why tell that tale about a fall? Though of course she would deny it – and she's got a husband, so perhaps I'm wrong. But you would be surprised. I've seen such things before.' She shook her head. 'I never understand young women, nowadays. How can't they live with what the good Lord sends? And as for wanting votes and driving motor-cars – it isn't natural. Though what is, with this war? Now, here's the husband coming. Can you dispose of this?'

She gave the bowl to Martha, who stared stupidly at it as Ephraim came into the kitchen from the yard.

'What's happening?' He looked expectantly at each of them in turn.

Martha was relieved that the midwife took control. 'I'm afraid your wife has lost her little son, but she herself is out of danger now. I've left instructions – nourishment and rest – and done what I can for her,' she told him briskly. 'So I think I've finished here. You can go upstairs, she should be decent now – but don't stay long, you mustn't overtire her. I'll see myself out. Remind me to whom I should address the bill?'

Pattie was lying back on pillows, looking pale and weak, her long hair lank with perspiration round her cheeks. Dorcas – or somebody – had bundled up the bloodstained clothes and sheets into a heap, dropped them on the floor and replaced them all with clean ones from the cedar chest, so Pattie looked respectable enough.

When she looked up, though, her eyes were expressionless and dull.

'I killed it, didn't I? All that and it is dead?'

'You didn't mean to,' Dorcas comforted. 'You fell downstairs, that's all. An unhappy accident.'

Ephraim reached out and took his wife's two hands. 'God moves in a mysterious way. Perhaps it is His will that this burden has been lifted, and we should start again.'

Pattie pulled her hands away and put them to her face. Tears came seeping through her fingers as she began silently to cry.

Martha could bring herself to say nothing comforting. The dreadful secret weighed on her like lead. 'Pattie's tired. What she needs is rest.' She went into the corner and scooped up the bloodied clothes. 'Best thing I can do for her is take this washing home. Ephraim, can you find something I can put it in? And there's a bowl of stuff downstairs that wants disposing of.' She hesitated. This was difficult: Strict Adherents, unlike a lot of sects, held that the human soul entered the body with the breath – on the principle that after God made Adam from the dust, He 'breathed into his nostrils the breath of life and man became a living soul' – in that order and not the other way about. Ephraim had preached homilies about it more than once. So he might object to what she had to say, but she went on anyway. 'You might want to bury it a bit decently somewhere, where the dogs won't find it, and say a prayer or two.'

Ephraim simply nodded, to her great relief. 'I'll be back to see you, Pattie!' He bent to kiss his wife's cheek but she turned away from him, and he allowed himself to be escorted reluctantly downstairs.

He found a piece of canvas to wrap the washing in, and a piece of twine to tie the bundle up but he did it slowly and mechanically like a man who was walking in his sleep. Nor did he ask about the contents of the bowl, though Martha saw him with it, a little later on, out at the enclosure on the hill where (as Strict Adherents were not entitled to a churchyard burial) several of his forefathers had been laid to rest. He was digging a small hole there. Martha turned away.

Finally when she and Dorcas had finished cleaning round and Patience was – at last – exhaustedly asleep, Martha began to think of going back home again. There were eight other daughters there who needed her, and Toby – and Pru and Vee at least – would have to be told that the baby had been lost.

'Nothing more that you can do for Patience, for the moment anyway,' Dorcas said, consolingly, as they walked home together across the fields, she with her basket and Martha with the parcel of washing. 'You heard the midwife. What she needs is sleep.'

'And beef tea!' Martha snorted bitterly. 'Where does the woman think I'm going to get that from, with meat the price it is? Haven't seen beef dripping in our house for a year – let alone a piece of steak. Wonder that she didn't suggest a drop of brandy, too!'

Dorcas laughed. 'Might have done, at that, if I hadn't warned her that talk of alcohol would give Ephraim fifty fits. But don't worry about beef tea, lover, sieved rabbit stew will do. Easy to drink and build her up a bit. I'll make some up tonight – and no!' – seeing that Martha was trying to protest – 'it's easier for me. You've already got ten mouths to feed. I've got one man's wages coming in, and only two of us. So let me see to this. Besides—'

she gave a rueful smile – 'I've had a soft spot for your Pattie, in particular – same age as my own would be, if he'd survived.'

Martha (who'd had all the children she had wished – and more) knew when to retreat. 'Thanks, Dorcas. Bit of rabbit stew will do her good. That midwife would be pleased.' And never mind what Ephraim, Toby and Grandfather might think about 'consorting with backsliders', she added inwardly.

Dorcas opened a gate to let her through. 'Give that woman credit, though, she knew just what to do. Gave Pattie something to bring things on at once – and staunched the bleeding, more or less, when I was floundering. Most likely saved her life – though it's a shame about the child. Your first grandchild and all.'

Martha stood stock-still and looked at her. 'Might be a blessing, Dorcas, in disguise. Don't look so shocked – you must know what I mean. Pattie was well on – much more so than I thought – otherwise she wouldn't have had the trouble that she did. If that child had lived, nobody in Christendom would ever have believed that it was conceived in wedlock. As it is...' She shrugged.

'It's just unfortunate? Lost her first one, like a lot of women do?' Dorcas nodded to show she understood.

'No one's to know that she had such a time of it – without you telling them, and I don't suppose you will. Wonder what he makes of it?' She nodded to the hill, where the distant form of Ephraim could be seen, methodically filling in the hole that he had made, then taking off his hat – prayerfully burying someone else's unborn child.

'Proper stricken, by the look of him,' her sister said. 'Strange man, always has been, but I've come to the conclusion from what I've seen today that he's genuinely fond of Pattie in his peculiar way.'

'Bless you, Dorcas,' Martha said impulsively, as they parted at the gate. She aimed an awkward peck at her astonished sister's cheek. 'You don't know what a blessing you have been.'

Because – she realized with amazement – what Dorcas said was true. Ephraim did care for Pattie in his fashion, though it was clear that Pattie didn't feel the same way in return. Perhaps she'd learn to, given time. And there'd be time enough. When he married, Ephraim Tull had 'put his hand upon the plough', and nothing on earth would make him let it go again. Whatever happened he'd do his best by her.

That was a crumb of comfort to carry through the day.

–

Verity's mind was only vaguely on the mission to the shed. She really shouldn't be there, she should be on her way to work – but when Mrs Dawes insisted that she should come and look, and was taking such an interest in her tale about the man, it would have been ill-mannered to refuse. Just a quick glance to be polite, she told herself – though Mrs Dawes was right. She was so late already that five minutes wouldn't hurt.

Her hostess was exclaiming over something now. Vee put on a politely interested face. 'Where are these dust-marks you were telling me about?'

But her hostess shook her head. 'Never mind the dust-marks. Look what's over there!'

'You mean that cardboard box?' There was one in the corner standing on its own. It looked innocuous enough

– the sort of box that any grocer used – and loosely tied with string, like a big order ready for the delivery boy to take.

But Mrs Dawes was staring at it as if it might explode. 'Exactly! It isn't mine, and it wasn't here a day or two ago. So what is it, and how did it get here? Something to do with your suspicious bicyclist, I think.'

Verity felt a little shiver of excitement down her back, but she shook her head. 'He didn't put it there. His hands were empty, I told you that before. And there was nothing in the basket of his bike.' She walked over to the box. 'But, as you say, it's strange that it should be here. I wonder what it is? Perhaps we'd better open it and have a look.'

'Oh, don't do that – you never know…' Mrs Dawes cried in alarm. 'It might be explosives smuggled from the mine, or anything…'

But Verity was already pulling off the string. 'My dear life! Look, there's another box inside. And would you believe it, it is one of ours! One from the dairy factory, I mean – the kind I pack myself. Twenty tins of powdered milk for the army, it should be – I recognize the size. Yes, see, it says so on the side. And there's the wire round it, so it can be dispatched.' She picked it up and rattled it. 'You know, there was a lot of stuff went missing a little while ago…'

Mrs Dawes was frowning. 'From the factory? What sort of things? Tools? Oil? Machinery?'

'Heavens no – just food. The things that we produce. Powdered milk, whey powder, cheese, all sorts of things intended for the troops, including tins of powdered milk just like this… The police were called and for a while it stopped. I thought that it was somebody I knew, but it can't have been, because she's gone and recently there's been a few things missed again. You don't suppose…?'

Mrs Dawes was nodding. 'I think you might be right. I had it back to front. Your man didn't come to put anything in here, he came to pick it up. Though perhaps he stole it to begin with, and hid it here meanwhile – that seems quite probable.'

Vee shook her head again. 'Can't see how he can have done anything like that. The stuff's going missing before it leaves the factory – between the packing station and despatch, when they come to load the carts they find the order's short. Mind, I don't know how anybody could have managed that. Not with the new security they've introduced – everything has to be double signed for, all the way along. It's a system Sergeant Jeffries put in place. Worked very well at first. Wonder what they would say, if they knew that this had turned up here?'

'Well, I think you should tell them,' Mrs Dawes replied. 'You're going there anyway. Take it with you and explain where it was found. Go to someone in authority. I think Sergeant Jeffries will take an interest in your man, too, after this! Might even earn a commendation for arresting him – stealing food is a serious offence, especially when it is intended for the troops. Under the DORA regulations, there's a hefty penalty, I've heard him say as much.' She smiled at Verity. 'So there may be a reward – if so, you have it, all of it. No need to mention me. You were the one that first raised the alarm.'

Verity gave her an uneasy look. 'But suppose they don't believe me? You'll speak up for me?'

'In that case, Miss Tregorran, naturally I will. But of course they will believe you. You've got proof now, haven't you?'

Verity nodded. That was true, of course. And – if she could point the finger to the thief – maybe they'd even pay her for the hour she wasn't there. She scooped up the carton. 'I'll be off then, Mrs Dawes!'

'Can you carry that?' Mrs Dawes was anxious. 'Bit heavy isn't it?'

It was so funny that Vee laughed aloud. 'I'm used to it. At the factory we do it all the time. Bigger packs sometimes, depending what it is. No, don't worry, I'll manage easily.' And to prove it, she set off along the path towards the lane.

'Take care, then,' Mrs Dawes called after her. 'And whatever happens come and let me know!' And she stood waving and watching at the gate.

It wasn't all that easy carrying the box, though it was not the weight so much, it was the awkwardness. There was nothing to catch hold of, now the string was gone, and Verity had to carry it in both arms, like a child.

That thought reminded her of Patience. How was she getting on? Was the baby born yet, and was it a girl or boy? She was so busy with her thoughts she did not hear the cart until it was upon her, and someone shouted, 'Hey! You there! Mind out of the way!'

Verity turned and looked up with relief. She knew that voice, it was Mr Grey again, clearly on his way back to the factory. 'Mr Grey!' She smiled up at him.

The smile was answered only with an anxious frown. 'Of course, you're from the factory. One of the Tregorrans. I recognize your face. What are you doing out here at this time of day?'

'On my way to tell you why I'm late,' she said. 'Me sister's taken bad and I was sent for help. And then—'

she nodded at the box – 'I wanted to see you about this anyway.'

Mr Grey craned forward and took a closer look – it was too heavy for her to lift up for him to see – and instantly his manner altered totally. 'Where did you get that from? What's it doing here?'

He sounded shaken. Poor man, Verity thought sympathetically. He was responsible for second-signing things – he'd likely be in trouble, for not being vigilant. 'You'd never believe it, but I found it, just a moment since, in the garden of a cottage just along the road. And I think I know who it was put there for, as well. There's a strange man on a bicycle I've seen hanging round – I'm sure he would have picked it up if no one was around. You'd know the man, in fact – I heard you having an argument with him once out on the cliffs – something about him getting in your way...'

But Mr Grey was looking furious. 'I don't remember any such event. I think you made it up. And as for the story about discovering the box, I never heard such tripe. Caught you red-handed with it, haven't I, you thief! Always knew it was someone on the staff – though I never imagined it would be anyone like you. And you a Strict Adherent!! Well – we'll have you on the cart – come on, get up.' He reached out and grasped her roughly by the arm. 'And we'll see what your parents have to say about all this.'

He tried to pull her bodily up onto the cart, but Verity resisted. 'But you don't understand. I didn't take it – I just found it – honestly I did. And I daren't be any later into work than I already am.'

Mr Grey gave an unpleasant laugh. 'Work, is it? Well, young lady, you can think again – you don't suppose the factory will continue to employ a thief? You can consider yourself immediately dismissed. And that sister of yours too. Nothing but trouble, all the lot of you.'

'Dismissed?' A shock of dismay ran through her like a thunderbolt.

'What else do you expect? Caught you red-handed with a box of stolen milk. I shall have to tell the bosses and they'll inform the police – and count yourself lucky if you don't end up in jail. Now, give me that box and be on your way.'

He tried to grab at it but she eluded him. 'But Mr Grey…?' She wailed, still hoping to persuade him of her innocence.

'Let go of it, you vixen!' He got down from the cart to wrest it from her, brandishing his whip. Vee screamed and backed away. He followed, there was a moment's tussle – and then a figure on a bicycle came pedalling round the bend.

Three

Sergeant Jeffries hadn't really meant to come this way, not so early in the afternoon, but there was no sign of Martha when he'd called there earlier. Not even any of her girls – only the sound of Toby hammering at the forge – so he decided to patrol the cliff road for an hour or so.

And call in on Effie Dawes, of course. He hadn't been there since the time he'd cut the weeds – not to visit, though he'd ridden past each evening on his rounds. But today he had some news for her, about that bicycle. She wouldn't want it now, of course, but he'd heard of one for sale and that would give him an adequate excuse. He was dwelling on the prospect of a nice cup of tea, when from somewhere just ahead he heard a woman scream.

It was hilly here, but he put his head down and pedalled full-speed up the rise. It made his heart thump and he could feel his face was turning red, but he battled on – he could always coast a little on the other side.

But when he reached the corner he did not coast anywhere. The source of the disturbance was in the lane below – a man and woman were struggling in the ditch: he was lashing ineffectually at her ankles with a whip, while she was tussling with him, trying to protect a box – to the extent of biting at his other hand, which was attempting to tear it from her grasp.

Will was still puffing like a steam engine, but he had sufficient wit to dismount the bike and sit astride the bar, gather himself up and blow a shrill blast on his police whistle. It worked. The scuffling figures leapt instantly apart, looked up towards him and the man cried, triumphantly, 'Sergeant Jeffries! Now we'll see what's what!'

Will got off entirely and wheeled his bicycle towards them down the hill, surprised to realize that he knew both of them: Verity Tregorran and that fellow Grey, whom he'd encountered at the dairy factory. He put on his most official face, propped the bike against the hedge, and walked over with his notebook in his hand.

'Now then!' He licked his pencil stub. 'I am surprised at you two. Causing a disturbance on the public road. What's this all about?'

Both of them began to talk at once. Will held his hand up.

'One thing at a time. Grey, you are the senior person here, let's hear your side of things.'

'I think we've caught our factory thief, at last. This girl was missing from the morning shift, and I caught her red-handed out here in the lane carrying a box of stolen goods – tins of milk – the very stuff that was reported missing yesterday. Swears she found it somewhere in a shed and was returning it, if you ever heard such lies – but she won't get in the cart and fights like a tigress when I try to take it back.'

Vee had tried to interrupt this several times, but Will ignored her. Now he turned to her. 'Well, young lady, what have you to say?'

She was scarlet-faced and angry, and clearly close to tears. 'I've told him half a dozen times – I didn't take the box. I found it in a shed – exactly like he said – and I was on my way to take it back where it belonged. And if you don't believe me, you can ask that Mrs Dawes – it was her that found it really, I just happened to be there. It was her shed it was in. Well, her old pigsty really, but it's used for storage now.'

Will pushed his helmet back and scratched his head and even Grey had the grace to look surprised.

In fact, the man had turned an embarrassed shade of puce. 'So you are saying that there's someone can vouch for you? Then how didn't you say so, straight away?' He turned from her to Will. 'Even now, I wonder if it's true. More likely that she led the woman to the box by accident – and then pretended that she didn't know that it was there. And if she was so anxious to return the box, why did she refuse to hand it over when I asked for it? If was me she would have had to give it to, back at the factory – as the girl well knows.'

'Is that true?' Will said to Verity, and she nodded sullenly.

'But it isn't how he makes it sound at all!' she protested, angrily. 'If I gave him the box, I had no proof of anything I said. And he wouldn't listen – just said I was a thief and I had been dismissed. Never got a chance to mention Mrs Dawes. Besides…' She tailed off.

'What?' Will demanded, but she shook her head. 'Something I've just thought of – though I can't tell you now. And there's something else as well. I might be wrong, but Mrs Dawes would know.'

'Tell me and I'll ask her,' Will suggested with a smile. Another head-shake. 'I'd sooner talk to Mrs Dawes myself. Could you take me back there? And Mr Grey as well? Soon find out the truth of all this then.'

Grey was frowning. 'I'm very sorry, Sergeant, I can't agree to that. My absence will be holding up dispatch. They need my signature before the orders can go out.'

Will nodded. 'Yes, of course.' The system was his own suggestion, after all. 'But you could spare five minutes, surely? This won't take more than that.'

'Sergeant, these are urgent food supplies for our boys in the field. The factory's humble contribution to the war effort. Goods won't go out without me – and this girl has delayed me too much as it is. Take her with you by all means – she's no longer a member of my staff in any case, unless and until her innocence is proved, I've made that clear to her. But you don't have any reason for detaining me. I'm not the one who is accused of any crime.'

The policeman nodded slowly. 'I suppose you're right. But if you wish to bring charges…?'

'You'll know where to find me. Though it may be better to let it go at just dismissing her. This'll be in all the papers otherwise. Don't want to bring the factory into disrepute.'

'And if it's proved that she is innocent?'

Grey looked at Verity and shrugged. 'I'd need to be convinced. I still think she knows more about this than she'd like us to believe. But in that case, I suppose we'd have to think again. Thank you, Sergeant Jeffries, I'll take that parcel now.'

Verity surprised them. 'No! He can't do that. It's evidence. In more ways than you think. I'll show you – when we get to Mrs Dawes.'

Grey raised his eyebrows as if appealing to the skies but Will said, 'Yes, perhaps the girl is right. If there are charges to be brought, this box is evidence.' He could already see himself producing it in court, proudly labelled 'Police Exhibit A'.

Grey did not argue, but he was not pleased. He stumped off to his vehicle, untied the horse – which had been tethered to a tree – and disappeared so quickly that a cloud of dust arose. Will turned to Verity.

'Coming with me of your own accord, for questioning? I'll write that in the book. Saves me having to arrest you formally, on suspicion of a theft. Though 'tisn't like you, being who you are, so I'm happy to see what Effie has to say. Mrs Dawes, as I should call her properly. Now let me have that box. I'll balance it on the carrier and you can walk along with me.'

—

Effie was even more surprised the second time, to see Verity Tregorran at her gate – though now the girl had Sergeant Jeffries in tow and it was Amy who hastened to the door. Effie finished her letter and signed it hastily, but by the time she'd heated sealing wax and sealed the envelope, the maid was at the doorway of the writing room.

'That policeman to see you, madam, and that girl again. Says it's official business and he needs to talk to you. I've put them in the parlour to wait while you come down. Should I bring a tea tray?'

Effie shook her head. 'Not for a moment, Amy. If he's on duty, it's not appropriate. I'd better deal with this. I'll call if I need you.' She went down into the room.

Jeffries was standing by the fireplace with one hand behind his back, and the other cradling his helmet at his chest, while Verity Tregorran was sitting on the chair beside him, looking cowed.

She looked up as Effie entered. 'I'm sorry, Mrs Dawes – I was afraid of this. They think I stole that box. From the factory, I mean.'

Effie looked at Jeffries. 'How totally absurd. Didn't she tell you that we found it in the shed?'

'That's what I told him, but he don't believe a word – and Mr Grey's now saying that I must have put it there.'

Jeffries put his helmet down and got his notebook out. 'Mrs Ethel Dawes? An Dyji cottage?'

'Don't be silly, Sergeant. Of course that's who I am.'

He ignored this. 'Miss Verity Tregorran here has named you as a witness.' He cleared his throat importantly. 'She was found with a box of stolen goods in her possession, apparently taken from her place of work. She claims that she had merely found them and was returning them – and that you can corroborate the fact. I hardly like to ask you, but—'

'Of course I will. I took her to the shed, simply to show her some tracks that I had found.' She explained about the dust-marks and the stranger on the lane and the path that led to the shed across the field. 'I felt that we had rather undervalued what she said, the first time she reported it. And then we found the box, and saw what it contained. I think it rather looks as if Verity was right, and that man was up to something all along. Not spying, or even smuggling in the usual sense – but procuring stolen milk-products, presumably to sell. I imagine someone's making quite a profit out of it – he must have a supplier within the factory.'

Will licked his pencil and scribbled furiously. 'I see,' he muttered gravely. 'A serious matter that. "Black market-eering" they are calling it, and under DORA regulations, penalties are harsh. We'll have to find the weak link in the factory, of course, but when we do, and if we catch these fellows out, would you be prepared to testify in court?'

'Of course I would,' Effie said quickly, trying not to imagine what the family would say. Uncle Joe had hated courts and policemen all his fife – and Alex's parents would think it most unladylike. 'Though, as you say, you'll have to find who's stealing from the factory. That might not be easy.'

'But I know who it is. At least I think I do.' That was Verity. 'It's Mr Grey himself. I know it sounds preposterous, but once you think of it – of course it all makes sense. I saw him driving down the lane before the man appeared, towards Penvarris, which looked quite natural – but he must have stopped here to drop the parcel off.'

Effie saw the point at once. 'And when the man saw him further down the lane, he knew to pick it up? They would not have to communicate at all.'

'Exactly. And the first time that I saw the stranger on the cliffs I was only there because I couldn't speak to Mr Grey – he had gone out and wasn't at the factory.' She turned to Effie. 'I told you at the time.'

Effie nodded slowly. 'I believe you did.'

'I bet that they were doing something similar, back then. And then – that day I came to see you and was sent away – the man was here again, arguing with someone on the cliffs. I realized afterwards that it was Mr Grey – he had his pony-trap, and I thought he was angry cause he'd nearly had a spill. But when I think about it, it wasn't that at all. Mr Grey was saying that they'd have to stop – because of the new security I expect – and that it was dangerous to be "careering on the cliffs" because other people used the lane – meaning that they were likely to be seen. And it did stop for a while – but it's begun again.'

'But Mr Grey's a very senior man, and in a post of trust. Surely…?'

'And he's the one who has to double-sign the chits. So he has his hands on everything that leaves the factory.'

Will Jeffries made a disbelieving sound. 'But he only double-signs them. Someone else has got to witness it as well. How would he get round that? Sounds fanciful to me. And there's not a shred of evidence, as far as I can see. Of course the man has business calls outside the factory – arranging contracts and taking money to the bank – the bosses know it and he makes no secret of the fact. And as for this business of the argument – even you thought it was about something different! It seems to me he's been behaving entirely properly. You're making something out of nothing – like you always do.'

'Then how did he know what was in that cardboard box? Tins of milk, he told you – and that was right, of course. But how did he know it? It's written on the inner box, but that was covered up – as you can see. And I didn't tell him. He didn't give me a chance. Soon as I realized that, I knew it must be him – or he knew more about it than he should have done. That's how I wouldn't let him have the box.'

Effie looked at her with some surprise – and admiration, too. The girl had more intelligence than she had supposed.

But Jeffries was scornful. 'Just knew what had gone missing yesterday, I expect, and worked it out. Man like him would have his finger on the pulse. Guessing what was in it doesn't prove a thing.'

Verity was not abashed at this. 'Maybe, but how did he know that it was hidden in a shed? He mentioned that as well – before I said a word. No amount of guessing could have told him that!' She shook her head. 'But of course he'd say I told him – it's his word against mine. And who'd believe me? You don't, even now! That's why I wanted to talk to Mrs Dawes. She told me once her husband was keen on fingerprints. I wondered if there might be fingerprints to find.'

Will Jeffries was stroking the ends of his moustache. 'Hard to get them from a cardboard box. And – even if we could – it won't prove anything. He would have handled the factory parcel when he signed it out, and I saw him with my own eyes tussling with you, so his prints will be all over the outer box as well.' But he was taking this whole matter more seriously now, you could see that at once.

Verity looked downcast. 'Then what about the string? That wasn't on the box when we were in the lane – and it must be round here somewhere. And – according to his story – he hasn't handled that!'

The Sergeant looked contemptuous. 'We're not magicians, Miss Tregorran. We are just the police. We can't conjure fingerprints from little bits of string.'

'But I wonder if Mr Grey knows that?' Effie put in thoughtfully. 'If you were to tell him that the police were collecting fingerprints – including from the string – and then ask him for his own, I wonder what he'd say? If he is guilty, that would frighten him, at least, and he might betray himself. Though, wait a minute!' A sudden thought occurred to her. 'What about the shed? He must have touched all sorts of things in there – and there might be boot prints in the dust, if we had thought to look.'

Sergeant Jeffries nodded enthusiastically and puffed out his cheeks. Effie had seen him wear that look before – it meant that he was thinking of shining in his job. 'Now that's a different matter. There might be prints in there. If we can match them, it's proof that Grey was there – and there is no reason why he should have been, except to leave that box.'

Effie said sharply, 'Quite the opposite in fact – he should not have been there and neither should his friend. Trespassers, the pair of them, and that would be the proof.'

'Supposing that we find their prints, that is,' the policeman said, lugubriously. Then he brightened. 'Though that's another point. If we could find the other fellow's fingerprints as well, we'd have the both of them.' He bestowed a smile on Verity. 'Thank you, Miss Tregorran, a very good idea.'

She shook her head. 'But the thin man didn't get there, I saw him go away. And if he learns from Mr Grey that the parcel isn't there, he won't come back again.'

'Great Heavens, girl, you're right. I'll get over to the factory as fast as possible – make sure that Grey does not have an opportunity for sending messages. In fact I think I'll take him in for questioning. I haven't taken fingerprints from anywhere as yet, but – just as you suggested, Mrs Dawes – it might be helpful to let him think I have. In the meantime, you keep a watch out for the man.'

'And what do you suggest we do if he comes back again? We're only women and he might be dangerous,' Effie said, with some asperity. 'Certainly I don't think we could keep him here, if he was determined to break free and run away. Though…' she broke off.

'Though?' The Sergeant prompted.

'You might just ask the farmer who owns the property. He's a big fellow, and he's got a gun. Uses it for rabbits – I know, he brought us one last week, help eke out the rations when my folk were here. More than a match for your suspect, I should think.'

Jeffries nodded. 'Another good idea.' He gave her a patronizing smile. 'Perhaps we could do with you ladies in the police – they're starting to have them in London now, I hear. Well, I'll call and ask your farmer. Can he watch from here? I would prefer it if he wasn't stomping round the shed – just in case I do require to take some fingerprints, or boot-print casts, if that's appropriate. But if I mean to catch up with Grey in time, I'd best be on my way.'

Effie rang for Amy (who must have been listening at the door, she came in so quickly) and the policeman was escorted to the door. Effie turned to Verity. 'Well, it seems that the police are listening to your concerns at last. At any minute we shall have the farmer here – I'll take him upstairs to the writing room to watch. In the meantime, would you like some tea?'

–

Nobody had ever offered tea like this before – outside the family, and that didn't count – and Vee was not sure if it was proper to accept.

But she said politely, 'I could do with some. Truth is, Mrs Dawes, it's been an awful day. Then I suppose I'd better run off home and see how Pattie is – seeing I haven't got a job to go to any more.'

And that would be more trouble, she thought bitterly. Doubtless Prudence would have turned up at the factory by now, but what would happen when Mr Grey got back? She would be thrown out on her ear, like Verity herself – so any moment now she'd be going home with the news. 'Be all round the factory that I'm a thief, by now.'

'I'm sure they'll reinstate you,' Mrs Dawes replied, ringing for the maid again and ordering the tray. 'If you want to go back to work there, that is. I suppose you do? Might be a bit awkward if it comes to trial and you have to testify against a former boss.'

Vee hadn't thought of that. 'It won't be very pleasant. The place is a nest of rumours as it is – first it was Pattie, now it will be me. But, I suppose I'll have to. What else would I do? Pa wouldn't have us go as bal maidens down the mine – rubbing shoulders with young men, he says, and godless, some of them. And he wouldn't like us going in private service, either, where there might be men about – too many temptations, I've heard that many times.'

'What about a female household?' Mrs Dawes enquired.

Verity shrugged. 'Where would you find one?' she said bitterly, and then realized that it sounded like a hint. 'What I'd really like, though,' she went on, trying to change the subject as fast as possible, 'is to go into a shop. Milliner's or something – where only women go. Like you used to do, I suppose…' She broke off as the serving-girl, Amy came in with the tray, and Vee watched in silence as she poured the tea, remembering not to seize the cup but wait till it was passed.

'Funny you should say that,' Mrs Dawes remarked, picking up her own cup with enviable grace. 'I was in the act of answering letters when you came – including one from a solicitor – and something's just turned up. I've got to go to Falmouth in a day or two – to sign a lot of papers and that sort of thing. But, if it all works out as I expect, I might just know of an opportunity…'

Vee nearly dropped her teacup. 'In a shop you mean? Not in Falmouth surely?' She shook her head. 'Pa would never hear of such a thing – away from home and guidance

– and, in any case, who'd have a girl like me? All tongue and no judgment, my mother always says.'

'I don't know about that. You seem to be a girl of some intelligence. And it's not in Falmouth, this would be much nearer home. Though it's not certain yet. In the meantime, would you like a temporary post, just for a day or two? It isn't onerous. I have to go to Falmouth, which means going up by train, and as a recent widow I can't well go alone. Would you care to travel with me? I would pay of course – not much, but a little. What would you say to that?'

Vee's head was spinning. 'Well, I'd love to go, of course. I've never been further than Penzance in all my life. But if you need a companion, how don't you take your maid?'

The woman laughed. 'You're very sharp, young lady! I could do that, of course. But there are two reasons for asking you instead – first that the day concerned is Amy's half-day off, and that would mean she didn't see her family and, second, that I'll have to change at Truro on the way. I have friends there and I thought that I might break my journey for an hour and call on them. Amy has no special reason to welcome such a thing, but – according to Crowdie – it might appeal to you. Free time to walk to anywhere you choose. I understand you have a friend who's in a hospital nearby.'

Go and visit Ned Chegwidden? Was that possible? Vee knew her eyes were shining but she shook her head. 'Pa won't allow it, I can tell you that. In fact…' She put her cup down with a clatter as she spoke, 'I ought to run off home. You've been very kind to me, and I appreciate the fact – but there'll be all sorts of trouble and I'll get a larraking, for people even thinking that I might be a thief

– let alone getting fired and losing Pru her job as well! Pa will likely skin me before I get the chance to speak.'

'Not if I come with you,' Mrs Dawes replied. 'Wait while I get my bonnet.'

And that is what she did.

Four

Martha was putting Pattie's washing in the tin bath to soak – milk and salt were good for shifting blood – but lighting the copper would have to wait until another day. She was still shaken from the day's events.

So she was hardly in a state to cope with visitors, but there was blessed Verity coming through the gate and a strange woman with her. Somebody well off, too, by the look of her. Someone from the factory perhaps – might be, but you couldn't ask Prudence, because she wasn't here.

Martha ran her fingers through her tousled hair and tried to straighten her pinny to look respectable, then she hurried from the wash house to greet the newcomers. 'Afternoon… I suppose it's afternoon by this time,' she began.

Verity was looking terrible, she thought. All flushed and worried like the dear knows what. 'Anything the matter? Who's this lady then?'

The stranger smiled and held out her hand. 'I'm Ethel Dawes. Perhaps you've heard of me?'

'Lady who gave the crates to Pattie,' Verity put in. 'How is she, anyway? Have I got a niece or nephew?'

Martha shook her head. 'Neither one, I fear. Midwife came, but Pattie lost the child. She's weak but pulling through. Ephraim's down there with her, but I said I'd go again. Thought I might send Prudence, where is she by the way? Not come home with you?' As she spoke she led the way into the house. Kitchen was an awful mess – what would this stranger think? 'Bit early aren't you?' She glanced towards the clock. Somehow today she'd lost all sense of time – it seemed a hundred hours since Ephraim had arrived. 'Girls aren't home from school. Something happened down the factory?'

Verity said, inexplicably, 'You haven't heard the news then?'

Martha's knees betrayed her suddenly, and she found that she was sitting down instead of standing up. 'Not our Prudence too? Nothing's happened to our Prudence?'

Mrs Dawes and Verity exchanged a glance, but it was Vee who answered. 'Not the way you mean. You sit there a minute, and Mrs Dawes here will explain. Oh, and here's Constance coming with the girls – they'll have to hear as well.'

So they were all in the kitchen when Sergeant Jeffries brought Prudence home with the welcome news that he'd caught up with Mr Grey. 'I've got the other fellow under lock and key as well. He turned up at your pigsty, as we thought he might – good job that the farmer had a gun! Blaming each other, he and Mr Grey! Oh, and old Mr Radjel says your jobs are safe!'

And Toby chose that moment to come roaring in, and the whole story had to be repeated for his benefit. But his reaction startled everyone.

'Well, whatever Radjel says, that's the end of that! How dare they believe that my daughter is a thief! Dismiss her would they – and call her a liar too? They change their minds about it, now, but how did they ever credit a single word of it? Well, none of my girls will ever work for them

266

again! Sooner have them breaking tin stones down the mine. Anything but down that wretched factory!'

'In that case,' Martha murmured – seeing an opportunity, in front of witnesses, 'you wouldn't mind if Verity went to work for Mrs Dawes? She's very kindly offered her a little job – as a sort of companion to begin with, so I understand. Quite a vote of confidence in Vee's integrity.'

And Toby – who had always held that a Strict Adherent must stick strictly to his word – found himself unable to demur.

-

It was two days later that Will brought the bicycle. Effie had agreed to have it, once she heard, because it would be useful for Amy, after all.

Amy was delighted, and – with Effie's blessing – tried it out at once, though clearly it wasn't as easy as the vicar's daughter made it seem. Several times the girl fell off into the weeds and scratched herself quite badly, but she persevered and slowly began to get the hang of it.

'Be able to ride home, see Mother, very soon,' she said, delightedly – though with more hope than promise, Effie thought. 'Save me twopence for the horse-bus every time. And I can go whatever time it suits, stead of waiting if it's late.'

Effie had to smile at her enthusiasm. It helped to make up for leaving Amy at home and taking Verity to Truro on the train. Truth to tell, she would be glad of lively company – and Verity was so excited she could talk of little else. Though there would have to be a sober conversation soon. There was a business proposition to discuss.

It had been a shock to get that letter from the solicitor. It should not have been, perhaps. Major Dawes had made a point of telling her that he'd put some money by in trust for Alex when they wed, and that she would get it – but that was at the funeral and she hadn't really been in a state of mind to take it in. Not a fortune, as he'd told her, but a tidy little sum. And she had decided what she'd like to do with it.

Rescue Weston's Haberdashery. She could do it, she was sure of it. Miss Pearl would have to be consulted, naturally enough, but she'd already spoken of a lack of capital. And once Effie had acquired an interest in the place she could make the improvements she had always wanted to.

Not that she'd be able to do it all at once. She was still in mourning, so she could hardly work herself – but she knew a girl who might. And she could oversee it and work behind the scenes. Still live at An Dyji, which she'd come to love – get a man, perhaps, to come and clear the grounds, if she could find one, with the lack of manpower these days.

And there was another idea she might suggest to Verity! She laughed a little at her own enthusiasm for these schemes – but she felt as if the girl had brought her back to life. Taught her that conventions could be fought against, as well. She'd never met a family where so much was frowned upon – much worse than Alex's mother, even, she thought with a wry smile.

It was thinking of rebellion which gave her the idea. It was preposterous, of course – a woman of her age, and still in mourning too, but once she had thought of it, she simply had to try! And this was the moment, if it was ever to be done. It was very early – even Amy wasn't up, and it was barely light. There was nobody about.

The bicycle was leaning up against the shed. It was the work of a moment to tiptoe out to it, wheel it to a smooth part of the lane, put a foot onto the pedal and…

'Effie? Miss Pengelly? I mean, Mrs Dawes…?'

The voice was coming from nearby, behind the hedge. A man's voice, and incredulous – though more amused than shocked. Effie's cheeks burned scarlet – imagine being seen! – and she attempted to turn the bicycle away and hurry back to the safety of the house. In her haste she failed to free her long skirt fully, and it caught against the pedal shank. It jerked her over, and she gave a shriek and sat down with the machine on top of her.

'Not hurt, are you?' A man came rushing from the next-door field. Someone in uniform, with chevrons on his sleeve, who was lifting the bicycle and bending over her.

She was too embarrassed to even look at him. 'I'm perfectly all right. Please leave me, go away.' She couldn't for the life of her imagine who it was.

'Effie! I'm sorry. I should not have come. They've sent me back to take a training course – and I've got two days' leave. I took the night train down – going to see the family, but I'd heard that you were here. I had to come and see if I could get a glimpse of you. I didn't mean to bother you, of course – though I heard about your husband…' There was an awkward pause. 'I'm very sorry. It must be terrible.'

She raised her eyes but she'd already realized who it was. Peter Kellow. Smart as Christmas in that uniform.

'What do the stripes mean, Peter?' As if she didn't know. But she let him offer her his hand and help her to her feet. It was oddly comforting. And it didn't matter how unseemly she must look – this was only Peter, and that didn't count.

'They've made me a Lance Corporal, lowest of the low. But if I do well this course, they'll make me up again, they say. Might even rise to a commission – the last man to do my job got to be Lieutenant in the end, before he died. I'm training other miners – and they've got some new explosive they want to introduce.'

'Couldn't that be dangerous?' She didn't like the sound of that Lieutenant's death – however much of a promotion it might be.

'Stand me in good stead. Might get me recommended as mine captain one day – when the war is over, if I survive so long.' He shrugged and gave a laugh. 'Now, shall I wheel that bicycle back in for you, or do you want to try again?'

She shook her head and found that she was laughing, too. 'Shouldn't have tried the first time. It's far too soon for that. One day, perhaps, I'll dare to pedal it again – but probably I won't. I've learned my lesson – and bumped my elbow too.' She rubbed it ruefully.

But Peter Kellow wasn't laughing now. He looked at her. 'Don't close your mind to it. There are lots of things that you might learn to do, with time. Don't you think so?' And he clearly wasn't talking about the bicycle.

She shook her head again. 'I don't know, Peter. I don't know at all.'

He made a rueful face. 'Well, you go in now. I'll put this away. Put butter on that bruise. And forget you've seen me. I shouldn't have been here.'

Amy was up by now, and looked surprised to see her mistress coming through the door. 'Oh, sorry madam. I've not even made your tea.'

'I woke up early. Stepped out for some air. I'll have it in a moment, in the middle room.' She looked out through the window. But the bicycle was out there, leaning on the shed, and Peter Kellow was nowhere to be seen. She kept an eye out for him, but he did not appear again – and then his leave was over, and she knew he must have gone.

-

Ned was feeling better. Much, much better now. Well enough to take part in an egg-and-spoon race in the yard, where he hobbled well enough to beat Fred Wills – and everybody else – though it was clear he'd never walk without a limp again.

He was cock-a-hoop about his victory, till the medics called him in.

'You've made good progress. We're very pleased with you. But we're getting to a point where there's no more we can do.' They were beginning to talk about discharging him.

It hit him like a hammer. In here, he was fine. He could do as much as anybody else, very often more, and if he was slow and awkward – well, so was everyone. Ma came to see him sometimes, and that was wonderful – but what would happen when he had to go back home? She'd have to see for him, and wash his clothes and all the rest of it – and she'd see the leg, which she'd never really done. And he would be underneath her feet – they wouldn't pass him fit to go back underground. 'Fresh air and gentle exercise, that's the ticket, man. Get your strength back slowly, and you'll be right as rain. But we can't have you crawling down tunnels in the mine.'

And it was true, of course, he couldn't crawl at all. He couldn't do anything very much, but limp about and play stupid childish games, like egg-and-spoon races and draughts. He quite upset Fred one morning, when he refused to play again – just when he'd been getting good enough to win from time to time.

'Don't know what's got into you, Chegwidden,' Fred Wills said, crossly, sweeping up the draught set and making off indoors. 'Winning races seems to make you sour.'

'Find someone else to play with!' Ned retorted. 'I've got real life to think about.' And he sat at the table, huddled in his coat, and contemplated all the things he couldn't do: run, walk any distance, kick a ball about, even change his trousers without sitting down. He was sunk in gloomy silence, when he heard a nurse's voice.

'Somebody to see you.'

That would be Mother – though this was not her usual day. He looked up listlessly. 'Come twice this fortnight?' But the words died on his lips. 'My dear life! Verity!'

She was prettier than he remembered. More grown-up looking too. But she still had that sparkle and that delightful smile. She was smiling this minute. 'Ned. How are you?'

'What are you doing here?' He looked around as if her father might appear and march her off at any minute.

She shook her head and laughed. 'I asked you first. How are you? You are looking well. Better than I expected, from what your mother said.'

He made a face at her. 'That's what they're saying here. Threatening to discharge me soon and send me home.'

She sat down opposite, where Fred Wills had been. 'That's wonderful. Or don't you think so? Doesn't seem so from your face.'

'Oh, I dunno. What am I supposed to do? No use for anything, the way I am.' He looked into her eyes.

They were tawny, dark and very beautiful – even more beautiful than in his dreams. 'Couldn't, for instance, think of marrying. Even if your father would have let you – which he won't.'

'Marry me, you mean?' The eyes were misty now. 'That's what you'd like to do? Oh, don't shake your head like that, just tell me that it is.'

'Well, of course I would – if it were possible. But it never would have been, I suppose in any case... and now...' He shook his head. 'You wouldn't want me, not the way I am. Find yourself a proper man who can take care of you.' She didn't answer and he went on bitterly: 'They talk about heroes, but I'm nothing of the kind. Made into a cripple by a bit of wire.'

'You'll need to be a hero, if we're going to fight my pa!' She bit her lip and there were teardrops in her eyes, but she was smiling all the same. 'We'll find a way, Ned, if that is really what you want.' She put out a timid hand and sought his own. 'It's what I've always wanted, all along. And things are different now, with Pattie. You heard what happened there?'

'Heard she'd married, and then lost a child. Must have been upsetting.'

'It was worse than that. She had to get married – your ma explained it all, though I didn't really understand at first. Fair broke Pa's heart it did, and Pattie's too, I think. She was proper poorly, and she's not really better yet. Doesn't make an effort – that's what Prudence says – as if she's given up and doesn't want to live. Pru has gone over to stay with them in fact, try to give a hand and nurse Pattie back to health. You heard that we're not working at the factory?'

He looked at her, surprised. 'I thought that was all sorted out? Ma said so, any rate. It was Mr Grey himself who had been stealing things – police got his fingerprints and he broke down and confessed.'

Verity gave a peculiar little laugh. 'Well, after a fashion. He certainly confessed. I could feel quite sorry for him, really, when it all came out. He'd got talked into stealing very early on, just little bits of things, but the man that he was dealing with had got his claws in him by then – threatened to expose him to the police if he didn't go on stealing and supplying things, bigger and bigger orders as it went along. Then I gave him a bad fright myself, I think, telling the police I'd seen a stranger on the cliffs, and shortly after that there was a dreadful fuss – the books didn't balance – and the bosses called the police.'

'That must have given your Mr Grey a scare!' Talking to Verity, he felt more himself – taking an interest in the world again.

'He tried to stop it, but the fellow wouldn't go away. And in the end the law caught up with him.' She shrugged. 'I think it was a relief to him, if anything. He'll go to jail, of course, but he's turned King's evidence against the other man, who had a huge black-market system going, apparently – all over the country, not just locally. Hundreds of parcels passing through his hands – and not simply milk and butter, either – boots and kerosene, anything that he could find a market for. A proper criminal.' She grinned. 'Your ma tell you they gave me a reward? Five whole guineas, what d'you think of that!'

It was enough to start your married life on, that was what she meant. But he refused to dream of such impossibilities. In any case a man could not allow himself to be supported by his wife. He said, 'Generous of the factory! But you've not gone back?'

She shook her head. 'I've gone to work for Mrs Dawes instead. That's what I'm doing here. She's come to sign some documents, some money from a trust that comes to her now that her husband's dead. She's going to invest in a shop in town – she's been to see the woman and it's all agreed – and I'm to have a position in the shop, just helping to begin with, but she says we'll see.'

'How are you going to travel to and fro like that? Take all your wages just to pay the bus!' Why was he disappointed, suddenly? He knew they couldn't marry, he'd just been saying so. But all the same…

Vee was smiling at him. 'There's a flat upstairs there, and I'll be sharing that with the lady manager. Pa wasn't keen at first, but Mrs Dawes persuaded him that Miss Pearl was very strict – and she ought to know, because she lived there once herself. I'll get alternate Saturdays, so I can go home weekends, and still get to chapel with the family.'

'Well, things have worked out very nicely for you, I can see,' Ned muttered bitterly. 'Just as well we don't have any other plans.'

She twinkled at him. 'Ned Chegwidden, don't be difficult. Of course we still have plans. Why do you think she sent me here today? Wants to know if you would be prepared to work for her as well – not in the shop, of course, but where she's living now. Got a garden that's a wilderness, and – with this money – she can afford a bit of help. Needs a man though – it's too much for her – and there aren't so many males available. So will you think it over?'

A great cloud of despair had lifted suddenly. It wasn't mine work, but it was something real. Arranged by the womenfolk, but he could live with that – better than being under Mother's feet all day, or taking some menial surface job down at the mine. He looked at her.

'You mean it?'

'So the answer's yes? I'll have to go soon, and she'll want to know.'

Suddenly he wished he'd spent this hour another way – telling her he loved her, that they'd struggle through and marry and never part again. And now she was leaving. He caught her hand and held her fingers tight.

'You think we can fight your father?'

He knew by her face that she had understood his thoughts. Her words confirmed it. 'I know we can, my hero. Or defy him if we must. Ma will take our part as well, and that will help.'

'Well, that's arranged then!' He pressed the fingers to his lips. He was absurdly happy, suddenly. 'Vee! Shall I write to Mother? She'll be thrilled, I know.'

She shook her head. 'Let's wait till you come home. We'll tell them together.'

'I can hardly wait,' he said, and it was true. When she was gone, a moment later, he went and found Fred Wills and trounced him thoroughly in a game of draughts.

Epilogue

October 1919

Verity was hurrying down the pavement in Penzance, worrying about the meat that she was taking home for tea – things were coming back but there were still shortages and she'd only managed to get mince. But a pinch of curry powder might cheer it up a bit – exotic foreign stuff, but Ned had tried it in the army and had got a taste for it.

'Verity! My dear life! If it isn't you! I haven't seen you since you wed. However are you?'

For a moment Vee did not recognize the voice, or the woman calling from the pavement opposite. But as the person crossed the road, she realized who it was.

'Gloria Tresize!' she cried, in genuine delight. 'How nice to see you. What are you doing now?'

'Oh, still down that wretched factory. Never been the same though, since that awful Mr Grey. Did you know he was forcing young Mr Radjel to sign for things he never saw, because he knew that Mr Radjel had been having an affair with one of the girls? Never found out which – though there are lots of rumours. You know what it's like. Nothing changes. But you – you're looking well. Marriage clearly suits you! Is this your little boy?' She nodded at the pram.

Verity smiled proudly. 'Little Toby. Three months old. And isn't he the spitting image of my Ned, as well?'

'How is your husband? Not down the mine, I know. Is he still working for that Mrs Dawes?'

'Doing very nicely,' Verity replied. 'Taken over from me in the shop, these days – people seem to like to have a man to serve them, now and then – though obviously there's departments that he doesn't touch. And Mrs Dawes is doing more and more herself.'

Gloria glanced towards the shop and read the lettering. '"Dawes and Weston: Haberdashery." It's got a ring to it. And it's clearly prospering.'

Verity smiled. 'That's all Effie's doing. If she hadn't put that money in when she did, I don't think the business would have survived the war. And she does all the window dressing and the shelf displays. Miss Pearl never really had an eye for it. Ned does the orders and that sort of thing, and Effie comes in once or twice a week… oh, and there she is. Still in half-mourning, but she's looking well on it.'

'Never really got to know her,' Gloria remarked. 'Nice sort of woman, Crowdie always said. Used to wonder if that Sergeant Jeffries would make a play for her – with her being a policeman's widow anyway.'

Verity laughed outright. She couldn't help herself. 'Shouldn't think so for a minute. Though I'd like to see her happy, she deserves to be. Happy as me and Ned are – if that is possible.'

There was a bit more gossip and then Gloria hurried off, but Vee stood for a moment watching Effie Dawes. Vee knew where she was heading – towards the horse-bus stop. And yes, there he was! A certain young mine captain with a mop of towsled hair, dressed up like Sunday for his meeting in town – twirling his best cap between his hands and waiting with a patient smile for Effie Dawes.

As he had been doing since they were six years old.

Verity smiled and hurried home to curried meat and Ned.